Facing Love

Written By

Laura Powell

Cover Design: Pixel Studios

ISBN: 978-1-7353597-1-7

FIRST EDITION

Acknowledgments

Thank you to Glen Sheets and Alyssa Funk for their insights into the social work field. Your work, past and present, with families and children in need is admirable.

Springfield not only is home to the capitol of Illinois, it also has amazing businesses and organizations, a few of which I feature in *Facing Love*. Thank you to Café Moxo and Incredibly Delicious for allowing me to feature your fantastic restaurants. The local area hockey team, the Springfield Junior Blues, is also highlighted.

Finally, thank you to the James Project, a not-for-profit Christian ministry that provides home and support for fostering families in Sangamon County. Readers will find one of their many services touched upon in the pages ahead, and their vision is Biblical and commendable.

Dedication

God gifted me with the love of writing. My fourth-g
teacher, Deborah (Harding) Welch, and my seventh-grad
English teacher, Tammy Eaton, gave me great opportuni
explore words on paper. Dave, my husband and best frie
and sweet son, Joshua, supported my dream of seeing th
novel become a reality, and I am truly thankful.

My gratitude also extends to the fantastic team of
and beta-readers that helped shape this story. Anne and
Engelhardt, thank you for being such supportive parents
great proof-readers. Becky England, I appreciate your e
friendship and talent for editing.

Finally, dear readers, I am sincerely grateful that y
choosing to spend a few hours reading and that you sele
this book. When I started writing, I knew I wanted to cre
clean Christian content that would highlight Biblical conc
and bring glory to God. I pray you would enjoy *Facing L*
and know Immanuel is truly God with us.

TABLE OF CONTENTS:

Acknowledgments

Thank you to Glen Sheets and Alyssa Funk for their insights into the social work field. Your work, past and present, with families and children in need is admirable.

Springfield not only is home to the capitol of Illinois, it also has amazing businesses and organizations, a few of which I feature in *Facing Love.* Thank you to Café Moxo and Incredibly Delicious for allowing me to feature your fantastic restaurants. The local area hockey team, the Springfield Junior Blues, is also highlighted.

Finally, thank you to the James Project, a not-for-profit Christian ministry that provides home and support for fostering families in Sangamon County. Readers will find one of their many services touched upon in the pages ahead, and their vision is Biblical and commendable.

Dedication

God gifted me with the love of writing. My fourth-grade teacher, Deborah (Harding) Welch, and my seventh-grade English teacher, Tammy Eaton, gave me great opportunities to explore words on paper. Dave, my husband and best friend, and sweet son, Joshua, supported my dream of seeing this first novel become a reality, and I am truly thankful.

My gratitude also extends to the fantastic team of editors and beta-readers that helped shape this story. Anne and Jerry Engelhardt, thank you for being such supportive parents and great proof-readers. Becky England, I appreciate your enduring friendship and talent for editing.

Finally, dear readers, I am sincerely grateful that you are choosing to spend a few hours reading and that you selected this book. When I started writing, I knew I wanted to create clean Christian content that would highlight Biblical concepts and bring glory to God. I pray you would enjoy *Facing Love,* and know Immanuel is truly God with us.

Chapter One

1,440 minutes, the measure of each new day. Danielle's minutes were mostly spent working, which meant the extra boxes from her recent move were still stored in the one-car garage. Maybe her morning would have started better if she would have taken time to scrape the latest snowfall off her car. But instead, as she backed out of her drive, the pile of snow that had been resting on her roof slid down the rear windshield like frosting on a hot cupcake.

No longer able to see where she was going, the pretty blonde stepped on the brake. Not soon enough according to her nettlesome neighbor, Hawk. Although there was no visibility out of the back, through the driver's side mirror she clearly saw him give her the middle finger. Then he stepped on the gas and fish-tailed down the snow-covered road, leaving her shaking her head at his impatience.

Danielle sighed and blew out a burst of air in frustration. Welcome to Monday morning, she thought. Contorting her body to reach the back seat, Danielle grabbed the ice scraper before opening her car door. And once she stepped outside, getting solid footing while wearing fashionable knee-high black boots proved to be less difficult than she thought. She quickly pushed the white mess off the rear window and onto the ground.

She always tried to be an hour early to work, and even though the weather would cause a slight delay, she trusted she would be able to type up her case notes from the day before by the time her co-workers arrived at nine.

Because of the transient nature of her job, Danielle liked morning structure. Up by five-thirty. Prayer time until six. An exercise video next. Coffee, breakfast, feed the cat, and take a shower. Out the door by seven-thirty, she always listened to a Christian radio station on the short drive to the Child's Advocacy Center.

Most mornings ran smoothly, and the little incident with Hawk wouldn't phase her. The intense situations she faced daily as a social worker for the Illinois Department of Child and Family Services made getting flipped off seem as friendly as a wave from the postman.

Nine years with the agency meant Danielle knew to expect the unexpected. Yet, Hawk had proved predictable in the three months that they had been neighbors. He was callous, ill-tempered and reclusive.

Danielle's encounters with Hawk had been few and far between, since he was rarely outside. Joanne, her sixty-year-old neighbor, stopped by when she was unloading boxes back in October. She told her not to expect to see Hawk often, even though their houses were next to one another.

Then she lowered her voice, whispering that Hawk had a hideous purple face and kept odd hours. Working in the backyard after dark and unloading groceries before dawn seemed unusual, but Joanne said what she feared the most were the weird noises that came from behind the fence. In a whisper, Joanne said that she had been brave once, slinking over to his house after she saw him drive away, but tall hedges and a six-foot fence bordered the whole property, making visibility impossible.

That wasn't the worst of it, Joanne explained. He was mean. Once Joanne passed him while she was walking her tiny Yorkie. She said hello, and he muttered a not-so-neighborly greeting that told her in no uncertain terms to mind her own business. Joanne suggested avoiding him at all costs.

But Danielle didn't do that. Christmas had passed just a few weeks earlier, and she made Joanne and Hawk each a plate of cookies. After dropping off Joanne's, Danielle arrived at Hawk's doorstep, one wintry afternoon. She saw the lights on in his house and heard music playing when she approached, but although she rang and knocked past the point of appropriateness he never answered.

However, Danielle wasn't fazed. She was used to people hiding from her. It occasionally happened with her job when she went to do surprise home visits. There would be rustling activity in the house but getting someone to come to the door would be impossible.

Hawk hadn't welcomed her house call, and as she backed out of her drive, she had already dismissed Hawk's rude gesture and was thinking about her new case at work. After thirty years with the agency, her mentor, Paul, decided the blue-green water of a Destin beach was his new office, so Nevaeh's case was passed to her.

The first write up in Nevaeh's file was from a nurse at Heartland Hospital, who assisted with her birth. Nevaeh's doped-up dad claimed she was conceived in a cemetery. He said she was cursed, and he wouldn't take care of her.

The next investigation was filed when she was three. A neighbor reported seeing her standing outside in the snow, dressed in a threadbare nightgown, for over twenty minutes. The file lay dormant until Nevaeh started Kindergarten this past fall. Her teacher reported that no school supplies were sent, and she wore the same, overly small outfit every day for two weeks. Mrs. Birch also reported that Nevaeh fell asleep at her desk every morning, and she had trouble interacting with the other kids in healthy ways.

When Danielle picked up the investigation, she learned Nevaeh was often absent, and when she was present, she seemed to cower when corrected. Mrs. Birch noted she sucked her thumb, and one day she noticed five red blistering, circular dots on the same appendage. She suspected cigarette burns. But the biggest concern for Mrs. Birch came one day at recess.

Nevaeh was playing with a tiny plastic doll. She took small pebbles from the playground and piled them on top of the doll. Mrs. Birch overheard Nevaeh say quietly to the doll, "You were bad. Now we have to pile blankets on you. That's right. You can't breathe. You were bad."

As she carefully navigated the streets out of her neighborhood, she gave thanks to God for Nevaeh and asked Him to direct her in the investigative meeting with her parents that afternoon.

Newly elected Illinois State Representative, James Patton picked up his cell phone to call his mom. James talked to her at least once a day. When he began campaigning two years earlier, she had become his unofficial manager. She did everything from coordinating fundraisers to editing press releases. It was then the daily calls began, and after winning the election, they never stopped.

His dad had been proud of his achievement, but Karen Patton displayed an emotion even stronger than pride. James wondered if she'd be as exuberant when she had her first grandchild. He speculated that his win felt personal to some degree. Karen Patton taught political science courses at a junior college, and she loved to talk about his success with her students.

Either way, he was thankful for her support and counsel, even if she did get pushy with her opinion at times. While he waited for her to answer, he pulled his laptop out of the computer case and sat down on the black leather couch in his living room.

"How'd your lunch go with the Retired Teachers' Association?" Karen asked as soon as she picked up the phone.

James used his right dress shoe to pull at the heel of his left shoe. Then he opened his laptop and typed in the password, as he held his cellphone to his ear.

"Well, hello to you too," he chuckled. "It went fine, Mom. They just wanted to make sure I was going to work to protect their pensions."

"Did you reassure them you'll do all you can?" his mother pressed.

"Of course," he laughed. "Are you still enjoying your winter break?"

"Absolutely. Your sister and I went to breakfast at Le Peep Bistro, and I finished a book I was reading."

"A book you were reading for fun or for work?" he replied, as he clicked on his email account.

"Work. It's about the electoral college. I may want to add it to the required reading list for my freshmen classes next year. Oh, and the president sent me an email today asking if I could line you up to come and do a talk for our political science majors next fall."

"I'd be happy to, Mom. Requests from Professor Patton get top priority."

"So, what's on your agenda for tonight?" she asked.

"Finding a date for the inaugural ball. You do realize it's in two and a half weeks, and I don't have a date," he sighed.

"Why don't you take Teresa?"

"My campaign fundraising director? Didn't you know she already has a boyfriend?"

"Oh, I thought she was on your team because she thought you were cute," she teased. "Okay, so she's out. What about Amanda?"

"Amanda Biltmore? We haven't seen each other for a year. I don't think she even sent a text to congratulate me on my win this fall."

"Well, she must still be mad that you dumped her."

"Mom, I didn't dump her, we broke up amicably. Last I heard she decided to go to grad school at Valparaiso."

"How about you take Kira?"

"Don't you think it would look funny to bring my sister?"

"Would you rather bring me?" Karen chuckled.

"Mom, do you remember Danielle Davison?"

"Who?"

"Danielle Davison, one of the girls I went to high school with?"

"James you went to high school with about five-hundred other kids…Oh, wait, I do remember Danielle. She beat you out for salutatorian, didn't she?"

"Well, I was taught to let a lady go first," James smiled.

"Danielle ousted you by 0.05%," his mom continued, missing the joke.

"I remember," James sighed.

Rolling his neck from side to side, he decided it was time to get some dinner. Setting down the computer, he headed into the kitchen and opened the refrigerator.

"A few months ago, when I was visiting with some old high school friends at our class reunion, someone brought up Danielle. Anyhow, she's living in Springfield now. I was thinking I might ask her."

"Really?" his mom questioned. James could picture her raising an eyebrow. He grinned to himself, as he looked at the restaurant containers he had to choose from. Pasta sounded good. He opened the cabinet and got out a plate.

"What's wrong with Danielle?" he asked.

"Nothing. I just haven't seen her in years. She was cute in high school, but who knows if she's gained weight, or dyed her hair purple, or…"

"Or gotten married," James interrupted. "Wouldn't that be the more important concern?"

"Well, now that you mention it, yes."

"Then you should be happy to know she's still single. At least according to her best friend from high school. She doesn't have a Facebook page, Twitter account, or Instagram, so I haven't seen any pictures of her, but when did you become so concerned with outward appearance?"

"James, all sorts of reporters will be there snapping pictures. You don't want to ruin all the hard work you did to get elected by bringing some girl you don't really know anything about. Plus, how would that look to your constituents? They like that you're focused on your job. If you want to go on *The Bachelor*, send them your resume. You're working for the state, you don't have time to date."

"I can see where I got all my catchy, political slogans," he said, as he dumped the rest of the leftover spaghetti onto the plate and put it in the microwave. "Maybe I'll just text Kira tonight."

"That sounds like a good plan, honey. Oh, your dad is beeping in. I better go. He probably wants to know if he should pick up dinner or if I'm cooking. I'll talk to you later, son."

"Love you, Mom."

Hawk's fingers flew. When he took the typing test to become a medical transcriber five years ago, his score was fifty-eight words per minute. Now, just from sheer repetition and the use of expanders, which typed out simple phrases for him, he was able to master over seventy words per minute and do it with accuracy. But just because he was good at his job didn't mean he enjoyed it.

The luster of learning about new medical procedures, medications, and patients' treatment plans had become one-dimensional. A string of words flowed into his headphones, through his fingers, and onto the screen. His sharp memory meant he rarely had to look up terms, or spend time searching for the correct spelling in his medical dictionary. However, the pay was decent-better than his last job as an overnight janitor at Walmart. But the best benefit was that it allowed him to work from home, which was worth far more than the paycheck.

Hawk finished typing, "*has a fifteen-year history of hypoglycemia*," and took a deep breath as he pushed pause on the virtual tape-recording device that blended in on the left-side of the screen. The clock on his laptop told him it was noon, but his stomach had told him it was lunchtime fifteen minutes earlier. Getting up from the swivel chair in his sparse office, his movement woke Chewy, the bronze-colored cat that had been sleeping on top of a blanket near the floor vent.

"Hey, Chewy," he said, bending down to stroke the large cat's fluffy mane. "You want to go with me to get some lunch?"

Chewy followed Hawk out of the office and down the hall into the kitchen. None of the rooms in the tiny bungalow were large, but the space suited Hawk fine. It was clean and people-free, just the way he liked it.

After he grabbed a banana from the fruit basket on the counter, he opened the freezer and pulled out a microwave meal. Chicken pot pie sounded good, he thought. He sat down at the kitchen table and opened the landscaping book that was lying where he had left it at breakfast.

Pulling out the bookmark, he used his hand to crease the pages to keep it from flying shut. "Look at this, Chewy," he said as he peeled back the yellow skin of the banana. "These lady ferns can grow in places that don't get sunlight, and we have plenty of those nooks and crannies in our backyard."

"Maybe we could also try coleus this year under the dogwood tree. Look at that rich, purple hue." He took a bite of the soft fruit. "I can't wait to get out there again."

He looked out the patio door. "It's too bad we can't see all our hard work. It's buried under the five inches of snow, Chewy." Hawk spent hours over the summer creating a stamped concrete patio. The internet claimed it wasn't a do-it-yourself project, but that didn't stop Hawk.

The microwave's alarm beeped, and Hawk thought about the horn blast he gave his neighbor this morning. He didn't know her name, but she sure annoyed him. The first time he saw her was when she was moving in. She was a petite, blonde-haired beauty. The type of girl that would be kind to him on the surface but make fun of him behind his back. They could never be friends. Then again, he had never really had one, so what did he know?

He rose to get his pot pie, still thinking about Danielle. The next time he saw her, she was raking the brown leaves that had collected on *his* front lawn. At first, he was infuriated, not that it took much, but why did she feel the need to rake *his* leaves? Yet, after pacing his hallway for ten minutes trying to decide if he would go out and stop her, he decided it saved him from doing the job in the dark, which was the way he had done it ever since he moved in ten years earlier. She unwittingly rescued him from being seen, which suited him fine.

Then she moved his garbage can from the roadside back to the garage door *every* week, until he snuck outside in the daylight to do it himself. Somehow, her kind gestures were annoying. What did she want from him? Perhaps she hoped to woo him outside, so she could see his face. He had long been tired of the constant stares he got because of the port-wine stain that covered his right cheek, nose, and forehead. Hawk's mom had told him the marks were angel kisses, but he had read enough medical literature to know it was a discoloration of the skin caused by a vascular anomaly.

He was thankful he didn't have Sturge-Weber syndrome, which often accompanied port-wine stains. He had read stories about people that suffered with convulsions, seizures, and even paralysis because of the accompanying syndrome.

Pulling back the plastic cover on his microwave meal, he blew on the flaky crust. Maybe he shouldn't have flipped off the neighbor girl, he thought, but she hadn't been paying attention. He did see that her rear window had been covered with snow, but she could've hit his car. Who cares, he thought. He had learned from experience that people generally avoided anyone angry, so that's the shield he wielded.

Chapter Two

Danielle was glad she had worn layers. The office was freezing. She went to the break room and turned up the thermostat, before sitting down at her desk to go through emails.

The James Project, a local Christian not-for-profit, was going to deliver some clothes to siblings at a new placement. Callie, a fellow social worker and close friend, wanted to spend a few minutes with her to talk about a case that was causing her frustration, and a foster mom was having trouble with a teen recently placed in her home.

After writing down action items for each email, her mind went back to Nevaeh's case. At home, she had listened to her voice messages. Nevaeh's foster mom, Debbie Worthington, called concerned that she was having horrible nightmares, waking everyone two or three times a night with terrorizing screams. Danielle started an email to Debbie with some suggestions for a new bedtime routine, and a promise that she would call later in the day.

Danielle remembered when Nevaeh first entered foster care, four months earlier. She had been incredibly homesick. Nine years ago, when she first started her career, the bond between a biological child and her abusive parents seemed odd. Over and over again, she had witnessed children expressing a terrible longing to be reunited with their abusers.

For these poor souls, their home situations were all they knew, and the loyalty to their caregivers was fierce. Danielle had learned that, for better or worse, the ties to the past were a part of the child, and when they were severed the child felt like she was losing a part of herself. The goal for every social worker was reunification with a biological parent, but Danielle knew that didn't always happen.

The first time Danielle met Nevaeh, at her elementary school, it was a warm fall morning. They found a quiet space, in the school counselor's office, to talk privately.

Danielle brought her bag of toys and books along. Nevaeh chose Candyland, but didn't really understand the concept of colors, so she dove back into the bag and found a collection of dolls with easy-to-put-on outfits.

Danielle's broad smile and friendly, easy manner made her a kid-magnet. Even the tough ones usually ended up thinking she was okay, and Nevaeh was no different. Nevaeh's straight dark hair was long, and her bangs had grown out over her eyes. She spent much of the time pushing her bangs behind her ears. She had dark brown eyes, so dark they were almost black, and her skin was pale white which gave her a haunting appearance.

As Nevaeh put a yellow dress on the plush doll, Danielle positioned herself to make eye contact, and casually began to ask her questions. *Are there ever times where you can't find food in your home? Have you ever been left home alone? Do you know what drugs are? Have you seen your mom or dad take drugs? Do you feel safe?*

Nevaeh's answers were quiet, often in short phrases, but certainly clear. Unfortunately, Nevaeh's parents left needles lying around the house and frequently drank too much. Their addictions caused them to neglect Nevaeh, treating her worse than a household pet. She didn't always have food in the refrigerator, there were rarely clean clothes, and when her parents were binging, she could be left home alone for hours. But the worst abuse occurred when they got high in front of her and then proceeded to make fun of her, lock her in a closet, put her outside, or share their frightening hallucinations aloud.

There was no doubt in Danielle's mind that Nevaeh would not be going back to the same address as her parents that night, or any other, until they could make life-altering changes, starting with getting clean and sober.

That evening Chris and Debbie Worthington took over Nevaeh's care. With one son in college, and another son who was a freshman in high school, the Worthington's decided to pursue helping children in the foster care system. Debbie had been a stay-at-home mom since her two boys were born, and she wasn't ready to be done parenting. Both parents were excited when they received the call asking them if they would take Nevaeh.

However, the honeymoon phase wore off six days after the placement had been made. Nevaeh went for her first supervised visit with her biological parents, and like many children, her emotional stability flatlined. Danielle was glad to see Layla and Booker show up for the visit, since they cancelled the first one, but as she sat in a corner of the playroom in the agency's office, she could read the signs of fear through Nevaeh's play.

While Booker sat in a chair in the opposite corner of the room, scrolling on his phone, Layla looked anxious and uncomfortable as she tried to find ways to engage with her daughter. Nevaeh bashed the wooden blocks together with force and laughed. Then, she started throwing the blocks, and when Booker shouted at her to stop, she cowered and obeyed.

Halfway through the visit, Layla nervously stepped out for a smoke break, leaving Booker alone. Danielle's job was to write observations for the case file, and she remained poised to jot down something positive as she waited to see if Booker would show a desire to connect with Nevaeh. But instead of initiating conversation or play, he just tapped his foot up and down and continued to be engrossed in his screen.

Nevaeh continued to play independently on the floor with a doghouse and little pet animals. When she couldn't get the door to the doghouse open, she picked up the toy and took it to Danielle, not to Booker. Layla came back in, twenty minutes later, reeking of tobacco.

The potpie had been decent, but it had been a long time since anyone had cooked for him, so he didn't have very high standards. He tried to think back to the last time his mom had made him a meal. For Christmas day, she had ordered from Bob Evans. Thanksgiving was County Market's turkey and sides. Hawk always paid for the take-out. He knew that he made more as a medical transcriber than she did as a Walmart cashier.

Scratching Chewy's neck, Hawk saw the drift of snow on his back patio and knew he had to shovel. He had left the job undone the last two storms, and there was a bank of snow at the end of the drive that was becoming a barricade when he backed out. He also knew if he didn't do it the new neighbor would, and he hated when she did things for him. Like the time she pulled his emptied garbage can from the curb to the garage. What if it hadn't been empty and she peeked inside? Why did she feel the need to be so nice?

After all, he wasn't incapable, and he liked being outside. He just didn't like being seen. Hawk felt like his birthmark appeared darker in the sunlight, and the morning clouds had rolled away, bringing in a brilliant winter day.

Because he still had forty-five minutes before his self-appointed lunch hour ended, he decided since the street looked devoid of human activity, he would tackle the project. After he put on his heavy winter jacket, a hat, and a pair of insulated gloves, he grabbed a snow shovel from the detached garage before trekking to the front yard.

As he rammed the shovel down into the large drift near the road, he instantly regretted that he had let it get out of hand. Now the first seven inches were hardened and icy, so all he could do was push off the fresh flakes. Beginning near the mailbox, he had barely done two swipes back and forth when he caught sight of a car careening at him as it rounded the corner.

Kira, I will pick you up on Sunday at nine a.m. James texted from his downtown Naperville office. After he won the fall election by a narrow margin, he had been exhausted. The campaign for state legislator of District 41 began two years earlier. Then thirty-two, he was young but not inexperienced.

Graduating with a law degree from Northwestern University, he went on to become an attorney for the Naperville School District. His first run for office came when he vied for a spot on the Naperville Park District Board and won. After serving four years, he ran for a position as a City Councilman, and again he saw his challenger topple.

James would humbly say God did the work, he just showed up. But his mom would counter that God gave James a charismatic personality, drive, and an honesty that was hard to match.

Cleaning out a fund his late grandfather had set aside for him, James had seed money for the state legislature's seat. He was adamant about not having his loyalty bought, and he campaigned with such a promise that was backed up by funding himself and working hard.

Breakfast meet and greets, lunch appointments, and dinner fundraisers had filled his calendar. This was topped off with knocking on doors and trying to catch every farmer's market, summer parade and festival, so he could come in contact with carloads of constituents. And he still worked for the school district. As his mother said, he had drive.

While he had prayed that he would win, he knew God was sovereign, and James recognized it wouldn't matter what *he* had done. He understood he could get his horses ready for battle, but the Lord alone would give him victory.

The day of the election was electric. He was anxious, excited, and energized, all at the same time. The results rolled in slowly during the late afternoon, but it wasn't until ten o'clock that the contest seemed to be breaking away in his favor. In the end, he had beaten the incumbent by 2.04%.

Now, all that he had dreamed was becoming a reality, starting with the Governor's Inaugural Ball, and he couldn't believe he was taking his sister. How pathetic, he thought. Why did he listen to his mom? Danielle kept crossing his mind. Why hadn't he called her? A simple search on the internet helped him find her work phone number. He was surprised to learn she had become a social worker. The last he could recall she was going to become a lawyer.

In high school, she had been an equal match on the debate team and a valuable partner for their scholastic bowl meets. But they had never been more than acquaintances. She dated "bad-boy Brad Rollins" for a while, and she never seemed interested in James, not that he had given any hints that he was attracted to her. Of course, he looked considerably different twenty years ago.

One of the pictures in his yearbook captured him putting up posters for the senior class officer election, which he still regretted losing to Daniel Stevens, the school's star baseball player. His long legs were accentuated by the black dress pants he wore most days. As long as he could remember, he liked to look professional. The style seemed to work better now that he was in his thirties. His sister, Kira, sent him an article after the election claiming he was the most eligible bachelor in the greater Chicago area.

In high school, he was respected by his classmates, but he was very shy when it came to pursuing women. Never having a date for any of the school dances didn't stop him from going. He was far too involved with school activities to stay at home, but instead of dancing, he'd be busy taking the students' tickets or serving concessions. His mom often told him that one day his intellect and maturity would be attractive to women. Achieving a law degree seemed to help, but then he got too busy with campaigning to pursue a love life, which was probably why he didn't have any options for the weekend ahead.

Glancing at the calendar on his computer screen, he looked at his schedule for the week. Monday was the inaugural ball. Tuesday his sister left on the train to get back to her classroom, and he had his first mandatory training sessions as he became a state employee. Wednesday meetings. Thursday he'd be done by noon. It wouldn't hurt, he rationalized, to catch up with an old friend. Lunch wouldn't be too intimidating, he reasoned.

But how would he motivate her to say yes? It wasn't like she had been waiting fifteen years for his call. While he'd done hundreds of cold calls for his campaign, this one felt awkward.

The office was quiet. His administrative assistant had gone home already. He sat back in his chair and tried to come up with a good excuse to reconnect with Danielle. Drumming a pencil against the desk, his face wrinkled in deep thought. Then, like a car's high beams cutting through the dark night, inspiration came upon him. James picked up his cell phone.

Chapter Three

The headlights caught Hawk like a deer frozen in his tracks. Two seconds later, the car swerved to the left, throwing loose snow onto his jeans. Gaining control of his senses, Hawk shouted some choice four letter words and raised his shovel towards the car. As the vehicle slowly backed up, Hawk recognized the driver.

Danielle rolled down the passenger side window. "I am *so* sorry. I'm not having too much success today as a driver, am I?" she asked, sheepishly. Hawk put together a string of cuss words in response, and he noticed her attractive face looked remorseful.

"I was hurrying to get home to pick up something for a client on my lunch hour, and I wasn't paying attention. It's no excuse, but I really feel awful." As much as Hawk wanted to let a few more explosive jabs fly, there was something about the girl that made him want to control his tongue.

She reached across the steering wheel and offered a gloved hand. "I'm Danielle Davison. I moved in next door in October. Actually, I've wanted to meet you for months. I'm just sorry it happened like this."

Hawk just stood where he was.

Danielle slowly pulled her hand back and set it on the steering wheel. "Well... I better go in and get what I came for. If there's anything I can do to make it up to you, please let me know. I promise I'll be more careful." She rolled up her window and slowly inched her old gray Toyota Camry into her driveway.

Hawk listened to the crunch of the snow beneath the car's tires. Then, not knowing what else to do, he spun on his heel and hightailed it back into his house, regretting she had seen his face.

Danielle thought about her unusual interaction with Hawk as she opened her hall closet and pulled out the blue plastic tote labeled, "Social Work Supplies." When people from her church family gave her items for clients, and they didn't have a specific place to go in the supply room at the office, she stored the leftover items at home. After pulling out a backpack and a stuffed animal, she pushed the container back into the closet and shut the door.

Hawk's birthmark covered his forehead, eyelid, left cheek and nose. It was hard not to stare, so she had tried to focus on his hair. It was dark, slightly wavy, and long. He also had a scraggly beard, and the facial hair made his purpled left side look dirty and smudged. His face was handsome and well-proportioned beneath the purple stain, but his attitude was atrocious.

Danielle had hoped for nice neighbors, but she should've prayed more about the outcome. *God, why did you put me next to him? He's so rude, and you know I deal with hard to handle people all day long. Help me be patient with him.*

Her stomach rumbled, and she was glad there were a few pre-made salads left in the refrigerator from her weekend food preparation. Pulling out a clear square container filled with an organic spinach mix, cucumber slices, and crumbled feta cheese, she sat down at the table, fork in hand.

She had just finished a short prayer of thanks when she heard her phone buzz against the wooden tabletop. Swiping the screen to unlock it, she checked the number. It wasn't one she recognized, but that wasn't anything new. She sighed, wishing she could be eating instead of answering.

"Hello, this is Danielle Davison."

Danielle? This is James Patton."

Danielle wracked her brain trying to think of how she knew someone who fit the deep, confident voice.

"We went to Naperville North together. We were on the debate team and Scholastic Bowl together. I went to Northwestern. You were going to go to Columbia University, if I remember correctly."

Connections with James Patton came flooding into Danielle's mind. She recalled his tall lean frame, carob-colored hair, bushy eyebrows, and respectful manners. He was one of the smartest young minds that came out of Naperville North High School, and she had to study long hours to beat him out for salutatorian.

Neither James nor Danielle could beat out valedictorian Aayush Ganesh, but from their sophomore year they battled back and forth for the second-place spot. She chuckled cynically to herself, remembering how hard she worked to earn that honor to impress her parents. Parents that couldn't be impressed.

James would have given a better speech at graduation, she thought. Although being on the debate team had given her practice speaking in front of others, he was always the best when it came to delivering powerful prose.

"James," Danielle's voice indicated her recognition, "How have you been?"

"Well, thank you. And you?"

"Same. How long's it been?"

"This fall we had our fifteenth high school class reunion. We missed you."

"That's not my kind of thing."

"That's understandable," he said kindly. "I don't mean to bother you. I'm sure you are busy, but I have a favor to ask."

"Okay."

"I was recently elected state representative, and I'm in need of some input on how well school systems are supporting social workers. Molly…you remember Molly Turner, right? She was at the reunion, and she mentioned you were a social worker, so I thought I'd see if you could help?"

Danielle got up from the table to get salad dressing out of the refrigerator. Molly Turner had been one of the few girls from her high school that attended the same college. Although they hadn't run in the same social circles, she must have been aware of her career path.

"I don't have time right now to answer any questions, James, but I could put something on my calendar," Danielle replied skeptically, feeling caught off guard. It sounded like a waste of time to her, but she didn't want to be inconsiderate.

"Actually, I'm going to be in Springfield this week, and I was wondering if you would like to do lunch on Thursday?"

"I'll need to check my schedule. Could I text you later?"

"Absolutely. The number I called from is my cell, so feel free to just shoot me a text, either way."

"Okay, will do."

"Thanks, Danielle. I hope it will work out. Meeting with you would be a great help."

As they hung up, Danielle stood with the refrigerator door open, forgetting why she had come. She shook her head to clear it, picked out a balsamic vinaigrette, and sat back down at the table. The call had come out of left field. She didn't have many thoughts on the school system's influence on her work. Certainly, there were lots things she would want to change about her job, but the school system's role wasn't one of them.

Thoroughly hungry, she stuck her fork into the mixed greens and took her first bite. Why did he call her? Didn't he know any other social workers in his district? He had to still be in Naperville, she thought.

Curiosity got the better of her, and she spoke his name into her phone to see what an internet search would uncover. Reading the first bolded headline, "James Patton wins District 14 election for State Representative," she clicked on the newspaper article.

In an instant, a picture at the top of the page captured James raising his hands in victory as he stood in front of a podium wearing a dark suit and tie. Danielle was taken aback at how handsome James had become. The wrinkles by his dark blue eyes told of many spent smiles, his once overgrown eyebrows were tamed, and his brown hair was cut in a fashionable style with short sides and small spikes on top.

Her stomach rumbled, and Danielle realized she had forgotten to keep eating. Glancing at the time on her phone, she realized she needed to get back to the office. The background check on James Patton would have to wait.

"Mr. Patton, your one o'clock appointment, Mr. Kevin Banks called. He's running a few minutes late," his secretary, Wanda, shared through the phone's intercom.

"Thank you, Wanda," he echoed back.

James was not looking forward to seeing Kevin Banks. The Harshaw Petroleum Company had formed a Political Action Committee, and the slick talking greasy rat, Banks, led the pack.

Although Banks had offered to sponsor three different fundraisers for James over the course of his campaign, he had politely turned him down each time.

James didn't accept any money from Political Action Committees. He made that clear at the beginning of the campaign. Too many politicians, who began their careers with good intentions, were bought with strings attached.

He noticed, when he did an internship on Capitol Hill, that at least a third of the politicians were swayed heavily by interest groups, and some groups were even said to write the policies that became law.

Yet, raising over a million dollars to promote himself wasn't easy, and he knew he had taken a gigantic gamble when he took the $200,000 his grandfather had saved for his future so he could level the playing field. But the time seemed right. He had prayed for God's approval, and three times in the week following, random people told him he should run for state representative. So, he began the process to get on the ballot.

Financing the television ads, mailers, and yard signs came from holding barbeques and formal dinners, and aside from his main base of support from family and friends, he had the largest income from small donors that any candidate had seen in the last twenty years.

The *Daily Herald* reported that James Patton was the "honest Abe Lincoln" of the twenty-first century. He was lauded as intelligent, creative and independent. His love for the education system won teachers over, and his innovative policy ideas for reform in the schools scored with voters. Finally, his call to balance the budget was a plus for people who had watched the state of Illinois spiral into more and more debt, having one of the worst financial futures in America.

Still, Kevin Banks was a constituent, and his office was open for anyone to come and speak with him. James opened a desk drawer and retrieved a box of Tic-Tacs. He heard Wanda talking with someone, and concurrently the office phone buzzed again.

"Mr. Patton? Mr. Banks is here to see you."

"Thank you, Wanda."

James got up and straightened his blue dress shirt with his hands. He anticipated an intense conversation, so he did what relaxed him-organize. Putting two pens back into his desk, he then straightened a stack of papers before making sure the guest chair was properly parallel to the desk. Taking a deep breath, he went to open the office door.

"Mr. Banks. Welcome. Come on back," James said ushering Banks in.

"That was a good campaign slogan," Banks said, pointing to the poster on the wall, as he walked in.

"Thanks," James replied. "My mom's idea."

"Is she in marketing?" Banks asked as he slid into the blue leather chair across from James.

"Actually, she is a college professor, but she's the type of person that is good at almost everything. Except golf," he chuckled, remembering being stuck in too many sand traps with her at one of his fundraising outings.

"Well, then it sounds like you're a chip off the old block," Banks smiled. "Good at everything."

James groaned inwardly. He had become accustomed to people trying to win him over with flattering words, but he still didn't like it.

"What brings you in today, Mr. Banks?" James said, sitting forward in his chair and clasping his hands on the top of his desk.

"To cut to the chase, James-I can call you James, right? I know we didn't see eye to eye during your campaign, but now that you're who we've got, I want to make the best of it. So, I've come to make a donation towards your next campaign, and I wanted to bring my check in personally." Banks reached for his jacket pocket and took out a check.

"I'm not campaigning for the next election, Mr. Banks. In fact, I don't even get inaugurated until next week."

"Well, son," Banks replied, setting the check on the top of the desk. "You can never start too early. As you know, you only hold your position for two years, and you need to make every connection you can… *if* you want to make this a career. And, you do intend to make this a career, don't you?"

"Sir, I am working for a High General. He gives the commands, and I follow. Right now, my order is to do the best with these two years, and I'm sure He'll let me know what's going to come next."

"High General?" Banks said, raising an eyebrow.

"God, sir."

"Oh," Banks coughed in discomfort.

"Well, son, this check is blank. What is the limit for individual donors these days?"

James knew Banks would have the answer down as clearly as he did. The Harshaw Petroleum Company could give a large amount, while an individual had a smaller limit. He also knew only a handful of donors, in his last campaign, offered that kind of support. Banks had decided to dangle a carrot in front of him.

Chapter Four

Danielle put the stainless-steel tray into the middle of the oven. She hoped Hawk liked slice and bake chocolate chip cookies. When she lived in an off-campus apartment during her graduate-degree years, she liked to bake cookies from scratch. Now she was too busy, and she also carefully selected what she ate. She had read too many studies about the link between stress and nutrition, and she had enough stress without adding anymore due to a poor diet.

Chewy cookies took eight minutes, so she set the timer accordingly. She liked her cookies chewy. Hopefully Hawk did too. While they were baking, she sat at the kitchen table and opened her laptop. Tinkerbell, her furry white cat, brushed against her leg before jumping up to lay on top of the computer. Laughing and setting her aside, she thought about the close of her workday.

The last appointment involved making a visit to a family that was under investigation, and it had not gone well. She was cussed at and threatened, although the threats were empty. The cops would be on her side, so there would be no use in the clients calling them even though they said they would.

Looking up more about James Patton would be a good mental distraction from the day's events. Since the random phone call, she had been intrigued. While the cookies baked, Danielle scrolled through newspaper articles about his campaign and learned that he wanted to see the education system become less about testing and more about play-based learning at the early levels, mentoring in the teen years, and teaching real life skills as they got older.

She liked his ideas, and he had certainly grown up to be better looking than he was in high school. But he still wasn't her type. The "nice guy," especially one wearing a suit, never had been. Her dad had ruined that for her. He wore suits, too, and could be charming as charismatic in public, but behind closed doors he was an alcoholic with a wicked tongue.

James was a lawyer, just like her parents, so that was two strikes against him. For a moment, she thought about how much her dad had wanted her to become a lawyer. After she turned sixteen, he had her work as an assistant at the firm where he worked. Back then, she thought the prestige of the title would make her happy. She also knew lawyers loved to manipulate words. She had a few former boyfriends who did too, and for those reasons she was thankful her life had taken a different direction.

Politicians also liked to wax and wane with words, but it looked like James also liked action. One article said he used his law degree every summer to offer pro bono services to people in his community that couldn't afford legal advice, and he had taken short-term trips to serve the people in Haiti and the Dominican Republic in the same way.

Danielle thought he would have made a good Boy Scout. In high school, he was that kid who said "please and thank you" for everything and greeted parents with a handshake and a hello. Back then, his actions seemed old-fashioned. She wondered if he would still seem that way.

To find out, she would have to meet with him and that would take time. And she didn't have extra. Doing her job well meant working long hours, even on the weekends. But she had been in the field long enough to know that it needed major changes so good workers would stay on board, rather than abandon ship because the rowing got hard. She had seen five colleagues leave her office alone in the last seven years because of the mental and emotional demands as well as the excessive workload.

Perhaps James would have a sympathetic ear, even though her concerns didn't involve the school system. And although he wasn't her representative, he had a voice. Jolting her back into reality, the buzzer rang.

Danielle pulled the hot pan out of the oven with a flowered potholder and set the steaming tray down on the granite countertop. One of the features she loved best about the house was its updated kitchen.

With stainless-steel appliances, sleek black counters, and faux wood floors, it was a space that had helped sell the home. She also loved that it had a garage, even if it was detached. The only problem was she hadn't made time to clean out the boxes that were being stored there since the move. Maybe if she had her car would have been spared of snow and she wouldn't have almost run into Hawk…twice.

As she waited for the dozen oozing circles of dough to cool, she texted James.

Hi James. It was good to hear from you today. I would be happy to meet with you on Thursday. My last appointment ends at five. Would you have time to do something after that?

Hawk was sprawled out on the couch, Chewy curled up next to his legs, scrolling through the new property listings on the Re/Max website. He had typed in his usual perimeter for land, fifteen to twenty acres. For the last ten years he had been saving aggressively for his dream, setting aside ten-thousand dollars a year. Living in the country would be ideal for many reasons, and as his doorbell rang, having no neighbors seemed like reason number one.

Who could be stopping by on a cold January night at eight o'clock? Certainly not lawn maintenance salesmen, Christmas carolers, or Girl Scouts. He got up from the couch and walked to the door. Peering out the window, he recognized Danielle shivering in a red winter coat and cashmere hat. If her gloved hands hadn't been holding a container, he would have let her ring the bell to her heart's content. However, Hawk sensed she would keep coming back until she made the hand-off. Two chimes later, he opened the door. Let's make this short and sweet, he thought.

"Hi. Sorry I rang so many times. Your lights were on inside, so I thought you were home," Danielle said with a small smile.

Hawk just stood there, feeling the cold air rush in around him.

"Do you mind if I step inside for a minute? I don't want to let out all your heat."

"Yes, I do mind," Hawk said, regretting how rude it sounded. But it was the truth.

"Oh," Danielle replied, slightly flustered. "Well, here," she continued, handing him the silver tin with green Christmas trees on it. "Sorry it's a Christmas tin. That's all I had to put these in. They're chocolate chip cookies. Not homemade, unfortunately, but they are still warm."

She smiled again, and Hawk noticed she had straight teeth to go with the blonde hair and big blue eyes. She had probably been a cheerleader in high school, he thought.

"Joanne told me your name is Hawk, right?" she asked, as her breath made white clouds in the dark air.

Hawk said nothing. At least she wasn't staring at the purple birthmark. He always knew when someone was trying to take in his whole hideous face.

"I just wanted to apologize again," she continued. "I will do my best to be a more careful driver. Okay, well I guess I'll go. Have a good night," she said, turning to leave.

Hawk watched Danielle trudge through the layer of snow that still covered the ground between his house and hers. She never looked back.

Hawk took the cookies into the kitchen, and Chewy, who had found a hiding spot under the couch, came out to follow him. He opened the tin, and on the top of the cookies was a thin piece of paper that said, "I'll be watching out for you," signed Danielle, in wide, curvy letters. The paper had absorbed some of the grease from the cookies.

She would be watching out for him. He chuckled cynically. No beautiful angel ever had before. Hawk took out a cookie. She had laid them in threes, between pieces of parchment paper.

Danielle looked like one of the popular girls from his high school, Reese Prader. Reese had a locker next to his freshman year. She would actually talk to him before and after school, when they were loading and unloading their bookbags.

Nothing major, of course. Just the passing niceties, but that was a startling change from silence, staring or mean jokes made by most of his classmates. Looking back, he couldn't believe he really had a crush on Reese.

That all changed one day when he overheard her talking to her friends as he passed by her table at lunch. She said the principal had talked with her before school started and told her what Hawk would look like. He asked her to be kind to him, and she reassured her friends that that was the only reason she acted like she did around him.

After that, he stopped talking to her, and like most others, she came to believe he was mean-which was fine by him. The two years he spent in public high school were miserable. He found eating alone at lunch lonely, so he joined Mike, the janitor, in the hall closet that had become his office.

It seemed that even after the initial shock of his appearance wore off, no one desired to be around him. Being invisible may have been worse than being a monster.

He was forever grateful that his mom let him switch to being homeschooled for his junior and senior years of high school. Upon graduation, he worked the night shift as a stocker at the same Wal-Mart where his mom worked. But even then, he didn't enjoy interacting with people. When he saw an ad on his computer for medical coding, it was the perfect solution for a life of solitude, and he'd make much better money than loading shelves for minimum wage.

Chewy had jumped onto the counter and was swiping at the tin with his apricot-colored paw. "No, Chewy," Hawk said, taking another cookie out before putting the lid on the tin and setting it on the top of his refrigerator.

Why had he been so uncivil with her? After all, she was trying to make amends. Maybe next time he would let her know his name. But she said Joanne already told her his name. His heart began to beat faster. What else had the nosy neighbor, Joanne, shared with sweet Danielle?

Joanne was a pest. He had seen her eyeing his backyard. Maybe this spring he'd have to install barbed wire at the top of his fence. The "private, keep out" sign obviously wasn't working.

"Mom, he was trying to bribe me," James said into his cell phone, as he threw his keys on the counter. The clock on the microwave read nine o'clock. He was thankful that traffic on the way home from the meeting with the Lutheran Schools Association was light.

"Honey," his mom replied, "you're going to have to get used to people giving you money and then wanting their interests supported. Just because you won't take donations from Political Action Committees or lobbyists trying to buy your vote doesn't mean you can't take donations from individuals."

"Are you saying I should've taken Banks' money?"

"Of course, you should have," his mom replied.

"I thought you were on my side." James sat down on the couch and began to take off his dress shoes. It had been a long day, but if it hadn't been it wouldn't feel normal.

"I'm *always* on your side, James. This is about you building a fund to get re-elected."

"Wow. I just didn't think-"

"Didn't think I would be for it?"

"Yeah," he sighed. "Banks will expect something from it."

"You don't owe him anything."

His phone buzzed by his ear, indicating he got a text.

"Well, Mom, I just got home, so I'm going to turn on the news. Tell Dad hello."

"Will do, son. Love you."

"You too, Mom."

James reached for the remote and turned on the nine o'clock news. As the television came to life, he touched the button to pull up the text.

Do you think I should wear a pants-suit or a dress? Kira had texted.

Dress. He replied. Then he saw that he had another unread text, this one from Danielle. She wanted to meet on Thursday evening. That would mean he would have to stay an extra night in Springfield.

He'd leased a downtown apartment for the next two years, so that wouldn't be a problem. Like a majority of the state representatives, he'd be splitting his time between his home base in Naperville and sessions at the state capitol.

James swiped the screen of his phone to locate the calendar. Pulling up the following Friday's office schedule, he saw he had a nine o'clock meeting with the Naperville Association of Builders and Contractors. That couldn't be moved, he reasoned. No matter, he could get up by four-thirty and be there with plenty of time to spare, not accounting for any major snowfalls. Would the lack of sleep be worth the reunion?

In high school, Danielle had reminded James of Cinderella, with her blonde hair, blue eyes, and petite frame. However, people change, and not just physically. He wondered what she was like now.

Back at Naperville North she had been a rival, someone with goals and dreams and drive. What made her become a social worker, he wondered? She had always been kind-hearted, but she had seemed set on becoming a lawyer.

Whatever the answer, it would be nice to have a friend in Springfield.

But Karen Patton didn't need to know he was widening his circle, which meant he certainly wouldn't be sharing any details about this date with his sister, Kira. That was a surefire way to have it get back to his mom in a hurry.

It would be great to reconnect with you next Thursday evening. If you have a favorite restaurant, let me know. Otherwise, I can ask a colleague for a suggestion. I'll be in touch. Have a good night.

Chapter Five

Danielle stared at the color-coordinated sections of clothes in her closet. She had a light blue terry cloth towel wrapped around her slender frame. Her half-hour "Cardio Blast Interval Workout" soaked her t-shirt with sweat, even though the temperature outside was minus three degrees. Danielle thought of her mentor, Paul, who was probably picking up seashells with his wife. She missed him.

Paul had been instrumental in helping her become a strong, confident and compassionate social worker. He also had been the one she would go to when cases got tough or to vent her fears and frustrations. Since she hadn't spoken to her dad for fifteen years, Paul had also secretly become a father-figure. If only he was available to help her with Nevaeh's case.

Nevaeh's mom, Layla, was trying to make strides to clean up her life so she could get her back. Unfortunately, Booker wasn't helping. He was angry and belligerent about the process. The last time she had gone to pick them both up for their counseling session, he had cussed Danielle out and threatened to send his gang-member cousin after her, so Layla went alone.

Danielle had worked long enough in the field to know that if both parents are addicted, it's very difficult for the pair to get clean unless both are committed to the process. She prayed Layla would be strong enough to change even if Booker didn't.

As she thumbed through her clothes, she settled on black pants and a cream turtleneck sweater. Danielle had learned to dress modestly on the job, but tonight she was meeting James, and she wanted her outfit to be appropriate for both functions. She had decided upon Café Moxo for dinner. It was one of her favorite spots to eat downtown because she loved their chicken and white bean chili. Plus, it closed at sixty-thirty, which meant they would have to leave at a set time. She didn't want their meeting to go on forever. This was business for her.

The last time she had met a guy for dinner was only weeks earlier. Callie, her newest co-worker, had set her up with a date for New Year's Eve so they could double with her and her boyfriend. But Stephen was too nice, and she never trusted nice guys. People always thought her dad was nice too, but she knew better. Sometimes she'd ask her mom about him, but since they were divorced, her mom didn't keep tabs on the man she was named after.

Danielle checked her watch and noted that she only had a half hour to finish getting ready for work. She needed to stop by a drug store to pick up batteries for a toy computer they had in their parent-child playroom. It was a favorite, and when she had checked the supply room for more the day before, she found the double A battery box was empty.

She pulled the sweater over her head and then used the mirror in her bedroom to fashion her hair into a messy bun, pulling out little stands around her face. Then she quickly finished off her usual make-up routine with light blush, lip-gloss, mascara and eyeshadow. Knowing she wouldn't have time for oatmeal, Danielle grabbed a Larabar from the cupboard and snatched her lunch bag out of the refrigerator.

As she opened the front door to leave, Tinkerbell ran past her legs and darted outside. Danielle called her to come back and jingled her keys, but seeing those techniques of retrieval weren't working, she jumped into the snow to run after Tink.

The silly cat fled from her and shot into Hawk's backyard through a small triangular crevice between two boards in his fence. Danielle groaned. Looking at her watch, she realized she had no time to deal with this dilemma, but she couldn't leave her cat in the cold. The trip to get batteries would have to be skipped.

Was seven-thirty too early to knock on a neighbor's door, she wondered? Hawk already hated her, so she figured she'd try calling to Tink from the fence. Crunching through the snow she called out to Tinkerbell. As she neared the tall, wooden boards, she heard a booming voice.

"Get away from there," Hawk yelled from the driveway.

"Oh, so sorry," Danielle replied. "My cat went through that opening," she pointed to the Hershey Kiss-shaped spot.

"I'll get your cat for you," he complained through gritted teeth. "Just move away from my property. See the signs?"

Danielle now noticed the "Keep Out. Private Property," warnings in red. As she turned back to talk with Hawk, she realized he had disappeared. Moving towards his front door, she felt the icy air with each inhale. There was a wind-chill advisory today, and she needed to get Tinkerbell back home. Hawk opened the front door a crack and peered out.

"Your cat's leg got cut, probably going through the opening. I'll bandage it."

Danielle moaned. "I have to get to work. I have an appointment this morning, and I can't be late. A client rearranged her work schedule to be able to come in at eight, and I can't miss it. Could you keep Tinkerbell with you today? I can pick her up later tonight."

Hawk snorted. "Fine."

"Thank you so much. I work until five, but I can get her right after I'm done."

Hawk was silent.

"Will that be okay?"

"Fine."

"Thank you, again," Danielle gushed. "I really appreciate it."

James was always early, and Café Moxo was quiet when he arrived at 4:45. His training had finished at noon, and he had spent the last three hours at his apartment reading pre-session house bills. He was a fast reader, which was one of the skills that helped him through law school. He also recognized this would come in handy as a state representative. Bills could be hundreds of pages long, and they could get boring, just like many of his law textbooks. At the moment, he was thankful for a diversion from the reading, and he looked forward to a good dinner.

Café Moxo was trendy, with its exposed brick walls and high ceilings. Since he had his choice of seats, he picked a table far away from the front door, which let in cold air when it was opened and closed. He had already looked at the online menu and knew what he would order, so he went through his mental inventory of questions to ask Danielle.

Throughout the week in Springfield, he second-guessed his decision to delay his return to Naperville just to meet Danielle. Somehow when he was contemplating a "plus one" for the inaugural ball it had seemed like a good idea, and he wasn't one to back out of a commitment.

James didn't date much, although meeting Danielle wasn't a date he reasoned. After he graduated from law school, it was hard to meet anyone who met his standards. With his sights set on becoming a politician, he also knew that whomever he dated had to be ready to live a very public life, and that requirement attracted two types of attention. Sometimes women went after him hoping he could offer something flashy and powerful, other times ladies seemed to think he was independently wealthy as a lawyer with political interests. James didn't want to be coupled with either type.

A woman had never intrigued him so much that he wanted to spend the rest of his life with her. Sometimes that worried him. After all, he was thirty-four. But his mom and dad never pressured him, and he had been too career-driven to think much about dating. However, after he won the election, the victory seemed empty.

The night the results came in, the staff that helped him get elected celebrated at a local restaurant. Afterwards, he went home to his empty house and couldn't sleep. At first, he was too hungry. In the anxiety of waiting to find out his fate, he'd lost his appetite, but it came back with a vengeance after he'd changed into sweatpants and a t-shirt. When he'd finished some leftover takeout, he spent the next hour scrolling the internet, reading news stories of different wins around the state.

By three o'clock in the morning, he thought maybe he should pull a Jerry Maguire and write a manifesto of all the things he wanted to accomplish in office. But he knew he'd already done that, and it was listed on his website. Then he thought about calling his mom. After all the hours she'd put in to help him, he felt like the accomplishment was as much hers as it was his. But she had been with him all night, and there wasn't much more to say.

It was at that moment he wondered if he'd ever have someone to share his triumphs with, besides his mom. And it was the first time he'd felt so alone. It was the first time his career didn't seem to be enough.

As the minutes at the restaurant ticked by, James made friends with his food server and with the husband and wife who were visiting the state capital as they passed through for a friend's wedding. Looking down at his watch, James noticed it was 5:10, and there was no sign of Danielle. He checked his cell phone to see if he had any messages. As soon as he glanced down at the screen, he sensed movement out of the corner of his eye.

"I'm so sorry for being late," Danielle gushed as she bounded over in her red winter coat.

She was still captivating, he thought as he took in her sophisticated appearance. "No worries," James replied. "I just made a few new friends," he said, as he waved to the married couple that was getting up from their table to leave.

"You were always good at that in high school." Danielle said as she set her purse under the table, at her feet. "I didn't mean to make you wait. I don't like being late. Unfortunately, in this profession getting done by five is practically unheard-of. I had an appointment with a foster family at three-thirty, and I just got done fifteen minutes ago."

As she sat down, James suddenly felt nervous. All of the prepared questions flew out of his head at the sight of Danielle. She had been cute in high school, but now she was model material.

Feeling anxious was foreign to James. He was used to the pre-speech jitters before a big crowd, but he thrived on being around people and rarely ran out of things to talk about...with anyone. He felt his underarms begin to perspire, and he wondered if he remembered to put on deodorant before he left the apartment.

"If you don't mind, Danielle, I'm going to go to the restroom. I've already decided what I want to eat, so it will give you time to look over the menu. I'll be right back," James smiled and excused himself. He had located the bathrooms on the way in, and he headed to the back corner.

Danielle wasn't apprehensive at all. That only happened when she was around guys she wanted to impress. Seeing James in person reminded her how unappealing those in business suits were to her. The guy she saw behind the counter, with his muscled arms filled with tattoos had been her style in the past. Yet, she'd been burned too many times by that type, so for the past few years she had found contentment in her solitary lifestyle.

She felt tired from the stress of her workday and was hopeful that this reunion would be short. A few of the ideas she wanted to share with James about reforming the foster care system were rolling around in her head, and she hoped he would be receptive to them.

As she looked at the menu, she was disappointed to see that the chicken and white bean chili was only available on Tuesdays. Today's soup was loaded baked potato, and she decided to order that with a turkey cranberry waldorf salad.

Back in the bathroom, James wiped his armpits with a paper towel to remove the perspiration and spoke to himself silently. *James get it together, bro. You've been around beautiful women before. Why, you saw about five lovely ladies at the inaugural ball three nights ago. This is no different.* He checked out his hair in the mirror and blew into his hand to see if the mint he had put into his mouth was doing its job. Walking back to the table, he asked God to help him with the conversation. Danielle was checking her phone when he sat back down.

"Did you decide what you wanted to eat?" he asked.

"I think so. They don't have my favorite-chicken and white bean chili, so I'm going with a salad."

As if she heard their conversation, the food server appeared at their table within seconds to take their orders. As the young server walked away with their menu, James twisted the white paper from the straw.

"So, we have a lot of years to catch up on? Don't we?"

Danielle smiled. "We sure do. I heard you are now a state representative. That's really impressive."

"Thanks. It was a long road to get here, but after getting sworn in on Monday, I can tell you I've never felt more ready to begin a job."

"What's it like? Getting sworn in?" Danielle asked, as she leaned forward towards him.

"It was very patriotic, actually. I don't tear up very often. The last time was probably when my grandpa died seven years ago, but there was a high school band playing "America the Beautiful," and it just hit me. How many people have stood where I stood and have had the privilege to represent the people of our great state?"

"I happened to find my old yearbook, and I read that even back then you had aspirations to become President."

Danielle thought about his tiny rectangular picture. Back then, his hair had been darker. Now his lighter brown hair was styled in a trendy cut featuring short sides and a spikey top. Someone must have told him to wax his once bushy eyebrows, as they were now very tame. There was no doubt about it, he was handsome. Even his ears, that happened to stick out slightly more than average, added to his cute factor.

James grinned, and his left cheek dimple appeared. "Oh my. I haven't looked at my yearbook in a long time. Have you kept in touch with anyone since high school?"

"No, how about you?"

"Well, one thing campaigning does is that it keeps you in touch with people. Many of our classmates stayed in the area. Do you remember Nicole Hodges?"

"Wasn't she on the debate team, too?"

James nodded. "She was on my fundraising team. She's a teacher now. Married with two kids. Nice family. Are your parents still in the Naperville area?"

Danielle fiddled with the fork that lay on the table. "My Dad is, but I haven't seen him since I graduated from high school, but my mom and my step-dad are."

"Wow. That's a long time not to see a parent."

"It makes my life more peaceful not to have him in it," she said, grateful to spot the server headed her way with a drink.

Chapter Six

"Do you mind if I pray?" James asked, after the soups, salad and sandwich had been delivered.

"I would love that," Danielle replied sincerely. So, what's it like to be a state representative?" Danielle asked after the prayer, as she scooped soup unto her spoon and began blowing on the hot creamy broth.

"To tell you the truth, I don't know yet. I'm sure I'll find out more in the next few weeks. After the inauguration, we had training the rest of the week. We're state employees now, so it's mandatory. We have next week off, but we'll be back the following week to start legislative sessions."

"Can you tell me about your platform?" Danielle asked, and James noted that she seemed confident leading the conversation, which he found attractive. Everything she did made him like her, which was more exciting than it was scary.

"Well, I am hoping to make changes to the education system. Less testing, more hands-on projects, more help in determining students' gifts and talents at the beginning of high school, then a better direction of the type of classes they take. That kind of thing."

"Is your dad still a principal?"

"Yes. He's moved on from Meadow Glens Elementary. He's in middle school now," he chuckled. "I'm surprised you remembered his profession."

"Well, the article in the *Herald* helped me a little," Danielle said slightly embarrassed to admit she had been reading up on him.

"So, you did your research before you came?" James said, feeling impressed.

"It's not every day I get a call from a politician asking for a reunion," she said.

"Are you happy with what you found?" James asked quietly, looking down at his sandwich.

"Absolutely, you are a credit to our school."

James wished she would have had a different answer, but he didn't stop to dwell on it. With the food in his stomach, the questions he had prepared were coming back to him.

"I also did my research, and I found out that you have worked for the state as a social worker for almost ten years."

"Nice work," she replied, scraping the bottom of the soup bowl. "I started with the Department of Children and Family Services right after I got my master's degree. Been there ever since."

"It must be hard," James said, as he lifted his water to take a drink.

"It's never as hard as the situations I rescue these children from."

"Is it gratifying?"

"Some days. But mostly it's long hours, lots of stress, and lots of prayers that parents will desire to change so that these kids will be healed from their pain, with the ability to grow up to be healthy adults."

"The burn out rate must be high."

"It is. I recently read the statistics that indicate seventy-five percent of people entering the field will not stick with it."

"Why is that?" James asked, as he leaned back against the wooden chair, sincerely curious.

"Actually, I was hoping this would come up," Danielle said with an impish grin. "I have lots of ideas for reform. I'm not the only one who does, but now that I have a friend in the capitol, maybe some things will finally change."

"I'm a rookie, remember?" he grinned. "So, why's burnout so high?

"We come into the profession to help, and then we're constantly bombarded with negative situations. We need to have time built into our work schedules to decompress. We need ongoing personal therapy, to manage what we see and hear. We need lighter caseloads. Our system is seeing a record number of cases come in, and we don't have the funding to hire more staff. And, a lot of us think that the timetable for parents to make changes should be shortened. For some kids it can be three years of stress, not knowing if their parents will make the transformations they need to get them back." The words tumbled out with ease and passion.

"Wow."

"That's just the tip of the iceberg. I have so much more to share."

"Then we should do this again," James said, glad for the opening to pursue a second meeting, but also wishing it would have come up without the use of his government title.

"I'd like that," Danielle replied, surprised that she genuinely meant it.

Hawk glanced at his watch. It was 6:35. Danielle had said she would get Tinkerbell after work at five. Why was she over an hour late? He glanced at the cardboard box on the floor. Tinkerbell was still curled up inside on the blanket.

After he had bandaged Tinkerbell's back leg, he had let her roam free, but she kept hiding behind the curtains in his bedroom, so he figured she was scared. It was certainly understandable, he reasoned, she was in a strange home with a hurt leg. Once he made-up the box for her, she calmed down. And a few hours later the bleeding had completely stopped, so he carefully removed the bandage, only garnering a few scrapes on his arm and one long hiss. He knew that the wound needed to breathe. Hawk also trusted his instinct, which told him the cut wasn't serious enough to make a trip to the veterinarian's office.

Now what? He wondered. Should he go next door and see if she forgot to pick up Tinkerbell? Should he just dump the cat outside? That would serve her right for making him cat-sit all day and then not showing up on time. After walking the living room floor for a few minutes, he decided to go outside and look to see if the lights were on in her house. He put on his slippers and padded into the frigid air to take a quick peek.

The house was dark, so he quickly shuffled back inside. Sighing, Hawk turned on the television hoping that a game show would distract him. Flipping to the local news, he settled back against the faded navy-blue couch, and his cat, Chewy, jumped onto his lap. Chewy had been curious about Tinkerbell, but now that she was in the box, he left her alone.

When the news ended *Entertainment Tonight* came on. Hawk wasn't a fan of celebrity gossip so he flipped channels until he found a game show. A half-hour later when Alex Trebek announced a winner, the clock read seven. Just as he was about to get up for a snack, he saw car lights through his front window. He peered out the slatted blinds and confirmed that it was Danielle. Hawk picked up the box and carried it to the door.

"I'm so sorry," Danielle said as he opened the door a crack, still holding the box in one arm. Tinkerbell peered over the cardboard side and meowed with delight. Danielle leaned in to kiss her. "Are you okay?" she cooed at the cat.

"She's okay," Hawk said gruffly. "Just take her," he said, shoving the box into her, almost causing her to fall backwards.

"Whoa," Danielle said as she stumbled back, catching herself on the step below. "Look, I'm sorry I was late. I forgot I was meeting someone after work. It went longer than I expected. I would've called, but I didn't have your number."

Tinkerbell tried to jump out of the top of the box, and Danielle shut the two flaps that were dangling at the sides of the box.

"Her leg's fine. I took off the bandage around ten this morning. No need for stitches or to see a vet. Now, if you don't mind, I'd like to get back to my night."

Hawk started to close the door, but Danielle shielded it from shutting using the box as a wedge.

"What do you want?" he growled, adding in some choice cuss words.

"I just wanted to offer to pay you for your time and for the bandage. I know you weren't expecting to cat-sit today."

"I don't want your money, lady. Just go home."

Danielle withdrew the box from the door. "Well, for what it's worth. Thank you. I wouldn't have been able to go to work knowing she was out in the cold, so I really appreciate how you helped me get her inside and how you took care of her."

Hawk began to shut the door for the second time.

"You might just want to get used to having me as a neighbor." She tentatively smiled.

"Well, I don't plan to be here much longer," Hawk said, closing the door in her face.

Hawk was so tired of having neighbors. While he was only three months away from having enough money saved to put a down payment on the property he wanted in the country, it felt like forever. If his mom didn't live in town, he would've moved to Montana. He didn't mind the cold, and he loved the rolling prairie. Still, he mused, he could fulfill his dreams in the countryside of Pleasant Plains, and it was only a half hour from his mom's apartment.

As he sat back down on the couch, Chewy reappeared from under the sofa. "Come up here," he beckoned, patting the cushion. Why had he treated Danielle with such contempt, he wondered? He hated the way his face felt flushed when he interacted with others.

Hawk recalled the last night he worked at Walmart. A new girl had begun working the overnight shift. She was a talker, and even though she was supposed to stock home goods, she kept wandering over to the pet supplies aisle, where he was restocking dog food and cat treats.

Her name tag read Aliyah, and not only did she elaborate about her life, she asked about his. How did he get the big purple marks? Was he burned? Did it hurt? Had he ever tried to put make-up on it? Did he work nights because he was embarrassed?

He'd never had someone ask him so many bold questions. At first, he appreciated her curiosity. He'd rather have someone ask an honest question than to stare or snicker. He'd be happy to educate anyone interested about port-wine stains. But, when she questioned if he'd ever been kissed and how did his birthmark affect his love life, that's where he drew the line. Instead of putting away the rest of the cat treats, he'd gone on break and never came back. That was the catalyst that began his career in medical transcription.

On a night like tonight, when Hawk could not stop staring at Danielle's full red lips, he wondered what it would be like to be kissed. He shook his head, trying to free it from the images it was creating of kissing Danielle. A girl like her would *never* be with a guy like him. But if he didn't have the marks, would she at least look twice at him? Hawk opened his laptop which was resting on the end table beside the couch. Typing in "laser treatment for port-wine stains," Hawk scanned the list of articles that appeared from the search.

Chapter Seven

"Mom, I brought Popeyes," Hawk called as he entered her third-floor apartment.

"I'm in here," she replied, and he followed her voice to the living room where she was watching television, like usual. Suzanne had two modes- work and rest. During the latter, copious amounts of movies and television were viewed, and occasionally she did a puzzle at the same time.

Hawk put the brown bag of food, already getting grease stains at the corners, on the center of the dining table in the shared space and hunched to give her a hug around her shoulders.

"Was it slippery out there?" Suzanne asked as she muted the game show.

"Not too bad. Most of the roads are just covered with slush now." Hawk sat down on the wooden chair next to his mom so he could see the show too. He opened the bag of food and took out the stack of napkins.

"I'm glad it's warming up," Suzanne said as she grabbed for a spicy chicken tender.

"Me too, although we can barely call a thirty-six-degree day warm."

"Well, when it's been minus-fifteen, I think we can," she smiled.

"Did you get your haircut, Mom?" Hawk asked as he pulled out a container of steak fries. Suzanne's shoulder-length hair was dark brown like her son's. However, it was straight and thin, unlike Hawk's, which was thick and unruly.

"Just a little trim."

"Looks nice."

"Thanks, Ethan. How's your neighbor's cat?" she asked as she dipped her chicken into a tub of barbeque sauce.

"Fine, I guess."

"You mean you haven't been over to check on it?"

"No, why would I?"

"To be nice. Plus, you said that girl-what's her name?"

"Danielle."

"Yeah Danielle, you said she was good looking." Suzanne grinned and her brown eyes became crescent moons, due to the overuse of dark black eyeliner on her upper and lower lids.

Hawk sighed. "When has a girl ever given me a second glance." Then he snickered. "Take that back. Girls give me second glances all the time, just not for the right reasons."

"You really are handsome, son," Suzanne said sincerely.

"I've got a face only a mother can love," Hawk laughed cynically.

"Ethan, you've got the face of a model. The places where the angels kissed you only color it."

"I wish you'd stop telling me angels kissed this face," he replied disgustedly. "I don't believe in angels, and if I did, I'd tell them to stick to coloring books."

"Oh, Ethan. I wish I could've afforded the laser surgery when we first heard about it, ten years ago. But, working at the grocery store didn't pay enough."

"Treatment costs have come down, Mom."

"How would you know?" Suzanne asked, cocking an eyebrow.

"I've been researching a little."

"Really? You've never been interested before."

"I was just curious."

"Danielle must be pretty cute," she grinned.

"Mom," Hawk said with exasperation. "This is not about Danielle. I have some money saved up-"

"The money you're saving for the land?"

"Yes."

"Why would you want to do the treatments if you're just going to be a hermit living in the country? I thought the whole point of that was to get away from people so you could live the way you wanted?"

"That's not the *whole* point, but if I did the treatments it would only set me back a year or two."

"A year or two? You just got enough saved up."

Hawk ate a fry. "I know. I'm not saying I'm doing anything. Just thinking, that's all."

"Are you sure Booker won't go?" Danielle texted Layla.

"Yes," Layla replied. "*He says he doesn't need counseling.*"

Figures, Danielle thought. The few times Booker actually showed up for something he was either high or angry. He'd never hurt Layla or Nevaeh in front of her, but he was controlling, and his words were biting and harsh.

Layla had missed three of the last four visits with Nevaeh, but when Danielle was able to talk with her in person, one morning on a rare visit when Booker wasn't at home, she convinced her to keep up with the plan they had set for her recovery. Today was her fourth scheduled session with counselor Kathy Ferris.   She had missed two, but Danielle was always required to show up at her tiny rental house to get her, since Layla didn't have a car, or a driver's license.

"Well then, I'll be at your house by ten tomorrow morning. Just remember you can get healthy, even if Booker doesn't want to. His decision doesn't have to affect yours."

Danielle set her phone down on the kitchen table. The microwave clock read 8:45 p.m. If only the days weren't so long, she sighed as she stroked Tinkerbell's soft fur.

"We've got to get ready for bed, Tink. Five will be here too soon."

The chime on her phone indicated a text had been received.

"I hope Layla isn't cancelling," Danielle said to Tinkerbell.

"Hey Danielle. I'm going to be in town next week for session. Would you want to grab a bite on Thursday for lunch?"

Danielle had been surprised at how much she enjoyed her time with James, two weeks prior. She felt at ease in the conversation, and she appreciated that he really listened to her concerns about the burdens on social workers. After they had closed-down Café Moxo, Danielle had given James a ride - just two blocks to his downtown apartment where they talked in her car for a half-hour more.

She wasn't shocked that James was still single. The newspaper articles made a point to emphasize the laser-focus he had about his career. And his future was promising. If she lived in his district, she would have given him a vote.

However, she recognized with his good looks and his power he probably had many women who would long to share his last name. Danielle, on the other hand, had no plans of marrying. She was six when her parents divorced. Although that made the split final, there were problems long before the papers were signed. Yet, she speculated, it would've helped if her mom and dad had spent time together. As busy trial lawyers for two different firms, they worked long days and nights, and Danielle had consecutive nannies until she was old enough to stay home alone.

Once, when she was five, she remembered her parents taking a trip to Hawaii. When they came back, their relationship seemed refreshed and as glowing as their tans, but neither lasted. They fell back into the same grind at their jobs, and as her mom advanced, making partner in her firm, animosity grew in her dad's heart.

Neither parent had offered her a loving attachment, and she didn't really have any happy memories as a child, but she found life even more difficult when her mom moved out. Her dad tended to take his anger and frustration out on her, especially when he drank too much. And when her mom remarried a few years later, she rarely saw her daughter. No, marriage was not for Danielle. She had enough drama at work.

Did she want to see James again? She had told him in the restaurant that a second date would be fine, but after their half-hour conversation in the car, all of the information she wanted to share about social work reform had been covered, at least in a brief overview.

Pulling up her daily calendar, she saw that she had an appointment to take a client to the doctor's office at eleven-thirty. That made the decision easier.

Sorry James. I have an appointment during the lunch hour that day.

James sat at his computer, in his new Springfield office at the Stratton building. The more important and higher-ranking politicians got offices in the capitol itself, but being a rookie, he got the leftovers. Not that he minded. He was still in the honeymoon stage with the job and even a closet-sized space with his name on the door he found thrilling.

After two weeks in Naperville, legislative sessions in Springfield began. In the first three days, he learned a lot about decorum. Unfortunately, he accidentally reversed the order of operations of who to address and how to ask a question when taking a turn on the floor. He was thankful the correction from the Speaker of the House was gentle when they went on break.

Not as surprising was how many bills were required reading. When he spent time at Capitol Hill during an internship years ago, he saw the representatives go through masses of legislation. Now he was covering over two-thousand bills-including ones to increase minimum wage, raise salaries for state employees on maternity leave, and give low-income families more financial assistance for college.

Some bills he found dull, but others were ones he believed in. James hoped to be a champion for the education system and its reform. However, as he listened to Danielle talk two weeks prior about the demands on social workers, he had been given a glimpse into a different realm where he could enact change. Afterall, that was why he wanted to be a politician. Maybe he was naïve, but he believed he had the power to transform things that were broken.

The dinner at Café Moxo had been surprisingly nerve-wracking for the usually cool and collected man. Danielle had grown up to be strikingly beautiful. It was her eyes. Kind, welcoming, lovely turquoise blue with long lashes. Whenever he thought about her, which was often, he thought about her eyes, followed closely by her countenance. She was still as poised and confident, just like he remembered from the debate team.

Part of him tried to push away the thoughts. He didn't have time to date. At the last Patton family Sunday lunch, he was relaying the commitments he had for the week to his mom, and he reflected again that he didn't have time to go chasing a relationship. Yet, every night his feelings fluctuated when he flipped on the lights at home, and the stillness engulfed him.

James had been lonely before. In college, when others were out partying on the weekends and he was in his room studying, he felt the sadness of being disconnected from the life he heard echoing outside his door. Sure, he had friends, but they were in their rooms hitting the books too. Once he graduated, he found much of his free time spent at board meetings, and with the weekly Sunday lunches at his parent's house, he no longer seemed so solitary.

However, he could be in the same space with dozens of people and feel anonymous. There was a difference between knowing others and being known. And, now more than ever, it weighed on him.

Of course, his mom wouldn't approve of anything, or anyone, that took his eyes away from his position. In the past, they both agreed that politicians' families suffered because of the long hours the job required. But James rationalized that getting reacquainted with a friend from high school was a long way from settling down, and his mom didn't need to know *everything* he did.

When Danielle said she had a lunch appointment, he decided to stay in Springfield an extra night so he could see her for dinner. Somehow, she had agreed to a Chinese dinner, even though he had to ask twice. Now all that was standing between him and an egg roll was a quick video for his YouTube channel. Each week he intended to update his constituents on issues concerning their welfare. His stomach rumbled, and James decided an order of cashew chicken would go well with his appetizer.

Chapter Eight

Danielle pulled down the driver's side visor and slid open the light-up mirror. She dabbed at the places where her mascara had run as she had driven to the restaurant. It had been a hard day. When she arrived at Layla's tiny rental house, the front doorbell was broken, so she knocked to no avail. Even though she knew it wasn't the best idea for her safety, she wanted to make every effort to see if Layla was home. That meant a trip to the backyard to try the patio door.

Booker's gray pit mix was tied up on a stake, and as he lunged and barked, Danielle wondered how long the steel chain would hold. After five more minutes of rapping, she resigned herself to the fact that Layla was missing another therapy appointment, which made three weeks in a row of lost progress.

Later in the afternoon, she had an appointment with the Worthington's and Nevaeh. As Danielle held Nevaeh and read her a story, she noticed the girl's long lashes and how her thick, black hair looked so pretty tied up in the blue ribbon at the base of her neck. The little girl continued to warm up to Danielle, yet she wished the Worthington's were having the same success.

Unfortunately, Nevaeh continued to act out in their home. She wouldn't get near Steve Worthington, even though he had done nothing to harm her, and their freshman son, Aiden, was feeling neglected because of all the time they were putting into caring for Nevaeh. This brought a strain on the family's relationships.

The Worthington's weren't sure if they could handle the load. Danielle tried to reassure them that things would improve as Nevaeh felt assured of their love and stability. But they still said to look for a back-up, in case it didn't work out. She knew that would be detrimental to Nevaeh. Too many changes in placement really affected a child's ability to bond long-term.

Danielle felt discouraged, and the tears she had been drying threatened to storm again. She had thought about cancelling dinner with James, but then she remembered that he said he was going to stay in town just for their meeting. Dabbing her eyes one more time, she took the keys and headed inside.

James was waiting for her at a table in the back of the dimly lit tiny restaurant. A young Asian waitress was talking with James as she approached. "I think it's great your parents are doing so well here," she heard James say as she sat down.

"Danielle, this is Hua. Her parents are from Beijing, and they are the owners of China Star."

"Nice to meet you," Danielle replied, extending her hand to the fair-skinned, dark-haired beauty.

"What can I get you to drink?" Hua asked politely.

"Water would be great."

Hua hurried away, and James got up politely to help Danielle with the sleeves of her winter coat.

"Thank you," she said as James walked back to his seat.

"My dad always helps my mom with her coat."

"Does he open her car door, too?" Danielle said, trying to keep the smugness out of her voice.

"Absolutely. He even helps her grocery shop and unload everything. But-" James paused, "he's not perfect. They have two wingback chairs in the master bedroom, and he clutters them with dirty clothes."

"Do you follow that example as well?"

"Absolutely not," he replied emphatically. "I am a neat-nick. If you visited my apartment here or my house in Naperville, you would find everything in its place. My clothes are organized by season and color, on space-saving hangers, of course."

"Of course," Danielle laughed. "You're a smart politician, who makes friends with everyone, holds open doors, keeps his house clean and helps ladies with their coats. You might be the most eligible bachelor in Illinois."

"Oh, I have flaws. Plenty of them," James said, taking a sip of his water.

"Yeah? Name one," Danielle challenged.

James looked around suspiciously. "You're not with the press, are you?"

Danielle looked at him quizzically. "What are you talking about?"

"I can't let the secret I'm about to tell you leak out."

"Well then, it must be good."

James brought his voice to a low whisper. "If one day I'm going to be president," he said with a little mischievous grin, "I can't let this reach the public. So, if I share with you one of my *many* faults, you have to promise not to tell anyone."

Danielle leaned in, and replied with a whisper, "I promise."

"Okay...I'm afraid of heights."

Danielle leaned back in her chair and laughed. "Why is that such a big secret?"

"Think of where I work."

"So?"

"The state capitol."

"I know. So?"

"Have you ever been in it?"

"Of course. Quite a few times. And?"

James continued in a whisper. "Politicians are the only ones that can give private tours of the dome. Did you know that the ground to the dome it's 361 feet high?"

"Have you given a lot of tours?" Danielle whispered.

"Not yet, but I've only been at the capitol for two weeks."

"What are you going to do?"

"I've been giving that a lot of consideration, and I've decided I'm going to spend copious amounts of time praying that no one ever asks."

Hua arrived with Danielle's water and took their orders.

"So how was your day?" James asked as Hua walked away.

"Pretty rotten."

"Anything a politician could have made easier?"

"Not today…unless politicians can mandate world peace, take away human selfishness, and remove all temptations that cause addiction."

"I only know one government that can do all that."

"Me too. God's." Danielle smiled.

"You're a Christian?" James asked with hopeful eyes.

"My roommate freshman year in college took me to some Cru events with her. Then, we started doing a Bible study with some of the Cru staff members and girls on our floor. It wasn't something that happened overnight, but I learned a lot about Jesus and His teachings that year."

Danielle heard abrupt laughter from a table near the front, and they both looked to see a group of four ladies enjoying their night.

"The summer after my freshman year, my roommate and I went on a mission trip to Guatemala. I wasn't welcome at home, so I was looking for things to do. I had changed my major that fall from pre-law to undecided, because I knew I didn't want to follow in my dad's footsteps. When I got up the nerve to call my dad and tell him, he explained very clearly that I was a disgrace, and he didn't want to see me again."

"Wow," James replied. "I had no idea your dad would do something like that. What'd your mom say to his reaction?

"You remember my parents are divorced, right?"

James nodded.

"Well, she and I don't talk much. I don't think she knew, at least for a while. She's never really been involved in my life. Never wanted to have kids. But I was a surprise. Not a very welcome one, though. I guess I could've stayed with her and my stepdad that summer, but since we don't really have much of a connection, there was nothing to go home to."

Danielle rubbed the edge of her glass. "So, I was in Guatemala playing with orphaned children, putting on skits and playing games with them. I loved every minute. But one night, after we were all done with our nightly Bible study, I went outside and sat on a bench outside the building where we were staying.

I looked at the dark sky and reflected on God's character. If He was real, why would He put children in families where neither a mother nor father wanted them. That particular day at the orphanage, one of the young girls took a liking to me, and she wanted me to hold her the whole time. My heart broke for her, but I also was shaking my fist at God."

James was so engrossed in Danielle's story, he didn't see Hua approaching with their food. Hua slid the plates onto the table and asked if they needed anything.

"Anyhow, making a long story short," Danielle continued after Hua left, "I had carried my Bible outside. After I wept for a while, I opened it. Guess where it landed?"

"Where?"

"Though my father and my mother forsake, the Lord will take me in. Psalm 27:10. It's become a life-verse, and that night I prayed that God would take me in. He's been my mother and father ever since." Danielle gave James a warm grin and continued on as if she had not just shared such a powerful story. "Our food's going to get cold. Do you mind if I pray?"

When Danielle finished, she unrolled her napkin and took out a fork.

"That is a powerful testimony. It makes me wish my own was more interesting," James said.

"You were probably born into the perfect Christian family," Danielle replied with no hint of malice.

"Not quite. My parents are Christmas and Easter attendees. I had a neighborhood friend invite me to his church for a back-to-school-bash when I was in sixth grade. Then I started going to his youth group on Wednesday nights. Sometime by the end of junior high, I decided to ask Jesus Christ to be my Savior, and I've been following Him ever since, albeit imperfectly."

"Albeit! That's an obscure word," Danielle laughed.

"I'm talking with a former scholastic bowl teammate. I can throw in my big vocabulary."

"Is that how all politicians talk?"

"No, but the bills read like a dictionary at times."

"I saw in the paper that you were a lawyer before you became a representative. I bet you'll keep up just fine."

"Thanks for your vote of confidence. The job certainly provides me with extensive amounts of reading material."

Hawk was looking at videos on YouTube while Chewy slept on his lap. The couch was their favorite place to rest after a long day of transcribing. Hawk wished it was warmer out, so he could move his body more. Sitting all day at work and then sitting all night made him feel restless.

He hoped that March would be warm, and he could get to work on all the backyard projects he had planned. Sometimes the inactivity in the winter made him want to get a gym membership. But the twenty-four-hour place where he used to work out in the wee hours of the morning when no one else was there had closed.

All the more reason to get to the country, he thought. The sooner that dream could be actualized, the better. Then, even in the winter, he could be working in his large work shed he already drew up plans to build. Cold weather didn't bother him, and he didn't even mind shoveling snow. He just didn't like people.

"Chewy, look at this," Hawk said pointing to a picture of an outdoor trellis on the screen. "Don't you think that's the perfect design?" He jotted down a note on the pad beside him.

Hawk looked at his watch. It was eight o'clock, and the snow that had fallen earlier in the afternoon needed to be removed from his drive. He didn't want Danielle shoveling it again. The last two snowfalls she had done his driveway because he hadn't made it outside before her.

The sky darkened almost three hours earlier, but he never risked being outside when she would get home from work. He wanted to avoid conversation at all costs.

"Chewy, I'm going to go shovel," Hawk said as he rose from the chair, the cat gracefully glided to the floor in the process.

Chapter Nine

"So, you have excessive paperwork, there is a high turnover rate, there are limited opportunities for advancement, and there needs to be more ongoing training as well as more safety measures put in place for home visits." James looked down at his notepad. "Did I get those last few points down correctly?"

"Absolutely. Good summarizing," Danielle replied.

The restaurant had quieted as the four ladies left, and Danielle and James remained sipping chamomile tea while talking about reform for social workers. Danielle had hoped James wouldn't be bored by the conversation, but he seemed engaged, almost energized, while they talked about the changes that could be made to help the struggling system.

"Wow, I can't believe it's almost nine o'clock," Danielle said, looking at her watch. "What time do you have to be back in Naperville tomorrow?"

"I probably should get going," James replied reluctantly, shutting his notebook.

"Since you carefully avoided the question like a good politician, I'll sadly assume that means it's going to be an early morning."

Sheepishly James shrugged. "I've got a nine a.m. meeting."

"Yikes," Danielle replied. "You've got a three-hour drive in the morning."

"This was worth it," James said sincerely, grabbing the paper bill left in a brown plastic tray on the table.

"Why don't you let me get that? It's the least I can do for taking up so much of your time talking about my own interests."

James put the bill in his pocket, to take to the front. "I've got it. It's been a pleasure reconnecting with you, and I thoroughly enjoyed listening. I only wish I could've heard more about your journey since high school. We still haven't really caught up," James continued.

"I'm sorry about that."

"Nothing to be sorry about. I hope that means I can see you again. I don't have many friends in Springfield, and it would be nice to have one here."

"Well-" Danielle said with reservation in her voice. "It's just that I'm so busy all the time with work. And I know you are too-"

"But even two workaholics have to eat," James grinned making his left dimple appear.

"And they also have to sleep," Danielle replied. "Tonight, I'm keeping you from that."

"Time with you was a good trade."

"You're very sweet," Danielle said politely as she stood up. "Thank you for dinner, and I hope you have a safe trip tomorrow morning."

Danielle wished she had all-wheel-drive, and she said a silent prayer that roads would be less icy in the morning for James' drive back to Naperville. During the day, the temperature had warmed to above freezing, but as the night fell, the thermometer dropped, causing layers of ice to form on the roads.

As she waited at a stoplight, she thought about how her dinner with James had taken her day from awful to exceptional. Maybe if he wasn't such a gentleman, she would change her mind about being the marrying type. But her dad was nice, too, just like James. Only his cordiality was the kind a chameleon would wear. Dan Davison would change colors to fit his environment.

Danielle didn't want to reflect any part of her phony father, but she couldn't help carrying his name. When she was born, her mom decided to name her after her dad. Danielle figured that even back then, her mom didn't have time to care enough to come up with something more creative.

Sometimes she wondered if her dad was still drinking too much, or if he had found someone else to verbally berate now that she was gone. What had puzzled her was why he was so welcoming to everyone in public, but in private he was a serpent with a poisonous tongue.

Maybe it had been bad before the divorce, too. It was hard for Danielle to recall. After the divorce, Danielle became Dan's pin cushion. He was always sticking her with mean comments. "You're not smart enough to take that class. Why didn't you get an A+? That shirt looks horrible on you. You're worthless. Only salutatorian? If you hadn't come along, your mother wouldn't have left me. It's because of you that she doesn't spend time with either of us."

After her trip to Guatemala, and her new relationship with God, Danielle began to take all that hurt to her heavenly Father. He led her to a good Christian counselor her sophomore year. By the time she graduated with her bachelor's degree, she knew she wanted to help children who were wounded like she had been.

She also knew that God's love was strong enough to heal and restore her broken spirit, and she was thankful she saw many children go through the same transformation in her years at the Department of Children and Family services, but she still didn't trust "kind" men. Too much could be hidden behind the friendly façade.

The light changed from red to green, and as she eased forward, she felt her tires spin. The car worked to grip the ground, and it finally found its traction. If she *did* like nice guys, James would be at the top of her list. Handsome, outgoing and smart, he was a man that was going places in life. She wished that she had gotten to hear more about how his past shaped who he had become, but she didn't have time for a casual friendship.

As she rounded the bend onto her street, she made sure to take the curve slowly. Almost hitting Hawk had been enough of a scare. Her headlights illuminated Hawk's driveway as she turned the wheel to the left, but what was that on the ground?

Putting her car in park but keeping the lights pointing towards the drive, Danielle stepped out and immediately heard curse words intermixed with cries for help.

"Hawk," Danielle exclaimed as she saw him writhing in pain in the middle of his driveway.

"Call an ambulance," he gasped between groans of anguish.

Danielle ran back to her car to grab the cellphone she had left in her purse. As she hurried back, she dialed 911.

"My neighbor fell on the ice," Danielle said calmly. All her training dealing with intense situations paid off in moments of

72

crisis. "Address? 31 Wydown Lane," she replied briskly, looking at the number of the front of Hawk's house. As she hung up, she knelt next to Hawk. "Do you have a blanket in your house, or should I go get one from mine?"

"On the couch," Hawk panted, half gesturing with his hand towards his house.

Danielle walked briskly to the front door, but found it locked.

"I went out the back," Hawk yelled. As Danielle started to head that way, Hawk grunted, "Don't go in my backyard!" he exclaimed, and then let off a string of curse words.

"Okay," Danielle replied calmly, "I will go get one from my house."

By the time she arrived back at his side, he was shivering and sweating at the same time. His head was against the icy concrete, and Danielle could see that his right leg was contorted. Carefully lifting up his head, she put one blanket under it, and she covered his body with a large, lilac comforter.

"How did this happen?" Danielle asked, kneeling again at his side. Tears streamed down his face, and Danielle wished she had her purse so she could get a tissue to wipe them. Pulling up a corner of the comfort, she dabbed the moisture from the hairline around his ears, where the tears were pooling. In pain and embarrassment, he let out a string of cuss words.

"I was shoveling. I fell on the ice. I think I fractured my patella."

Danielle was momentarily silenced by his word choice. Then she recalled that the patella was your kneecap, and she wondered why he knew the name of the bone.

"Could you call my mom?" he asked, still shivering and panting heavily.

"Sure. What's her number?"

Hawk gave her the digits, and as she dialed, they heard the wail of a distant siren. Covering the mouthpiece, Danielle asked, "What's your mom's name?"

"Suzanne," he groaned aloud, moving the parts of his body that weren't on fire to relieve the part that burned.

As the call went to voicemail, Danielle spoke, "Suzanne, this is Danielle Davison. I am your son's neighbor. We want to let you know that he fell on the ice, and I've called an ambulance. He thinks he fractured his patella…kneecap. Once I know what hospital they are taking him to, I will call again and let you know."

She hung up and asked, "Can I pray for you?"

"What for?" Hawk cried.

"Peace, relief from pain?"

Hawk just panted.

"Heavenly Father, I thank you that you are with us right now. Would you please give Hawk peace right now? Would you help the workers and doctors take good care of him? Please help him know you are near, and that you love him. Amen."

The roar of the siren became nearly deafening as the ambulance rounded the corner and pulled partially into the drive. After they loaded Hawk onto a stretcher, Danielle told him she would meet him at the hospital, but he cussed her out and told her not to bother. She gave the emergency technicians a pitying look, and as they shut the doors, she noticed the ambulance had drawn a small crowd. After Danielle told Joanne and the neighbor across the street all that she knew, she finally took her car out of park, and drove into her own icy driveway, thoroughly exhausted.

Chapter Ten

"With all due respect, Representative Patton," Kevin Banks said as he leaned across James' desk, "fossil fuels are not a problem for the environment. Those statistics are cherry-picked by people who are pushing an agenda."

"Thank you for sharing your opinion, Mr. Banks," James replied. He was tired from the almost five-hour drive home. The icy road conditions meant that traffic was moving slower than normal, but the time with Danielle had been worth it.

"I trust you won't be throwing any power towards these new proposals to make Illinois essentially a solar-powered state by 2050?" Banks asked.

"Mr. Banks, is there a specific policy you're here to contest?"

"Every one of these inferno proposals," he said, throwing a stack of papers onto the desk with force.

"I can assure you, Mr. Banks, that I have read each of those, and I will be weighing the facts."

"You do know that we pumped $100 million into the last presidential election, correct?"

"Yes," James replied calmly. "I am aware that the oil and gas industry has strong interest in the choices that are made by the state and national government."

"I'm here representing thousands of jobs in this state. Keep in mind, if you place a vote for change, you will wipe out ten to twenty-five percent of the petroleum companies' jobs by doing so."

"How so, Sir?"

"By incentivizing alternative fuel choice, the demand will go down, and we won't be able to employ the same number of workers. There will be lay-offs, son. I guarantee it."

James' phone buzzed. "Mr. Patton, your ten o'clock appointment is waiting."

"Thank you, Wanda," he replied.

"I'd be happy to hear more of your thoughts any time Mr. Banks."

Kevin Banks leaned back in the chair and lowered his voice. "Son, you know Harshaw Petroleum would be happy to sponsor any fundraiser you'll be doing in the next year or so for your next campaign. Would you like my secretary to call you, and we can start setting one up?"

"No thank you, but I really appreciate the offer."

"Son, you had first-time donors and your Grandpa's money for the last election. You're not going to be able to succeed without big companies stepping in and giving you a hand."

"Well, Sir, I'm working right now to serve the people during my current term. I'm not concerned with the future. It will take care of itself."

Banks pounded the desk with his fist. "Patton, don't burn bridges. Someday you might need the path."

It had been a food day at Danielle's office, as was tradition the first Monday of every month. At the end of the day, each social worker picked a number out of a hat, and the person who drew the highest number got to take home the leftovers.

Danielle drew a ten. As she carried two bags of Olive Garden leftovers, snickerdoodles, butter cake and pumpkin muffins, she wondered what she would do with all the food.

Her heart's response was to share it with Hawk. He had been home for two days, and she had wanted to check on how he was doing, but she couldn't muster the energy. It was hard enough to have a job that required so much emotional stamina, but now to have a neighbor with needs, it was overwhelming.

"*God*," Danielle prayed as she set the food on the top of her car and opened the back door, "*Why me? Why did you place me right next to this man?*" Danielle's threshold for receiving insults and curse words was high, but she was not immune to feeling frustrated.

"*He's never kind, and to be honest God, because you already know my every thought, I don't like him very much. I'm tired. I'm tired of the cold days and dark nights and all the needs around me. I'll take this food to him, if that's what you want, but could you please show me your purpose here?*"

As she pulled into her driveway, she saw Hawk had a car in his. She had never seen him have a visitor of any sort. Maybe he's getting home healthcare, she thought. Putting her phone in her pocket, she grabbed a bag of leftovers and walked over to his house.

A petite, dark-haired woman in her fifties answered the door after the first knock.

"Hello," she said warmly.

"Hi, I'm Danielle, Hawk's next-door neighbor. I brought him some dinner."

"That is so nice of you. I'm Suzanne, Ethan's mother, please come in. I've been meaning to thank you."

Danielle tentatively stepped inside. She surveyed Hawk's living room, or was his name Ethan? The room was neat and tidy, although it was not well decorated. An old, brown couch, chipped coffee table and a small flat screen television took up the floor space.

"Can I take those for you?" Suzanne offered.

"Sure, I was just going to drop them off. I don't mean to intrude."

"You're no intrusion. You are an angel," Suzanne gushed, taking the two bags from Danielle. "I can't begin to tell you how grateful I am that you found Ethan last week. You saved his life."

"I don't know about that," Danielle replied, stifling a giggle at the extreme statement.

"Truly," Suzanne continued, "It was so cold out that night, and Ethan said he tried to pull himself back inside, but he was in too much pain. He was afraid he would pass out. If you hadn't come, he could have frozen to death."

"How is he doing?" Danielle asked, noting he was nowhere to be seen.

"He's resting in his bedroom right now, but I'm going to tell him you're here. Can you believe they already want him up and walking? I mean, not without crutches, but they want him to move the knee, even just a little bit, to help the healing process," Suzanne said. "Why don't you sit down? I'll go get him."

"Oh, that's not necessary," Danielle said, wishing she could make a swift exit. She had no desire to spend extra time with Hawk.

"I'm sure he'll want to thank you," she said scurrying down the hall to what Danielle presumed was his bedroom. As

Danielle waited for Suzanne to return, she surveyed the room with a keener eye. There were no wall decorations, but he had a stack of books by the couch. She sat down to get a closer look at the books as Suzanne burst back in.

"He's coming," Suzanne said happily, standing in the doorway.

"Hey," Hawk said tentatively, hobbling in. He handed his mom the crutches and he eased into the big Lazy Boy chair at the corner of the room. His mom pulled over the ottoman and put some of the couch pillows on in for his leg to rest on. Just sitting down caused him to break into a perspiration Danielle noticed. She also noted "Hey" was the politest thing he'd ever said to her.

"How are you feeling?" she asked.

"The pain is not as bad as it was the first few days, but it still hurts like-" Hawk stopped himself, in the company of his mom and Danielle. "It hurts."

"I'm sorry to hear that," she replied. "You'll have to just keep taking your pain medication as prescribed to keep it under control."

"That's what I keep telling him," Suzanne interjected as she stood behind Hawk's chair. "But he doesn't want to get addicted so he's not taking it as often as he should."

"Well, if you are worried about that, then that probably means you're extra aware, and you should be fine," Danielle said.

"So, was it a broken patella, like you thought?" Danielle inquired, noticing a brown-colored cat slinking into the room.

"Yes," Hawk replied. "Luckily it was a non-displaced, closed fracture, and it didn't require any surgery. I've got to wear this thing," Hawk said pointing to his knee brace, "for four to six weeks. Physical therapy will start somewhere around then."

"I plan to stay here at his place for a few weeks," Suzanne interjected. "I know he won't like it so much, sharing a place with his mom again, but he needs the help."

"That's really nice of you," Danielle replied. "Will you have to take time off of work?"

"Unfortunately, I can't. I work as a customer service manager at Walmart. Unless I want to take personal time, I just can't request a two-week break."

"That's too bad. How will you get around when your mom is at work?" Danielle asked, looking at Hawk, and trying not to stare at his face. It was the first time she was so close to him, and he wasn't moving away.

"I'll manage," he grunted.

Suzanne shot him a frustrated look. "Since Ethan works from home, he won't have to take much time off. I think he'll start working half-days at the end of the week. Isn't that right?"

Hawk nodded.

"What do you do?" Danielle asked curiously.

"I'm a medical transcriber."

"Oh," Danielle replied brightly. "So, you listen to doctor's notes and type them up?"

"Basically, yes."

"He could have been a doctor," Suzanne said, rubbing Hawk's shoulder. "He has always been very gifted. How about you, Danielle. What do you do?"

"I've been a social worker for the Department of Children and Family Services here in Springfield for the last nine years," she said as the cat jumped up onto the couch and laid down against her side.

"That's Chewy. Short for Chewbacca," Hawk said. "If you want him to get down, just nudge his back."

"No, he's fine," Danielle smiled.

"No wonder you are so kind," Suzanne said. "Anyone who works with troubled children surely is. And I want to thank you for helping Ethan. Even before his accident, I heard that you were raking leaves, shoveling, that kind of thing."

Hawk narrowed his eyes at his mother.

"Thank you for coming to his aid, calling the ambulance and letting me know about the accident. You have been such a lovely neighbor, and I'm really thankful for all you've done."

"You're welcome," Danielle said, scratching Chewy behind the ears.

"Would you like to join us for dinner, since you were kind enough to bring it by?"

"Oh no, that's okay. It's all yours."

"Well, then would you come over on Friday night, so I could cook a meal to thank you properly?"

"That's a thoughtful gesture, Suzanne, and I thank you, but it's not necessary."

"Oh, please, do come," she said with hopeful eyes and a pleading voice. "It would mean so much to me."

Hawk shifted his hip and gently moved in the chair. "I'd take her up on the offer. She hasn't cooked for me in years. We're an "eat-out" kind of family. So, this is kind of a big deal."

Danielle smiled inside. She felt a shift in Hawk's attitude towards her, just like she often felt with her clients. He had finally shared a whole sentence of dialogue and usually that would indicate the beginning of a fresh relationship.

"Okay," Danielle replied, thinking in her head that she would rather say no, but she was about to say yes. "I would be honored to try out your home-cooking, Suzanne. Thank you for the invitation. I should be done with work by five-thirty. Is there anything I can bring?"

"Just yourself, sweetheart. Thank you again for stopping by and bringing dinner. We really appreciate it." Suzanne looked at Hawk, as if to tell him to chime in his thanks.

"Thanks," he replied, getting the hint.

Chapter Eleven

The Worthington's kitchen was pleasant. Six white chairs lined the oval table, like soldiers. Debbie had a plate of homemade cookies in the center, and she returned to the table carrying a kettle of hot water. Danielle had chosen a lemon-ginger tea bag, and it sat in her cup waiting for the steaming liquid.

"I could never have imagined that this sweet-looking little girl could be so hard to raise," Debbie sighed as she sat down across from Danielle.

"What are the biggest daily challenges with Nevaeh, Mrs. Worthington?" Danielle asked, pouring a scoop of sugar into her cup and stirring lightly.

"You're supposed to call me Debbie, remember?" she insisted. "Well, she's still having night terrors, so I'm not getting much sleep."

"I'm sorry to hear that. It has to be hard to be sleep-deprived. Does your husband take a turn getting up with her, or is she still not allowing him to get close?"

"The latter, I'm afraid. And that's so hard for Steve because he always wanted a girl."

"What type of things are you doing when she wakes?"

"We put a rocking chair in her room, and I'm holding her. Rocking her. I try to tell her gently that she's okay, that she's safe. Of course, this is after she runs around the house screaming because of the night terror. Thankfully, my husband doesn't mind wearing ear plugs, and our son took his brother's room in the basement, since he's away at college."

"I have to commend you, Debbie. You are doing everything so well. It may not feel like it, but you're certainly showing patience and genuine love for Nevaeh."

A tear trickled down the side of Debbie's nose. "Thank you, Danielle. Your encouragement means so much. There will be moments where I feel like things are getting more stable, but for every break-through there seem to be ten steps backwards."

"That's normal, Debbie. Right now, you're building trust with Nevaeh. Every time she falls asleep in your arms as you're rocking her back to sleep, you're showing her you care for her. That you're consistent and stable. You're earning this relationship hour by hard hour, and the gift you're giving her of being able to attach with an adult is the best thing you can give this sweet child."

Debbie took a sip of her tea. "I wish that my husband and son could hear your words. I know this has been difficult on them too."

"What do you think could make it easier for them?" Danielle asked as she cradled her cup.

"I think our son, Dylan, could benefit from some time with just me and Steve."

"How would you feel about using respite care so you could do that?"

"That's where Nevaeh goes with someone else for a short time, right?"

"Yes, like a day or a weekend."

"I think that would be good. I just wonder if Steve and Dylan would like it too much, and not want Nevaeh back."

"What about Steve? What would help him?"

Debbie sat back in her chair and the February sunlight streamed in the patio door. "I don't know. Maybe finding something that he and Nevaeh could connect on. Something so he feels like he's making a connection with her. She's always clinging to me and won't be alone with him."

"Maybe you could play a board game and Steve could be her partner. He could give her high-fives. That would be a way to incorporate some physical touch that is non-threatening. Or, he could try to read her a book. Even if she won't sit with him, she may be listening even if she acts like she's not engaging."

"Those seem like doable suggestions. Thank you, Danielle."

"We're thankful for dedicated foster parents, like you Debbie. Thank you for all you're doing to see Nevaeh through this process. The love you're giving her is a selfless act."

"How are things going with her parents?" Debbie asked warily.

"Well, you know they've not been showing up for their mandated visits with her. Occasionally, Layla will go to a counseling appointment. She's doing just enough to hang on, but I'm not sure if she'll turn the corner and make the changes to get Nevaeh back, or if she will end up signing her rights away- intentionally or unintentionally."

James was frustrated. Banks posted on a social media page that the young politician was close-minded and wouldn't listen. He tried not to get caught up in nay-sayers' opinions of him, but a friend happened to come across the comment and forwarded it. Usually he wasn't pulled in, but he had foolishly gone online to read the comments for himself.

As he ate a bowl of wheat bran, he stared at the screen of his laptop and thought of all the retorts he could make on Banks' page. A blinking ad for Valentines' roses popped up on the side of the screen and he thought of Danielle.

She had turned down two chances to meet again. First, he had asked her to go to dinner on a Tuesday, when he was in session, but she said she had too much work to do. Then, he had asked if she would go to a Junior Blues hockey game on a Wednesday night, the following week.

The Blues organization had given tickets to all the representatives. He ended up going alone and sitting by the "other James" as he called him mentally. Jim, from District #12, wanted to talk about hunting and fishing all night, neither of which James knew much about.

Why did it bother him so much that she had turned him down, and why was he so drawn to Danielle? The three-hour drive back to Naperville each week gave him plenty of time to ponder those questions.

During the last drive home, he thought about the loneliness he had been feeling. It had been over a year and a half since he dated the ever-driven Amanda. He had met her at a presentation on the role of government in America at a university in downtown Chicago. They both had stayed after to talk with the speaker, and then they ended up sitting in the college café for another two hours discussing their views on every major political topic known to man.

Yet, Amanda desired a career path that would require long working hours, just like his. Her passion was to become the president of a university, and she decided to go to graduate school to get a doctorate degree in education. They parted easily, and James rarely thought about her since.

So, what was it about Danielle that would cause him to lose focus on his job when he was headed right up the ladder he had always wanted to be on? James thought about the way her eyes sparkled with life, her smile. But it was more. It was her kindness. Her heart for the broken. Her devotion to making a defective system better.

Most importantly, she shared his love for God. Some of the women he dated in the past had too, but they had been too shy, too timid, too relaxed. Too something. With the proposed projection of his political career headed upward, he needed someone who could keep up with him intellectually and spiritually. Danielle, he felt confident, could do both.

Over the years, James had developed discernment, and he knew whatever he was feeling for Danielle was not reciprocated. In college, he had fallen for Natalie Vitale their freshmen year. The red-head in his political science class had been full of fire mixed with equal parts of kindness.

Even though he had been pretty inept at flirting, he attempted it. Whenever he saw her in the cafeteria he made a point to go and talk to her, and he conspired with her roommate to pass the word along that he liked her. It didn't matter. Her roommate eventually shared that she just didn't like him "like that."

Thirteen years of life had matured him though, and he liked to believe he was a much better catch now. Even if Danielle didn't fawn over him like many women did on their first meeting with him, he knew never to underestimate determination. And on his last trip home, he had decided she was worth the effort he was about to make.

He didn't know how he would find time, but it was important to show Danielle that he desired to be her friend…and more. Valentine's day was only one week away, and he spent more than a few miles on the interstate coming up with the perfect gift.

"Come in, come in," Suzanne sang as she opened the door for Danielle on Friday night. "Let me take your coat. It sure is pretty."

Danielle wiggled out of the red coat and handed it to Suzanne. Hawk was seated in the same position where Danielle last saw him.

She laughed, "Have you moved at all this week?" Then she immediately felt bad. She wasn't sure how Hawk would handle the joke.

"As a matter of fact, I have been up and down the hall about ten times today," Hawk grunted.

"I can assure you, that is true," Suzanne said as she took Danielle's coat down the hall, presumably setting it on a bed in a spare room. Danielle scanned the room quickly and chose to sit on the couch. For a moment it was quiet, until Suzanne bustled back in. "I'm sorry we're going to have to eat in the living room. Ethan isn't able to get his leg propped up in the right position at the kitchen table, so we'll eat on tv trays." Then she scurried into the kitchen.

"We're fancy folk," Hawk said so straight-faced Danielle wasn't sure if he was teasing or not, until a small smile spread across his face.

"There's nothing wrong with eating in the living room. It just makes it more memorable."

"Are you always so positive about everything?" Hawk grumped.

Danielle paused for a second, looking up to the ceiling in thought. "Mostly...but I don't like waiting in lines. I get pretty impatient."

"I take it you're not a Black Friday shopper?"

"Well, you know you can shop online on Black Friday, and that doesn't require standing in line," she smiled at him. "But, to tell you the truth, I don't have that many people to buy for."

"Your list can't be shorter than mine," Hawk replied, shifting his weight with an unspoken groan.

"I don't spend holidays with my mom. She and my stepdad always travel at Christmas. My dad and I don't talk, let alone visit, and I don't have any siblings, so that leaves buying for myself and my co-workers."

"Yep, my list is shorter than yours. I only buy gifts for my mom."

"No siblings?" Danielle asked as she heard Suzanne banging cabinet drawers, looking for something.

"It's just me-as far as I know. My dad left before I was born, so who knows, I could have half-brothers or sisters." Hawk realized this was the longest conversation he had ever carried on with a girl since elementary school, and he began to feel nervous. What should they talk about next? Was she staring at his face? Why hadn't he trimmed his beard? "Dinner almost ready, Mom?" he hollered.

"Almost," she yelled back.

"Need any help?" Danielle shouted.

"Nope," Suzanne replied, sticking her head out of the kitchen. "I'm just putting food on each of our plates. If there's something you don't like, just don't eat it. And save room for dessert. I made my famous banana pudding."

"Sounds delicious," Danielle smiled. "Your mom is really nice," she said softly.

"Unlike her son," Hawk replied swiftly.

Danielle stayed silent.

"I might as well apologize now, since it seems like an appropriate time." He sighed and scratched at the top of his cast. "I am very sorry for all the times I was incredibly rude to you," Hawk said sincerely. "I know this won't come as a surprise for you, but I'm not much of a socialite. And to be honest girls like you-"

"Girls like me, what?"

Hawk hesitated and reclined his head against the faded maroon chair. "I don't know, girls like you just have never been genuinely nice to guys like me."

"What do you mean? Guys like you?"

"Oh, come on, the port-wine stain. The birthmark," Hawk said angrily. "It's quite obvious."

"I guess you assume all people judge others by outer appearance?"

"We all do, Danielle. It's impossible not to."

"What do you see then, when you look at me?" she asked, pulling one leg under the other on the couch cushion.

Hawk didn't know how to field that question. Should he tell her she was the most beautiful girl he had ever known? And not just because she was so pretty. That he wished, with all his heart, that his face didn't hold him back from trying to win hers?

He did the safe thing. He shrugged.

"Man judges by outward appearance, but God looks at a person's heart. You can judge me however you want to by the way I look, but your eyes haven't told you that I'm someone who's had to work through insecurity too. And, I probably know how you feel better than you think."

Just then Suzanne came in carrying a plate of food in each hand. Setting one on Hawk's tray and the other on Danielle's she said, "I'll be right back with mine."

Chapter Twelve

Hawk noticed Danielle stifling a yawn and wondered what he should say to break the momentary silence. When his mom told him about the dinner, he was adamantly opposed, but she coaxed him into agreement by promising to do all the work. Now he needed her to get back into the living room to make conversation.

As if on cue, she returned carrying a plate of food for herself. "So, Danielle, how do you like your new home?" Suzanne asked, as she sat down on a cushion away from her on the couch.

"It's nice. I love the kitchen. That's what sold me on the place. I do a lot of meal prep, so I wanted it to be a usable space."

"This is a nice little neighborhood," Suzanne replied, scooping mashed potatoes onto her spoon. "I was happy when Ethan moved and got out of his dingy apartment. How long have you been here, Ethan?"

Hawk set down his fork and balanced his plate on his lap. "Almost ten years."

"I was in an apartment before I came here, too. Paying rent got old, but my salary doesn't go far, so this was about all I could afford." Danielle pursed her lips. "I'm curious. Your mom keeps calling you Ethan, but our neighbor, Joanne, told me your name was Hawk. Is that just a nickname?"

"Oh, Ethan," his mom moaned. "I thought you were done with that ridiculous name." Suzanne turned to Danielle. "He came up with it in high school. He thought it sounded fierce."

"Mom," Hawk groaned, and Danielle stifled a laugh.

"Of course, then he stopped going to public school and finished his degree at home. So, I thought that name was done," Suzanne finished.

"I still like it," Hawk said plainly.

"Everything is delicious, Suzanne," Danielle said, changing the subject. "I especially liked the broccoli-rice casserole."

"Oh, I'm so glad. Ethan likes that too. That's why I made it."

"Thanks, Mom, everything is really good," Hawk said.

"So, what do you do besides work, Danielle?" Suzanne asked as she took a sip of her soda.

"Unfortunately, I don't have time for much else. I don't know how the social workers with families do it. Most weeks I work sixty hours, or more. But I do attend a great church. That's where I am Sunday mornings. Both of you are welcome anytime."

Suzanne and Hawk were silent.

"Do you attend church?" she asked casually.

"No," Suzanne said, quickly adding, "Not that I have anything against anyone who does. I just work retail, so I never really have the chance to go."

"And I don't believe in God," Ethan interjected gruffly.

"Well, you should come with me some Sunday morning. Everyone's really friendly."

As the room got uncomfortably quiet, Danielle switched subjects again. "So, how have you been juggling work and taking care of Hawk-I mean Ethan?" she asked, directing her question to Suzanne.

"So far, it's been okay, but I noticed next Friday I will have to work through the dinner hour. Would there be any way you could come check on Ethan after work. Just make sure he's okay?"

"Mom," Hawk objected. "I have a cell phone. I can call you if I need something."

"I know, dear, it's just that I would feel better if someone checked in on you since it will be my first nine-hour shift since your surgery."

"That's fine," Danielle replied. "I'll just do a quick check," she said looking at Hawk. "I'll make sure you're not sprawled out on the ground again without your cell phone," she smiled, hoping Hawk would sense her that she was teasing.

He gave a half-grin, which was enough for Danielle.

Danielle was spending Valentine's day eating lunch in the school parking lot, before going inside to meet with a child. As she ate her peanut-butter, honey, whole-wheat tortilla roll-up, she listened to some praise and worship music and thought about the dinner with Hawk and Suzanne. In a strange way she had enjoyed herself. She, woefully, thought she was going just to be kind, but as the hour passed, she found that the conversation flowed easily, Hawk actually laughed, and she wished that she had a mother like his. She was so warm and friendly and genuinely seemed to appreciate her.

Danielle had settled in her mind that her mom and dad just didn't have the capacity to love well, and through the years she had honestly come to forgive them. But waves of grief still came, and today they were breaking heavily.

Most days she tried not to feel sorry for herself. Every time she placed a child in a loving home or reunited a broken family, she felt a success, because at one point that could have been her. God, she resolved, used all circumstances for good, and because she knew what it felt like to be neglected, she was able to relate in some way to every child she met in the system.

Maybe Valentine's Day brought on the feeling of loneliness, she rationalized. The last time she had a boyfriend on this holiday was in college. But her most recent relationship had ended two years prior, when the ever-cheating Dylan left her for his latest obsession. Of course, two months later, he called to get her back. But she had finally had enough of the type she'd always been drawn to.

In the past, if a guy resembled her dad in any way- good looking, professional, outgoing- she ran. Instead, if a man would treat her rudely, put her down, or need to be saved, she would draw near. How many relationships had ended because she thought she could "win them to Christ?" but in the end they ran her into the ground?

She hadn't seriously dated anyone since Dylan, and work kept her busy enough to remedy any regrets. But on a day meant to illuminate loving relationships, she felt she had so few, and a deep despair filled her soul.

When her final appointment of the day finished, she headed wearily back to the office to type up case notes from the final three client meetings. As she entered the building, she saw her co-worker, Callie, leaving for the day. "Girl, you've got to check out your desk," she sang. "Some tall cute guy brought in a whole bunch of stuff for you. I didn't even know you were dating anyone."

"I'm not," Danielle replied, confused.

"You better tell me all about it tomorrow. I've gotta go, Robbie's taking me out tonight."

"Have fun," Danielle said as Callie pushed on the glass door to leave.

Danielle's heart did a flip-flop as she hurried back to her desk. There she found a wicker basket filled with shredded paper filling and three packages wrapped in heart tissue paper. A pink envelope was tucked into the side of the basket. Setting down her purse and bag, she plopped into her chair and opened the card.

You probably don't remember this, but when we were at the Scholastic Bowl meet, a group of us were walking down the hall to get to our homeroom. An elderly janitor was dumping a small trash container into a larger one on his push-cart. Some of the papers, tissues and water bottles fell out. We all kept walking, but you stopped to help him pick up the mess. That's the kind of heart you have. A special one. One that sees the needs of others. Today, I want you to know I see you. You're a world changer- one life at a time. Happy Valentine's Day. James.

Danielle felt warm tears well in her eyelids. She didn't cry easily, but words of encouragement were the fuel of her soul, and she had felt dry for so long.

Taking a deep breath, she opened the largest package. It held a coloring book and a tin of expensive-looking colored pencils. A note fixed on it said, "to relieve stress." Then she reached for the middle-sized gift. Inside was a clear jar full of scriptures typed out in different colored scripts and fonts. The note stuck to it read, "to feed you spiritually." The final package was the smallest one, about the size of a deck of cards. Quickly ripping open the paper, she discovered a cassette tape. Affixed to it was a folded piece of paper.

In high school, I always wanted to make a girl a CD. You remember those, right? Those discs with the compilation of cheesy love songs or favorite music someone burned for you? Somehow, you've brought that desire back to mind. This is to bring a song to your heart, and hopefully make you think of me every time you listen. P.S. I noticed you had a CD player in your car.

She smiled. Yes, her car was old enough to have a CD player, and now she was thankful she had hung on to the decrepit dinosaur for so long. She couldn't wait to pop the tape into the player on the way home.

It had been two-and-a-half weeks since Hawk's fall. He had cursed the patch of ice he slipped on many times since that night. As he sat in the Lazy Boy chair with his leg propped up, he relished the quiet. With his mom's presence came more noise. She was up early, puttering around the kitchen and turning on the television. Then, when she came home from work the same thing would happen.

After so many years on his own, he had become accustomed to his independent and quiet lifestyle. Plus, she was overbearing. Suzanne was always wanting to make sure he was keeping his leg elevated and asking if he was icing it as often as the doctor said he should.

Hawk wondered if she would have been a helicopter parent, had she been given the opportunity. Suzanne always had to work one or two jobs to make ends meet, so he was at daycare or home alone often as he got older. But he never doubted her love, and she gave it freely and easily, for which he was grateful. She was the one constant in his life.

Yet, for the last week, Hawk couldn't get Danielle out of his mind. She wasn't like anyone he'd ever met. How was it that she made dinner in his living room seem like the greatest night of his life? She had laughed at his jokes, and she seemed to genuinely enjoy the time with his mom. Not that that surprised him. His mom was really nice. It made him wonder how he had become so mean. But being called "purple people eater," "prune face," and "beast" jaded a person. In elementary school students said he had a constant case of "alien-cooties" and anyone he touched would scream and ask to go wash their hands.

In junior high, he was slammed into a lot of lockers, tripped, and joked about- sometimes behind his back, but more often it wasn't even that discreet. Then in high school there was isolation. Everyone seemed to have a clique, or at least a friend. He had neither and the loneliness was worse than the name calling. Withdrawing from the world became his answer. And it had worked, until now.

Now he had a stirring in his heart that called him out of his cave. The dinner with Danielle gave him hope, and her statement that she too had insecurities made him wonder if she could look beyond his appearance.

When Valentine's Day came, he seriously considered sending her flowers, but he couldn't muster up the courage, even though he debated it every fifteen minutes all day long. She will be coming over tomorrow, thanks to his mom. At first, he was angry that Suzanne had asked, but then he realized he could spend a few more minutes with Danielle. The hard part was coming up with a reason to make her stay.

Chapter Thirteen

We had a great day today. There were no night terrors last evening. She got plenty of sleep. It's amazing how that makes a difference for everyone. Nevaeh even gave Steve a high five before she left for school. I think we're making progress, and it feels good.

Danielle smiled at the text she received from Debbie Worthington. Wounded kids could adapt. They were resilient, and they could even learn to love again. While she savored the good news about Nevaeh, she was saddened that Layla and Booker continued to skip their drug treatment program on Monday nights. Booker wouldn't participate in the anger management classes he was assigned to and neither could show proof of employment, even though Danielle had attempted to take them to two job fairs and four interviews.

She looked at the glass jar on the corner of her desk, and she remembered that calling James to thank him was on her mental to-do list. With the amount of time she spent on the phone with clients, she had come to dread phone calls. But she loved the gifts. On the way home from work, the night before, she had listened to the mixtape. Two of her favorites, *Everything I Do (I Do it for You) and Kiss From a Rose* were on it, plus eight other "oldies."

He liked her; she was sure of that. However, Danielle couldn't allow herself to trust him. He was too much like her father, at least on the exterior. Right now, the tree looked green, but just as the seasons changed, the leaves would too.

However, the gifts were incredibly timely. She felt seen, and it had been a long time since she experienced that. Picking up her phone, she typed in James' name until his number pulled up. Hitting the call button, she waited for him to answer.

After six rings it went to voicemail. *Hi, this is James Patton. I'm sorry I'm unable to take your call. Please leave a message, and I will get back to you as soon as I am able. God's blessings on your day.*

Danielle waited for the beep. *Hi James, this is Danielle. I just wanted to thank you for the very thoughtful Valentine's gifts. I colored in the coloring book while I listened to some praise and worship music last night, and it was really relaxing. I have the jar of scriptures on my desk, and the mixtape is great. Thanks again. Talk to you later.*

Hawk dropped a pill on the kitchen floor, and then pushed it with his foot so it would glide under the cabinet. Then he cussed. He hadn't realized his floor was covered with cat hair. Having Danielle retrieve his medicine seemed like a good plan, in theory. Now his mom would have to get it for him.

He only had fifteen minutes to come up with a new idea to get Danielle to stick around once she came to check on him. Wracking his brain, Hawk realized if he put the canned cat food on a top shelf, he would need help reaching it. But how would he get it without hurting himself?

Filled with a moment of impulsiveness, Hawk decided to pull over a chair and stand on it. Then he used his good leg to step onto the chair's bottom, balancing all his weight on his good leg. Once the cat food was moved, he jumped down, jarring his good leg on the floor. Groaning in momentary pain, he was glad that risky move hadn't gone south. It had been dumb, and he knew it.

By five o'clock she hadn't arrived, so he turned on the television as a distraction. He had scripted a few questions he could ask her, to make casual conversation, and he went over them in his head. Having so little experience with someone from the opposite sex, he felt heightened anxiety. He hoped the undershirt he was wearing under the flannel top would absorb any perspiration.

Hawk heard her car pull into her drive at five twenty-five, and within a minute she was knocking on his door. He shouted to her to come in.

"Hey," he said as she opened the door.

"Sorry I'm late. I got a call from a foster family right before I was trying to leave," she replied as she entered the living room.

"Your job is pretty demanding," Hawk replied timidly.

"Yes, but it's Friday, so hopefully the weekend will be without any major crises, and I'll be able to relax."

"What do you do for fun?" Hawk asked casually, proud that he was able to think of an impromptu question.

"Well, I like to exercise, or read. Watch movies. Lately I've been coloring," she laughed.

"Coloring?"

"Yeah, in one of those adult coloring books, with the complex designs. It's relaxing. You should try it."

Hawk raised an eyebrow. "Do I look like the coloring type?"

Danielle giggled. "I was just thinking since you're stuck in a seated position for most of the day, it would be something therapeutic."

Danielle pulled at the neck of her coat. Hawk saw she was getting warm.

"You can take off your coat," he said gently.

"Oh, I'm not planning on staying. Just here on your mother's orders to check to see if you needed anything."

"Actually, I do need something," Hawk interjected. "Chewy needs to be fed, and I can't reach the cat food."

"I'd be happy to help," Danielle said, taking off her coat and setting it on the back of the couch. "Where do you keep the cat food?"

"It's in the kitchen," he said grabbing the crutches by the side of the chair and pulling himself to a standing position.

Danielle entered the kitchen first and was impressed by its cleanliness. "Is this your mother's handiwork, or do you always keep your home so neat and tidy?"

"My mom is a slob," he chuckled.

"How do you manage?" she asked, glancing at his leg cast.

"I can balance pretty well on one leg, and the crutches help. Plus, I'm supposed to be moving the joint."

"So, where is the cat food?" she asked politely.

Hawk nodded his head to a top cabinet, and Danielle dutifully opened it. Standing on her tiptoes she still couldn't reach it. So, she did what he had done…pulled over a chair. Hawk regretted the task, now seeing that she could fall. Thankfully, she managed to grab a can without any trouble.

"Okay, where's Chewy's bowl?"

"Over there," he said, pointing to the far corner where two bowls sat on a padded mat. "Would you mind filling the water bowl, too?"

"No problem," she said, striding towards the bowls.

"Danielle-" Hawk said.

"Yes?"

"No," Hawk said sheepishly. "I'm sorry I was just starting to say, Danielle, it's a nice name." After it came out, Hawk wished he had stuck to his scripted questions.

As she carried the bowl towards the counter, he saw her grimace. "I was named after my dad. His name is Dan, and let's just say he's not the nicest guy in the world."

"Well, I hope you have a nice mother then," Hawk said, leaning on his crutches, trying to recover the conversation.

"Not really," Danielle replied casually, as she opened the turkey and giblets dinner. "She didn't want kids. Neither did my dad. I was the surprise that ruined their marriage. She's remarried, and I see her once a year."

Hawk began sweating, even though he wasn't in physical pain. How could the conversation go so awry? He decided to try a compliment. "How'd you end up so kind?"

"Well, I'm glad you think I am. I seem to recall quite a few times that you couldn't stand me," she said as she looked down, dumping the food into the bowl.

"Have I said sorry for that?"

"Not that I can remember," she said, looking up at him with a mischievous smile.

"Well," he replied self-consciously, "I am. Really. You've been nothing but perfect-" he stopped himself, wishing he hadn't handed out such a forward compliment. "And, I've been nothing but awful. I'm going to try to keep my tongue under control around you."

"That I will appreciate." Danielle walked the food over to the mat and set it down. Then she reached for the water bowl as Chewy came slinking into the kitchen.

It was silent, and Hawk tried to remember what other questions were on his list. But Danielle filled the gap. "You told me once you weren't staying here long. Are you planning on moving after you're recovered?"

Hawk was surprised she remembered, but everything about Danielle surprised him. "That's the plan," he said, wondering how much he felt comfortable telling her.

"Where will you go?" she asked, turning on the sink and feeling the water with her fingers.

"There's a parcel of land about twenty-minutes west of Springfield that I'd like to buy. Ten acres. It's a beautiful piece of land. Little rolling hills, a brook running through it, it has a cornfield on one side."

"You must be a good saver."

"Let's just say, I've been setting aside part of my paycheck for many years to afford it."

"Have you always wanted to live in the country?"

Hawk hesitated. What should he tell her about his plans for the land? "For a good while, yes."

"How about you?" he asked. "Ever wanted to live in the country?" He hoped her answer would be affirmative.

"Well, with my work right here in downtown Springfield it wouldn't be very convenient, but the setting sounds really peaceful." Hawk was happy she wasn't completely opposed.

Danielle carefully carried the bowl of water to the floor, and after setting it down she declared, "I guess my work here is done. Unless there's anything else?"

"No, I think that's all. Thanks so much for stopping by. I obviously needed the help."

"Call if you need anything. You have my number, right?"

The nights had been long. James had hosted two town hall meetings, one on Tuesday night in Warrenville and the other on Wednesday night in Naperville. Then on Thursday he had back-to-back meetings until nine p.m. It was nice to be back in Naperville, but everywhere he went busyness seemed to follow.

As he drove home on Friday afternoon, the phone's Bluetooth registered it was receiving a call from his mom.

"You did a great job this morning on WLPR, James. I enjoyed listening to you on my way into work."

"Thanks, Mom."

"I thought you handled that question about the trouble with balancing the budget really well, and I learned something new. How come you didn't tell me you were on the committee for Adoption and Child Welfare?"

"I don't know, it never came up?"

"How'd you get on that committee? I thought you were trying to focus on education?"

"I am, Mom. You know I'm on the Higher Education Committee and the School Curriculum and Policies Committee," James replied as he maneuvered to the right-hand lane.

"Did you get appointed to it- the Adoption and Child Welfare Committee?"

"No, I'm sponsoring a bill."

"What?"

"It's come to my attention that the system needs reform, so I just wanted to help."

"How'd you get to know so much about social work?"

"Oh…you know…I'm good at talking with people, finding out the issues," James smiled to himself.

"Well, I'm just giving you some friendly, motherly, political advice. Don't let it get you sidetracked from where you're really trying to make a difference. You're looking to reform the school system. You want to be known for something. And you campaigned on that promise."

"Thanks, Mom, for the reminder," James said, trying to reign in his sarcastic tone.

Chapter Fourteen

James had been showering Danielle with small gifts for weeks- a new umbrella as the spring season entered with torrents of rain one week, a tulip-scented jar candle the next, and most recently a cup of chai tea and a cinnamon crunch bagel delivered to her work. James didn't do the delivering personally—Amazon boxes came the first two times, and a driver for Panera delivered her mid-morning snack and drink.

Callie, who had recently broken up with Robbie, gave Danielle a good ribbing for not dating a man who would show her such admirable attention. It's not that she didn't like the gifts, she did. However, she didn't sway easily. Besides thanking James with a text or two, she enjoyed the gestures, but she still didn't want a relationship with him.

Danielle had a stack of case notes to type up, but she needed to call Layla and see if she or Booker would need a ride to the visitation with Nevaeh. Danielle always hoped for reconciliation with the family, but she realized that this case was headed towards termination of parental rights. When Layla didn't answer, she tried Booker. Trying to communicate in all ways, she texted them next.

I just wanted to remind you that you have a visitation with Nevaeh today at 3:30 p.m. Since I haven't heard from you saying you'll be there or that you need a ride, I'm going to call the Worthingtons and cancel the appointment. Just remember I'm here if you need anything.

Swiping her phone off, Danielle felt sorrowful over what Booker and Layla were losing because of the control their addictions had over them. Then her mind wandered to her own parents. They had chosen their careers over her. In some ways it wasn't that different. She said the same prayer she often whispered when she was grieving. *God, please help Nevaeh and I both understand how You fill in the gaps where our*

parents have failed. Help us both to know You don't turn away.
Help us feel your love.

Hawk was tired of sitting, and he was bored with his own company. Three more weeks with a leg brace felt like an eternity. Now that it had been a month since his accident, his mom had returned to her apartment. That he celebrated, but after having her around coupled with a few visits from Danielle, the house felt quiet.

He had spent a tedious day of typing up notes for doctors with foreign accents. Then he moved to the Lazy Boy chair that had become his second home. With his leg elevated, he put in a small order to Eden Brothers for some products he needed for an upcoming outdoor project, and then he began searching the internet for the perfect design for his latest build.

With March only days away, he felt the itch to get outside. Working in his backyard was the only thing in his life that truly brought him joy. His knee injury would delay his endeavors, but only by a few weeks. Knowing that he needed full mobility for the projects he wanted to complete, he had diligently done his physical therapy exercises at home several times a day, making stellar progress.

After a half-hour of surfing the internet, he looked out the window to see if Danielle's car was in the drive. Now that it was light out past five o'clock, he could easily see by looking out the front picture window. Her car was not in the driveway. Even if it was, what would it matter? It had been weeks since his mom had her check-in. Hawk had her number, but he never could think of an excuse to have her come over.

God, if you're there, give me a reason to call Danielle.
Just then his smoke alarm chirped once. He sniffed the air. He

knew he hadn't turned on the oven, and he no longer had the space heater running in his office. Hawk used his crutches to get out of his chair, and he looked around the house. Nothing was out of the ordinary, and by the time he eased himself back into a sitting position it had chirped two more times.

A low battery, he thought. *Thank you, God*, he said silently, and then wondered why he was thanking someone he didn't believe in. Now, he hoped Danielle would get home quickly so he wouldn't have to listen to the annoying alarm for too long.

After thirty more chirps, Danielle's car pulled into the drive. Hawk wondered if he should let her go inside. He didn't want it to appear like he had been watching for her, so he waited another fifteen chirps, and then dialed her cell phone number.

"Hey, Danielle," he said as she picked up. "It's Hawk, your neighbor." Of course she knows that you're her neighbor he thought, wishing he wouldn't be so awkward.

"Hi Hawk, everything all right?"

"Nothing major. Just a blasted smoke detector. It's running low on battery power, and I can't reach it. I was wondering if you could come help me change the battery before it drives me bonkers." Hawk put his hand to his head. Bonkers? He wished he could talk with a woman.

"Sure, let me put on my shoes, and I'll be over."

Within minutes, Danielle was in his living room looking professional in black pants and a bright pink blouse. Hawk had never seen her with her hair pulled back into a ponytail, and he thought she looked adorable. He wished he knew how to flirt. How was he supposed to get across the message that he liked her?

"Oh my. That *is* annoying," Danielle said as she stared around the room looking for the culprit. "Where is the noise maker?"

"In the hallway," Hawk replied, "but you'll need to get the batteries. They are on the top shelf in the laundry room, which is in the basement."

"Just like mine," Danielle replied. "Is the entrance to the basement in the kitchen?"

"Yes," Hawk said. Then he realized he hadn't closed the blinds on the patio door. "Would you mind trying to see if you can stop the chirping by pushing the button in the middle while I go to get a screwdriver?"

"Sure," Danielle said, heading towards the hallway while Hawk went to the kitchen, first to shut the blinds and second to grab a small screwdriver from his junk drawer.

"Okay, here's the screwdriver. You should be able to get the panel off so we can put in new batteries." The alarm chirped loudly in their ears.

"I couldn't reach it, so I pulled a chair from your office in this way."

"That one swivels," Hawk replied. "You could get hurt."

"Nah, I'll be fine." Danielle stood on the swivel chair and twisted the screwdriver around the two small screws until they fell into her hand.

"Here, can you hold these?" she asked casually, handing him the screws. As she dropped them into his hand, her fingers brushed his palm and her touch sent a shiver up his spine.

Stepping down carefully, she handed him the tool. "I'll go get the batteries now. This way, right?" she asked, heading for the kitchen.

When Danielle returned from the basement with the batteries a few minutes later, she found Hawk out of breath from changing out the swivel chair with a kitchen chair. "You shouldn't have gone to all that effort. I would've been fine."

"No use risking both of us having broken knee-caps," Hawk said with a sheepish grin.

After Danielle finished changing out the batteries, the quietness in the house echoed success.

"Thank you so much," Hawk said as Danielle carefully maneuvered off the chair and began carrying it into the kitchen. "Could I interest you in a dark chocolate truffle? My mom got me a box on sale after Valentine's day. They are really good."

Hawk knew he was desperate to get her to stay, and he hoped she would bite at the offer.

"Well, usually I would pass on sweets, but dark chocolate is my favorite."

Hawk's confidence soared as he hobbled on one crutch to the pantry and retrieved the box. Opening it, he explained which pieces had which fillings. Danielle chose a dark chocolate ganache heart.

"How've you been doing these past two weeks?" Danielle asked as she bit it in half.

"I'm not in much pain, but I am very bored," Hawk replied honestly, dropping his guard for the first time since she arrived.

"Do you read?"

"A little."

"I have a few books I could loan you," Danielle replied as she finished the other half of the candy. "What type of books do you like?"

"Umm, all sorts," he said, not wanting to tell her about the stack of gardening and outdoor design books he had in his bedroom.

"I have a few Christian classics. One is by C.S. Lewis called *Mere Christianity*. It's really good," Danielle said.

Hawk bristled inside. He didn't want to be proselytized. If there was a God, He certainly didn't seem to care how he had been treated by others while he was growing up, but he'd do just about anything for Danielle.

"I could try it," he said gently.

"Great, I'll bring it by sometime."

James couldn't believe the first two months of his work as a state representative had passed. He only had three more months before the summer recess. However, he still had to make it through March, April and May, and he was already tired.

When he was in Springfield, he spent time catching up on reading bills, writing emails and working on legislation for the committees he was on. There were only a few other representatives in their thirties, and they liked to go to bars after work. That wasn't his scene. He wished he could have been spending time getting to know Danielle. Two months had passed since their date at the Chinese restaurant.

Looking back, James couldn't really call it a date. Afterall, it had been guised as a work meeting. And it had paid off with the proposal of HB 4401. House Bill 4401 would offer social workers paid time off for personal self-care. The committee he was spearheading was still drafting exactly what that would entail, but it would be a win for those in the field, and he hoped it would mean the retention rate of good workers would increase-if it could pass, come May.

He only wished his attempts at softening Danielle's heart were going as well as the legislation. After his gift-giving spree in February ended with no date to show for it, he decided to finally talk with his sister Kira about what to do next. She encouraged him to give it one more try.

So, with a resurgence of hope, he bought a postcard of the capitol at the gift store and sent her a message that he'd like to take her on a tour. Unfortunately, all he got in return was a text that said, *"Thanks for the postcard. It's really busy right now at work. I'll let you know if it lightens up. Danielle."*

It all reminded him of Natalie Vitale a little too much. He pressed, prodded, pursued and she showed no interest. He had almost decided to give up the chase, when an outstanding opportunity arose. Governor Kirkwood was hosting a small dinner party at his mansion in Springfield to talk about services for children in the community, and one platform he wanted to touch on was social work reform.

Governor Kirkwood had gotten word that James had sponsored a bill about that very same thing. James could invite one guest to help him represent his agenda, and he knew the perfect person to ask. He didn't think Danielle would turn down the chance to advocate for change in her field, so when he called to personally invite her, he was happy that her response was positive. Secretly, he hoped that their night together would be the step forward the relationship needed.

Chapter Fifteen

It had been two weeks since Danielle received the postcard from James, inviting her to tour the capitol with him. She told him life was too busy. Truthfully, her job had been more draining than usual. However, Danielle didn't want to admit that the gestures from James were more welcome than she let on.

So, when he called to invite her to the Governor's mansion to talk about social work reform, she didn't hesitate to say yes. She had never been one to turn down an opportunity to advocate for her field. The only problem was she didn't have anything to wear.

Danielle hadn't been shopping for months. She was a minimalist when it came to her wardrobe, and she tended to cycle through the same ten winter outfits until spring came. She rarely had time to shop or had the extra spending money. However, she wanted to dress for the occasion.

After visiting three different stores at the local shopping mall, she managed to find the perfect jade green dress with a fitted waist. On the Wednesday evening of the event, she left work two hours early to get ready. After curling her hair, then piling it into a stylish updo, she slipped on her new dress that emphasized her fit figure. Then she slid her feet into taupe high heels, and loaded up a small purse with lipstick, cellphone, house key, and a packet of tissues.

James was picking her up at five-fifteen, and she managed to be ready and waiting by the front window before five o'clock. When Callie found out why Danielle was taking time off, she teased her for finally agreeing to go on a date with James. Danielle countered that it was all business.

He had asked her to prepare a short speech emphasizing the challenges of her work and the high burn-out rate of good employees. Danielle had worked on the speech every night for the past two weeks, saying it over and over again until it was memorized. Not normally nervous, Danielle felt her palms getting damp as she sat on the couch in the front room. *God, you know I am anxious. Would you please calm my mind? Help me to be clear as I speak. Guide my words and help me use my voice for good. I'm leaning into you, and I need your strength. Thank you for your willingness to use me. Amen.*

When she finished praying, she looked out the window again and thought about James. It wasn't the first time in their two months apart that he came to her mind. She seemed to have constant reminders of him. When she opened the umbrella, burned the candle, or glanced at the scripture jar, she thought of his kindness. But one thing that kept Danielle from burnout in her job was being able to compartmentalize her emotions. She had decided James wouldn't take hold of her heart, so she rationalized she could think about him with complete detachment.

And think about him, she did. Every time she got a new gift, she would spend the precious minutes before bed scouring the internet. She read every article she could find about him and his campaign. And she even looked at all his photos on Facebook, particularly eyeing every picture with him and any females, wondering if they were past girlfriends with great curiosity. She thought about him far more than she admitted to anyone. He had found a way past her impenetrable armor, but she didn't even recognize it...yet.

As she looked out the front window, she saw Hawk's front porch lights go on, and she wondered if Hawk ever had a girlfriend. There was something unique about him. She still saw the purple-coloring on his face when she looked at him, but the marks and his mean tongue weren't the only things that defined him now. Danielle could tell he was trying really hard to make conversation whenever they were together, but that made him more likeable.

Two weeks prior, she had brought him *Mere Christianity* and a few other books. She wondered if he'd read them and made a mental note to check in on him when she had the chance. She was surprised that her heart had grown soft towards him, when he had been so ill-mannered towards her until his accident. But in the weeks that had passed, he had become gentle, friendly, and even kind, as she had stepped in to help him when he called.

At five-ten, James pulled into Danielle's driveway in a sensible, four-door, blue sedan. She waved to him, and wondered if that was too girlish, as he walked up to the house. He looked very handsome in a blue suit, brown shoes, and a white Oxford. With his brown hair styled in a fashion-forward cut, she knew that most of the single, female population would be happy to be on his arm tonight. James rang the bell, and Danielle asked him to come in while she put on her coat.

"You look stunning," James said sincerely as she reached for the formal, taupe-colored, spring jacket on the back of the chair.

"Thank you. You don't look half-bad yourself," she replied.

James helped her with the arms of the coat, and then asked, "Are you ready for tonight?"

"I think so, although I have to admit I'm nervous."

James looked at her with kindness. "Don't worry. Your passion will just bubble over. You can't contain it."

"I'm praying so," she said as she grabbed her purse.

"I prayed on the way over, too," James replied.

"I'm glad we've got the power of God on our side," she said as they exited the house.

Four hours later, James and Danielle found themselves in the exact same position as when they started, in Danielle's driveway. The dinner had been a fantastic success, according to James. Danielle had managed to win everyone over with her sweet spirit and creative ideas.

"Danielle, you were incredible tonight," James said as he put the car in park.

"Thank you. God was good," Danielle replied, feeling flushed from excitement.

She had felt God's presence all evening, and James had treated her with such kindness and respect, she hardly knew what to make of it. He had introduced her to every one of the sixteen other guests personally, and found something different, but flattering, to say about her each time.

"You really helped everyone understand why it's so hard to stay in the field of social work, and I loved how you shared so many personal stories of redemption within the system," James said.

"I'm honored that you invited me. You could have chosen anyone to accompany you. I think my boss was a little miffed that she didn't get the opportunity."

"Maybe someday she can come and speak to the bill committee," James said as he looked at the front porch lights of Hawk's bungalow. Danielle's house sat dark in front of them.

"Well, thank you again," Danielle said. The cologne James' wore lingered in the car, and she liked its clean, woody scent.

"I think we were the only two not drinking," James said, making light conversation.

"I never touch the stuff."

"Danielle," James began, his voice becoming serious. "If you haven't noticed, I really like you." Danielle had noticed, especially as he had made the most of steering her around the room with the palm of his hand on the small of her back during cocktail hour.

Danielle looked at James. It was the first time all evening that she truly took in his face. It was etched with pensive worry. Guys like James had never been her type. So, she was taken aback with how attractive she found him.

"I'm sorry," she said, continuing to look at him. "We've been together all night, and I have forgotten to thank you for all the thoughtful gifts and that postcard. I've really been using the umbrella a lot."

"Glad to hear it," James said with a smile, and his dimple appeared. "Speaking of the postcard...Do you think you would take me up on that capitol tour? I'd really like to see you again- without it being worked related."

"Oh, James," Danielle said uneasily, "I don't mean to seem uninterested-"

"But you are?" James questioned.

"I just don't date guys that are," she paused, carefully choosing her word choice, "so put together."

James leaned his head back and laughed. "That's a first. What do you mean?"

Danielle was thankful he hadn't gotten mad, and she played with the wrist strap on her purse. "I respect you too much to be anything less than honest with you. Especially when you've been so nice to me. It's just that my dad was a lot like you."

"And that's a bad thing?"

"In this case, yes."

"How so?"

"Let's just say in public he was very impressive, but in private he had a drinking problem and a serpent's tongue."

"He was verbally abusive?" James asked in bewilderment.

Danielle nodded silently.

"I'm so sorry," James said softly.

"I have a really hard time trusting men that have a polished, professional image."

"Danielle, I would never hurt you in any way. That's not who I am."

"And I believe you," she said sincerely.

"Then give me a chance to prove it to you. Please let me get to know you, and you can get to know me. You can see that I am the same on the inside as I am on the outside. Well, maybe a little less energetic on the inside… a little more pajamas and slippers."

"You sound comfortable," she giggled.

"I am," he said with enthusiasm. "Please give me a chance," he said, taking a gamble and grabbing her hands in his. "Let me show you I can be trusted."

Hawk saw Danielle leave with a gentleman in a suit and pull back in four hours later. He knew he had competition, and he wasn't happy about it. He had been reading the book Danielle loaned him. But when they took off, he pulled out his laptop and researched laser surgery treatment for his scars.

Hawk reasoned it was his only way of having a chance with a girl like Danielle. Even then, he didn't know if it would be enough. He was so awkward and clumsy around girls. Life as a recluse would do that to you, he figured.

Unfortunately, his research showed that his insurance policy didn't cover the procedure unless he had recurrent bleeding, infection, pain or ulceration. For a brief second, he thought maybe he could lie and say he had pain. But he was too honest.

Out-of-pocket treatment would cost over six hundred dollars per surgery, and he was apt to need three or more. For two weeks, after each session, he read that his skin would look like he had a plague, riddled with purple dots in the places where the laser pulsed over the birthmark.

Sessions needed to be spaced apart, but after looking at some before and after pictures, he thought he would look remarkably better after just two. Could he stay away from Danielle for two months? He knew he wouldn't want to risk seeing Danielle with purple dots all over his face. The pictures he saw of the after-effect of the laser treatment looked worse than his skin's current condition. Was he willing to risk the guy in the blue car being alone with her while he was away? And would his mom take him in for a few months, so he wouldn't run into Danielle?

Finally, was a purple-free face worth the set-back of his country-living dream? He was so close. All he had to do was put in a call to his real-estate agent, and he could have the acres of land he had driven by so many times before his accident. He knew he couldn't make a decision about the laser treatment until his physical therapy was over for his knee, and that wouldn't be for another six to eight weeks.

Sighing, he closed his laptop and picked up *Mere Christianity* again. He was already on book three, out of the four books included in the collection. He had been taking notes, with the hopes that he could talk with Danielle about his questions. Hawk didn't plan on changing his mind about God, but it would open-up an avenue for conversation with his beautiful neighbor and for that he was grateful.

James' downtown studio apartment, near the capitol, was sparse. He didn't need much. Afterall, he was only there for a few days out of each week and a few months out of the year. And most nights he wasn't home long enough to do much more than sleep-like tonight.

He had just brushed his teeth, and was scuffling down the hallway to his bedroom, when he heard the phone ring. He hurried to the bedside table, where he had left his cellphone. It was his mom.

"Where were you tonight?" his mom asked, with concern, as soon as he answered.

"Good evening to you, too."

"I called at seven-thirty," she continued as he sat down on the bed.

"I was at a dinner meeting at the governor's mansion, if you must know."

"Really? Why didn't you tell me? You always let me know your schedule."

"I know, it's just that I didn't think the topic would interest you."

"Everything you do interests me. You should know that."

"Well, you certainly are my number one fan," James sighed.

"So, why were you at the governor's mansion?" she asked, not skipping a beat.

"I was having a delightful chicken dinner and talking about children's services in Illinois."

"How come?"

James pushed his pillow up against the backboard of the bed and leaned against it. "I'm a young and upcoming member of the legislator," he said with a lilt in his voice. "Why wouldn't I be invited?"

"You weren't talking about that social work reform bill, were you?"

"Why are you so against it?"

"I'm not. I just think you're getting off the platform you campaigned on, and that could be dangerous."

"How could it be dangerous if I'm making changes that help kids, Mom?" he asked with annoyance.

"Your constituents elected you to do one thing and you're doing another."

"I don't hear anyone complaining but you."

Karen groaned on the other end of the line. "Oh…"

"What?"

"I just put it together," she said, as if the sun had just burst through a window. "Back in January, you were looking for a date. You told me about that girl. That social worker in Springfield. You're seeing her, aren't you?"

James mentally noted that his mom was sharp. "Well, Mom, the *young woman* has a name, and it's Danielle."

"Are you dating her? Is that why you're doing all this?"

"No, Mom, we're not dating. Although I hope to be someday soon. I am pretty happy to be giving her a capitol tour next Tuesday." He knew that last statement would get under her skin, but he didn't care. She was being unreasonable. Politics didn't have to consume every minute of his life.

"For the record," she said with a huff, "you're messing up the best thing that's ever happened to us."

"*Us?*" he questioned with frustration.

"Maybe if you spent less time chasing a girl, you'd have more wisdom on how to spend your time in office now that you're *my* representative."

James didn't know what to say, so he said nothing at all.

Chapter Sixteen

It had been two months since Layla's last visit with Nevaeh, and in turn, Danielle now expected her to try to "clean-up" again out of guilt. Some cases were like this. Back and forth the parent would go, into and out of the dark cave of addiction. Booker no longer attempted to meet any of the requirements needed to get Nevaeh back, and he told Danielle that he would sign his rights away if Layla did. But she hung on.

In the foster home, the Worthingtons were continuing to make progress with the kindergartener. Debbie had offered to volunteer in her classroom three afternoons a week, which seemed to help Nevaeh feel less anxious about being at school. And the night terrors only came after a visit with Layla, which caused Danielle to wish she would pick a path and progress-one way or the other.

As Danielle had gotten to know Layla, her heart went out to the wounded woman, as it always did in cases like this. Like a majority of clients, Layla had been abused by family members herself which caused insecurity, depression and low self-esteem. When Danielle saw how much pain was caused through the cycle of sin, she tried to rest her mind on the hope of heaven, for there she knew brokenness would end.

The mid-March weather had been so unpredictable. And the night before her capitol tour with James, Danielle stood before her closet deciding what to wear. They were meeting directly after work, which meant whatever she chose had to fit both occasions. Slimming light gray slacks and a pink sweater seemed to suffice, so she hung the outfit on the handle of the closet in anticipation of the day ahead.

Lying in bed that night, she had a hard time falling asleep. Her thoughts drifted to her senior year in high school. She had just found out that she had earned the salutatorian spot, and she couldn't wait to tell her dad. When he finally got home from work that evening, it was nearly ten o'clock, but she heard him come up the steps and her light was still on. He peeked into her room, and she told him the news. With her graduating class having over four-hundred students, she expected congratulations, but she should have noted his mood.

Over the years, she had become accustomed to pretending she was asleep, tiptoeing around him, or retreating to the basement when he had been drinking. But her excitement had clouded her judgment, and as soon as she finished sharing the news, she saw his glazed eyes. The verbal beratement that followed for not finishing first in the class, and being worthless, left her crying into her pillow after he slammed the door behind him. She knew he would be mad if she cried aloud, so she hid her sadness.

After her graduation speech, he put his arm around her while she wore her cap and gown. He told everyone who stopped to congratulate her that she was headed to be a lawyer, like himself, and he almost seemed proud. When she changed her major, and he cut her off financially and emotionally, it had almost been a relief. The separation it created allowed her to get unstuck from the destructive atmosphere that had come from living with him.

Now, she wondered if James would turn out to be just like her dad. Would he win her over with gifts and kind words? Were his looks of admiration only acts? How would she ever know if he could be trusted? She thought about cancelling their date, but Callie would give her a hard time. Danielle had already mentioned she was going out with him, and she would never live it down if she broke it off with the "most eligible bachelor in Illinois." She could always make up an excuse saying she had to help Hawk. Afterall, it had been too long since she checked in on him.

Hawk was beyond frustrated. He needed to get to work in his backyard, but his knee injury was holding him back. When he first took off the leg brace he had been in for seven weeks, he was shocked. He had lost muscle, and the leg itself looked shriveled. But the doctor ordered him to try to move the joint, out of the cast, three times a day for ten minutes at each session. At first, he didn't know how he'd manage, since his leg felt as straight as a board.

For the next week, he groaned and cursed through the daily thirty minutes of exercise, knowing it wouldn't get better unless he pushed through the pain. Then he started physical therapy, and the agony only intensified. At his first appointment he could only move his knee thirty-five degrees, which was like having a wooden leg. The doctor had warned him that the scar issue could impede movement, and Hawk found that to be true.

Now, at the end of March, all the backyard projects he had wanted to start when spring had sprung were put on hold since he couldn't bend his leg well enough yet. With only two-weeks of physical therapy behind him, he hoped that by mid-April he would be able to start his first project. It was a big one, and it was for Danielle.

He hadn't seen Danielle in weeks, but it didn't stop him from thinking about her- all the time. Yet, even after he finished *Mere Christianity*, he couldn't invoke the courage to call her. Having her retrieve the book would have been a good reason for a visit, but after seeing her with another man he felt his chances with her were slim to none.

Laser surgery to remove his skin discoloration *had* to happen, and after he told his mom about the plan, she was thrilled. Even if it meant postponing his land purchase, Hawk reasoned it would be worth it. The pain couldn't be worse than fracturing a patella, and the money to buy land could be earned back in a few months of transcribing.

Since he couldn't go into his backyard, he figured he would spend time sketching drawings of his plans for the upcoming project. He couldn't wait for Danielle to see it.

She had her hair pulled up into a bun, and wisps of hair draped her neck and the sides of her face. James didn't know what the style was called, but he liked it. Then again, he hadn't seen Danielle ever look anything but beautiful.

Work had been long but being with Danielle brought new life into his weary spirit. Banks was on the rampage again to destroy his character, saying he didn't care about blue-collar workers in Illinois because he was going to side with clean-energy acts.

And unfortunately, Banks' influence was wide-spread, especially among those with deep-pockets. James figured most of his voters were the ones with shallow-pockets, so he tried not to be worried. He had been visiting in the lobby with security-guard Robert, as he waited for Danielle to arrive at the Stratton building.

He had always been good at remembering people's names, and that made him popular with people in his building. When Danielle got there, Robert gave her a light-hearted ribbing for not being able to make it through the metal detector on the first or second try. And James apologized for him, as they made their way down the marble corridors to his office. The tour had to start there, he told her.

The H-shaped building was eight stories tall and held offices for numerous representatives and senators. James mentioned it was poorly constructed, and it had been on the demolish list for years, especially since it was riddled with asbestos, but the current budget crisis didn't leave any leverage for changes.

As they passed other workers in the building, James stopped to introduce Danielle to each one. They took the elevator to the fifth floor, and after passing the main receptionist desk, which was now empty, they came upon a tall, slim, black door with the name plate, James Patton, inserted into the silver metal grooves on the door.

"It's not a glamorous office," James said defensively as he opened it, revealing a small space with a large window, two brown bookshelves with diplomas, pictures and knick-knacks, a desk and two guest chairs.

Danielle gravitated to pictures. "Is this your family?" she asked, vaguely remembering his mom and dad from scholastic bowl meets.

"Yes. This is my dad, Myron, my mom, Karen, and my sister, Kira," he replied pointing to each one.

"And who is this?" she questioned, picking up another small picture frame from the shelf.

"That's my grandpa. He's a big reason why I'm here. He worked as a supervisor in a factory for most of his life, but he saved a substantial amount of money for Kira and me. I cashed in my nest egg to campaign."

"I'm glad it paid off," Danielle replied, setting down the frame. "You've met President George W. Bush?" she exclaimed, glancing at the next photo.

"I did an internship during undergraduate school in Washington, D.C. I met him then."

"And look at these diplomas," Danielle smiled. "University of Illinois in Chicago with a political science degree,

Northwestern University with a law degree. You certainly are on track to be the next president."

Danielle sat down in one of the black guest chairs. "I think I remember reading in the yearbook that that was your future aspiration."

James sat down in the swivel chair at his desk. "My grandpa always said, 'you can get your horses ready for battle, but it is the Lord that gives you victory."

"That's from the Bible isn't it?"

"Proverbs," he replied, feeling excited to be showing her his world.

"Well, I think that's enough of my office, now it's onto the secret tunnels."

"Not so secret," she laughed. "They connect this building to the capitol, right?"

"Aww," he replied with disappointment. "How did you know?"

"I've lived in Springfield for nine years. It's common knowledge here."

"But have you ever been in them?" he asked with renewed energy.

"Actually, no. This will be a first. Lead the way."

After they passed through the underground tunnel, James led Danielle into the capitol. He showed her where the House of Representatives met when in session and took her to the seat he used on the floor. Danielle had lots of questions about the box at his seat, and he taught her what the function was for each colored button.

She gave him a good teasing when she found out the legislature only met from January to May and then came back for a veto session in the fall. But he reminded her when he was back in Naperville, there were local issues to address all year long.

Next, he took her to see where the Senate met, then showed her the forty-foot tall painting of George Rogers Clark enacting a peace treaty, before taking her by the Governor's office. Although it was locked, she got to see which wing it was in and how large the doors were to the grand workspace.

"Now for the most special part of the tour," James said. "Please follow me." They rode the elevator up two floors, and when they stepped off, Danielle could see they were on the fourth-floor rotunda, where only staff members, elected officials, and their guests were allowed.

"This is spectacular," she said looking around and then up at the magnificent dome. Then she looked at his face and saw he was putrid and pale. "Oh James," she gasped. "You told me you were afraid of heights. I thought you would never-"

James took a few shallow breaths, trying to get his bearings. He stood right by the elevator door and didn't risk moving an inch. "I did say I would never give a tour up here, but something-or rather someone-is worth the risk."

Danielle caught his remark, but didn't know how to respond, so she pulled out her phone. She craned her head upward and took a picture of the dome. "Okay let's get you back onto land, sailor," she joked, as she saw beads of perspiration form on his forehead. They walked back towards the elevator.

As they traveled down to the first floor, James's cheeks began to color again.

"That was really nice of you," Danielle said, leaning against the wall of the elevator.

"I wonder if that's how I'll feel if I ever pop the question?" he chucked, and then regretted his choice of words. He already would have proposed to Danielle, had he trusted she would say 'yes.'

Danielle laughed. "Probably, but maybe your girlfriend will ask you. Then you will be spared the agony."

Deciding to take advantage of the topic, James questioned, "Do you want to be married one day?"

"Well, we certainly are taking our sweet time picking life partners, seeing we're both single and in our thirties. Why haven't *you* gotten married? After all you're like the most eligible bachelor in Illinois…at least that's what my co-worker Callie says," Danielle said blushing.

"Do you ever remember me dating in high school?" James asked as the chime indicated that they had reached a new floor.

Danielle thought about it as they exited the elevator. "No. Not really."

"You are correct. And did I date during my undergraduate years?"

"Um, no?"

"Correct," James said, as he placed his hand on the small of her back to steer her towards the doors he wanted to exit. "In college, I always told myself that I had to keep my focus on my grades, extracurriculars, things I was running. When I went for my master's degree, I met Lisa Jenkins. She was getting a law degree, too. We dated for a year. Then, we both agreed we weren't a long-term match. After that, there was the occasional short-term girlfriend. But I've never met anyone I could really envision a future with…until recently."

Danielle understood exactly what he was saying. She was shocked. He barely knew her. She didn't know how to respond, so she decided to throw him off the chase. "Well, to answer your question, I don't think I ever will get married. I've dated too many cheaters and liars to believe that any good men are out there. You may be one of them," she said to ease the awkwardness, "but I am content being alone. I can eat cereal for dinner or leave my shoes in the middle of the floor, or pile dishes in the sink, and no one will care. Being single has its perks."

"Sure," James said as they walked down the marble corridor, his hand still on her back, to one of the many exits in the capitol. "But if you're alone, you don't have anyone to marvel at the color of the sunset, or cuddle with when you watch a movie, or listen when you have a bad day."

"I've got a cat," Danielle laughed. "Tinkerbell cuddles with me when I watch movies."

"You're a tough case," James said as they walked outside into the cool, darkening spring evening. "I have one more surprise back at my office, if you'll follow me."

Chapter Seventeen

"What's all this?" Danielle asked, in awe, as they stepped back into James' office, which was now aglow with candles, and there was a meal laid atop the desk.

"Two months ago, you happened to mention Café Moxo's chicken and white bean chili was your favorite, but they didn't have it that night. I figured a good tour should end with a good dinner," James replied, holding the guest chair out for Danielle to sit down.

"But how did you get all this set-up?" she said, flabbergasted, sitting down.

"Let's just say the night janitor and I are good friends, and a box of Fannie Mae chocolates goes a long way, too." James smiled, bringing out that charming left dimple.

Danielle had never had a man go to such lengths for her, and it stirred her heart in a deep place.

"Crusty bread, butter, wine?" she said observing the spread.

"We don't drink, remember?" he said sitting down in the swivel chair across from her. "It's sparkling grape juice."

"Oh," she replied, recalling how he also turned down mixed drinks and wine at the Governor's mansion. "That's refreshing. I don't think I've ever met a man that didn't drink, at least socially."

"I like to be in control of my mind, and if I'm going to represent God, I want to do it well. Mind if we pray?" he asked, and they bowed their heads as he said a prayer of thanks for the food and their time together.

"If you don't mind me asking, do you think your dad would have been kinder to you growing up had he not had a drinking problem?" James asked as he ladled some soup onto his spoon.

"I don't mind you asking, and yes, probably. I think when my parents were first married, he just drank socially. He seemed to get worse as my mom started out-performing him as a lawyer. Her career kept moving upwards, and his stayed stagnant. That's when it became a daily habit."

"What kind of contact do you have with your parents now?"

Danielle began buttering a piece of bread. "I haven't talked to my dad in fifteen years." Danielle stopped talking and sat silently for a moment. "Fifteen years…wow. It sounds so long when I say it aloud."

"It is long. I can't imagine," James replied, empathetically.

"My mom and I talk occasionally. Our worlds are so different, it's hard to find things to talk about for very long, but I pray for her and my stepdad. Maybe someday they'll become Christians, and then we'd have that in common."

"Your mom and stepdad are both lawyers?"

"Yes, they are both partners in the firm they work for." Danielle brushed some crumbs off her lap. "Did you like being a lawyer?"

"I did, actually. There was such a wide variety of issues I dealt with. Special education, school safety, teachers' salaries. I never got bored, and I got paid a lot more than I do being a state representative."

"Really?" Danielle asked, wide-eyed. "I would've thought a state rep made good money. I should've looked it up," she chuckled.

"I imagine some representatives probably have political action committees that create special slush funds, but that's not my style. I try to live a good deal below my means, so I can continue to save money for my next campaign."

"You already know you want to run again?"

"I think so. Even though I feel like the government is a slow behemoth at times. I can see how wise leadership effects change for people."

"What would you do if you weren't a social worker?" James asked, scraping the sides of his bowl clean.

"Oh, I don't know. Maybe be a teacher. I love kids."

"And you don't want to get married!" James exclaimed. "It sounds like you'd make a great mom."

Danielle shrugged. "Since my own mom didn't want kids, and I was an only... I don't know.... There's some fear in the thought."

"I can see we are about finished with the main course, so it's time for dessert."

"Oh my, there's more?" Danielle said with a smile.

"Now you get to try one of my favorite things in Springfield." He pulled out a small, clear plastic box from a desk drawer. Then he walked around to the chair next to her and offered her the first selection. "These are macarons. The best cookie in Springfield. Made by our very own local bakery, Incredibly Delicious."

The macarons were bright, solid colors. Danielle chose a pistachio flavored one with a St. Patrick's Day green coloring. James chose a blue one, which he told her was chocolate flavored. After they each finished off two cookies, leaving two in the box, Danielle leaned back in her chair and sighed contentedly.

"That was a great meal. Thank you so much. This was actually very fun. Thank you for talking me into taking the tour."

"My pleasure," he said sincerely, pulling his chair closer to hers. He studied her face. It was happy, and that made him feel amazing. He reached for her hands. They were soft and smooth. He rubbed the top of them with his thumbs softly. "I'd like to make seeing you a regular thing, Danielle."

Her expression changed, and she looked pensive, but she didn't pull her hands away. "I don't know," she said thoughtfully.

"Could you see a future with me?" he asked, not concerned about his boldness.

"I don't know. Maybe," she said, surprising even herself. The words had come tumbling out.

James leaned over the arm of his chair and took both of her cheeks into the palms of his hands. He stared into her eyes with such longing that Danielle wanted to look away. His emotion seemed so intense. Raw. Then he brought his lips slowly towards hers with confident intention. Gently he kissed her. Pulling away, he looked at her again. Sensing her readiness for more, he kissed her again more deeply.

This time Danielle pulled away.

"All that for a maybe," she said breathlessly, eyes closed.

"I'm just making sure we're working towards a yes," he smiled, and stroked her cheek.

"I can see a future with you, Danielle," James said softly, as she opened her eyes. "I want this to be the beginning of getting to know every part of you, and then one day, if we were to be married, I would want to know *all* of you."

"Married?" Danielle said, taken aback.

James kicked himself for saying too much too fast. How could he reel back the conversation? It had been going so well. "That came out wrong," he laughed, nervously. "I just wanted to explain that I want to get to know you more, but I want to guard our purity, so you won't have to worry about any pressure from me on that front."

"Oh, okay," Danielle said, slightly uncomfortable at the turn in the conversation, but secretly liking James' character, as his convictions came forward.

Danielle felt a tingly warmth inside as they walked to the elevator. She linked her arm in his. As they waited for the doors to open, they were contentedly quiet, taking in this new thing that had burst forth like the first spring morning after a long, cold winter.

As they stood silently by his side, she realized there was plenty of physical attraction between them. She thought about how she had welcomed his lips moments earlier, and she wanted more of his touch.

The doors opened, and they stepped into the elevator. The building was quiet as they stepped out onto the first floor. Not even the night janitor came out from the shadows.

"When can I see you again?" James asked, as his dress shoes clicked against the lobby's marble floor.

"How long are you in town?"

"Till Thursday afternoon… Evening, if it means I can spend time with you."

"Tomorrow I have a home visit to do in the evening, but I'm free on Thursday."

"Then Thursday it is."

Hawk saw Danielle coming and going with the same good-looking gentleman that drove the blue car for two weeks before he got fed up enough to make a move. His physical therapy appointments had been going well, and his flexibility of motion had risen forty degrees. He was halfway to full mobility.

His therapist suggested that he practice walking outside on the cement sidewalks, with supervision, to get used to different surfaces. The suggestion was a perfect excuse to ask Danielle for help. Within an hour of texting the request, she sent a reply saying she'd be happy to walk with him sometime.

The kindness she repeatedly showed him was one of the reasons he had been seriously contemplating the Christian faith. Her countenance was so different from his own. After he finished *Mere Christianity*, he asked his mom to buy him a cheap Bible at Walmart, and he read the book of John. There he found these words, "Whoever comes to me I will never cast out," and he couldn't get them out of his head. Maybe because he had been discarded so many times before.

The last few months had been incredibly hard and full of pain. He had feared, at one point, that he would never regain his mobility. And he was tired of needing help, being limited in what he could do, and frustrated about the medical expenses. His life had never been easy. Growing up without a dad, worrying about his mom working so much to make ends meet, dealing with bullies, and now years of isolation had made the wall around him thick. But a part of him wanted it to crack.

The book of John talked about how Jesus was the light of the world. There was a tiny whisper in his soul that the Light was trying to make it through the cracks in his armor. He just wasn't sure if he wanted it to penetrate his whole being.

Danielle had agreed to walk on Saturday at dusk, since Hawk didn't like to be outside in daylight. It only made his birthmark appear darker, and if he wasn't desperate to see Danielle, he wouldn't have concocted an outdoor plan at all.

When Saturday rolled around, the day dawned bright and lovely, with temperatures reaching mid-sixties by late afternoon. Hawk spent all day in his backyard, and even with the slight restriction of mobility, he was able to start the project for Danielle and also get to two others on his list.

He had taken a shower, changed into jeans and a flannel shirt, and cleaned up dinner when Danielle rang the bell at seven-thirty. Hawk felt nervous when he took in the sight of her in slim-fitting jeans and a coral spring coat.

"The temperature's dropping fast," she said, seeing his long-sleeve shirt. "You may need a coat, too."

"I'll be alright. Moving my knee works up a sweat."

"Oh, I didn't think about that," Danielle replied from the door. "Do you need your crutches?"

"Nope, I've graduated to this," he said, pulling out a cane from behind his easy chair.

"I'll have to call you Grandpa Hawk…although that just doesn't sound right," she laughed.

"I guess it will have to be Grandpa Ethan, then," he replied walking towards her.

"I know you said you picked Hawk as a nickname in high school, but how come you've stuck with it all these years?" she asked, easing down the front step to make room for him.

"When you don't want people to get too close, using a name that sounds intimidating keeps them away," he replied as he shut and locked the front door.

Carefully he stepped off the porch platform and groaned slightly. "Plus, I don't like being out in the daylight, and birds of prey hunt at night."

Danielle chucked. "Well, now I have to ruin your theory. Did you know that hawks actually hunt in the daytime?"

"What?" Hawk exclaimed. "How can that be?"

Danielle shrugged. "I was on the scholastic bowl team in junior high and high school. You have to learn lots of little facts. It's a little like *Jeopardy*."

"Well, I guess it really is Grandpa Ethan tonight then," he laughed. Danielle realized it was the first time she heard that sound erupt from him, and she liked it.

"Well, Grandpa Ethan, it looks like your therapy is going well," she replied as they made their way, side by side, down the cement driveway.

"That ** spot," Hawk said, then realizing he cussed, retracted his words. "That spot is where I fell," he continued, pointing with his cane to the place where the patch of ice tripped him.

"I can't imagine how hard this winter has been for you. It's bad enough we had so much snow and cold weather, but then you also had to deal with being stuck indoors, too. Although, now that I say that, you don't really like to be outside, do you?"

"Actually, I love being outside. I just don't like being outside where people can see me."

"How come?" she asked as they started down the sidewalk.

"Does that really have to be explained?" he asked gruffly, feeling embarrassed for the first time since their walk began.

"Sorry," Danielle replied. "I should've been more insightful. I guess I've stopped seeing your birthmark when I look at you."

"Really?" he asked, shocked. "That's what my mom says, too. Although I don't believe either of you."

"No, it's true. I mean, I know it's there, I see it, but at that same time, I don't see it," she paused. "I guess that doesn't make sense. Maybe what I'm trying to say is that it doesn't define you anymore, in my eyes."

"Wow. How come?" he asked as they passed another small bungalow and the sky's deep pinks and purples painted the horizon.

"I don't know you well, but I've gotten to know you better, and that helps. You should let more people in. I think you'd find your mom and I aren't the only ones that can see past the exterior."

"Ha," he grunted. "You should've gone to my high school."

"I think they are all probably the same. You've got your eclectic mix of a bunch of teenagers with raging hormones and insecurities trying to see how they can fit in with one another. It's not the easiest place to be when you stand out."

"You've got that right," he replied, feeling a twinge of pain in his knee and wondering if they should turn back. He'd already overdone it in the backyard all day. But this was his chance to talk with Danielle, and he didn't want their time together to stop. "What would you know about standing out? You're the type of girl who always fits in."

Danielle put her hands in her coat pockets. "When you have a dad who's an alcoholic and your mom has virtually abandoned you for her job and new husband, you don't really feel like you fit with Suzy Stephens, whose mom stays at home and bakes chocolate chip cookies for the basketball team, and her dad is a pastor at a church in town. Plus, my dad was really restrictive with how much time I could spend outside the home socially, so I was mostly a normal nerd, at home with my books."

Hawk shook his head. "It's hard to believe that, but then again you did just spout out a fact about hawks," he laughed, and she did too.

"Maybe we should turn around," Danielle suggested. "It's starting to get dark."

"My favorite time of day," he smiled. "Just a few more houses, please," he pleaded.

"Okay, but I don't want you pushing yourself too much," she said, without knowing how much he had already done.

"So, did you finish *Mere Christianity*?"

"I'm glad you brought that up, because I did, and I have a few questions to ask you about it."

"Great. Ask away."

"They're actually written down in a notebook, back at home, so maybe we can do that another day?"

"Sure. What was your biggest take-away?"

Hawk paused. He wasn't sure how much he wanted to tell her. Something was stirring, and it wasn't just the light breeze.

Chapter Eighteen

Two weeks had passed since James had taken Danielle on the capitol tour. In those two weeks they had gone to a movie, knocked over bowling pins, browsed a bookstore, and went out to eat. Every night he was in Springfield was spent with her, and he couldn't recall when he ever felt so happy.

However, it was only days away from the busiest month in the legislature-May. There would be long days and nights, as bills would either live or die, so James wanted to take Danielle out one last time before it got too crazy.

He had pitched a date at Nick and Nino's, thirty-stories up the Wyndham hotel, with stellar views of the city and equally good food, or so he had been told by some locals. But she said she'd rather walk at Washington Park and then go for frozen yogurt.

While the initial vision of grandeur left his mind, he was glad she felt comfortable making a suggestion. His mom, however, was not so comfortable with their budding relationship, and she took every opportunity to tell him. James didn't offer information, but now that she knew that he was serious about dating Danielle, she pestered him at every turn.

She thought his focus on his new girlfriend took away from his ability to do his job well. He countered that she made him better, because he could talk through issues with her, and she offered him a new perspective. He thought, perhaps, his mom felt left out. There had been less time for him to take her calls, and he sensed she didn't like feeling out of the loop. James figured it was high time his mother began to take a different role in his life. He was thirty-four, and he had been ready for a change, even if she had not.

When their walking date at Washington Park rolled around, the afternoon showers gave way to evening rain. So, he texted Danielle to suggest a change of plans. *Do you want me to pick up some dinner and bring it to your place since it looks like we can't go walking? Oh, and what's your favorite frozen yogurt? I'll pick some up.*

At six-thirty, James was glad the downpour had lightened to drizzle so he could get out of his car with dinner and frozen treats without getting soaked. There was no way he could balance an umbrella too, so his hair would just have to suffer. He had never been vain but getting loads of pictures taken for the campaign had caused him to reconsider his image. That was when he had decided to go with a trendy haircut and upgrade his wardrobe.

"Come in, come in," Danielle sang as she held open the door for James, and he rushed inside. Taking the bags from him, she ushered him into the kitchen.

"Cute place," he said as he pushed his fingers through his damp hair to make it go back in place.

"Thanks, I guess you didn't really see it much the night you came to pick me up a few weeks ago."

"No, just the living room."

"Do you want a tour? It's about as clean as it always is," she said, setting the food on the counter and putting the frozen yogurt containers in the freezer.

After she showed him the two bedrooms, guest bathroom, and tiny office, they walked back to the kitchen. "There's a basement, too. The laundry room is down there, but it's kind of dark and dingy. It's unfinished, but nice for storage."

"It's a great house," James replied, sincerely.

"Thanks, it was a good upgrade from apartment living. I was tired of paying someone else rent each month. And, I guess after nine years, I figured I was going to settle down here."

Danielle had set two floral placements on the table, along with plates and silverware. Now she started to take the containers of food out of the bag.

"Did you ever think you were going to settle somewhere else?" James asked as he watched her retrieve the salads, breadsticks and circular silver tins of pasta and sauce.

"I guess. Maybe part of me thought that I might move back to the Naperville area, or Chicago. Bigger city. More to do. And I might have, if I had reconciled with my dad."

"Do you ever think that will happen?"

"I prayed that it would, for a while. Now, I mostly pray that my dad would come to know Jesus. I can't imagine having a relationship with him if he's still drinking so much."

"Has he tried to contact you at all through the years?"

"No, but I have written to him a few times. Once, I just felt like the Holy Spirit was prompting me to share with him how I became a Christian, so I wrote about that. And I wrote to him when I graduated from college, and then when I graduated with my masters."

"And he never wrote back?"

"Nope."

James and Danielle sat down, and he took her hands in his. After only a few meals together, they had become accustomed to saying grace together before they ate. Then James scooped salad into their bowls.

"Does your mom keep in touch with him?" he asked, stabbing at a crouton with his fork.

"Maybe? Although I doubt it. I guess I don't really know."

"How about you?" Danielle asked, wanting to get the attention off herself. "What's your relationship with your parents like?"

"Good," James said, wiping his mouth on a napkin. "I used to talk to my mom every day."

When Danielle's eyebrows went up in amusement, he clarified.

"It started when she helped me with my campaign, and it just hadn't stopped- until recently."

"Why has it stopped?"

"I guess I've been too busy," he said. "Although, to be honest, it had gotten kind of annoying to run my schedule by her all the time. So, I'm glad there's been a little more distance lately."

"Must be nice to have someone who cares so much."

"I should be more grateful," he replied. "I imagine you'd love a parent calling."

"Yeah, but maybe not *every* day," she laughed. "Do you talk to your dad, too?"

"Not as much. My mom relays everything to him. His job is busier at night, during the school year. But we try to get together, my parents and my sister and I, on the weekends for at least one meal."

"That's awesome."

"I think you'd really like my sister. She's a fifth-grade teacher, and she loves kids, just like you."

After they finished their meal, and cleaned up together, Danielle suggested they watch a movie. She pulled out a few classics and a few romances. Together they decided on *Princess Bride.* As they sat next to each other on the couch, James put his arm around Danielle, and she didn't retreat. Halfway through the movie, James noticed Danielle was no longer laughing at the funny parts, and he looked down at her head on his shoulder, to see that she was asleep.

As he studied her beautiful face, he felt so blessed to be with her. James had never been one to go for the cutest or most popular girl. He cared so much more about a person's character. But here he was snuggled next to the prettiest woman he had ever dated, and it filled him with thankfulness. He only hoped Danielle felt as happy about their growing relationship as he did.

"I fell asleep on his arm. I probably drooled all over his shirt," Danielle gushed to Callie. They had finished a meeting with the staff fifteen minutes earlier, but they had stayed in the conference room to talk about a case, and Callie had taken the opportunity to sidetrack onto Danielle's love life.

"So, what do you think about dating someone from the 'light side?'" Callie asked.

"Is that a *Star Wars* reference?" Danielle laughed.

"Yes, he's not from the 'dark side' like Darth Vader and all your previous boyfriends, right?"

"He's totally different than anyone I've ever dated. To tell you the truth, I don't know if I am really comfortable with that yet. I keep waiting for the 'shoe to drop,' you know? For him to show his real colors."

"Maybe these are his real colors? I mean, you're the same inside and out, right?"

"I guess, at least I try to be."

"So, it's likely he is too. What would prove it to you?"

"I don't know. I guess I need someone who's going to be there for me consistently. And I want someone who's going to treat me really gently. Just be really kind."

"Isn't that what he's doing?"

"So far, but we've only been dating for a few weeks."

Danielle heard her phone buzz and looked down. It was a text from Layla. She wanted to go to her counseling appointment tomorrow. Could Danielle give her a ride?

"I need to get back to work," she laughed. "I need to let Layla know I can give her a ride tomorrow."

"I thought Layla was on one of her 'off' streaks again?"

"She was, so I guess she's trying to get clean again. At least she's trying. Booker isn't doing a thing."

"I thought that was good news, though?"

"At least I don't have to deal with his cussing, his hot anger, and his threats," Danielle said as she got up from the table. "I just wished he had cared more about Nevaeh and put her interests above his own."

"How is Nevaeh doing?" Callie asked as they exited the conference room.

"Really well. Debbie is still volunteering in her classroom, and she has her on a good, structured schedule at home. It seems to help Nevaeh's anxiety if they follow it. The only hiccups come when mom has a visit."

"I get that. You remember my client, Chenelle, right? Well, the same thing happens when her mom actually follows through with a visit."

"It's a tough spot to be in. We want the parents to get better, but we want the kids to get better, too."

"Exactly. And it seems like these two things work against each other at times."

James had been driving for three hours, and he couldn't get to Danielle's house quickly enough. The Sunday lunch with his parents and sister had gone smoothly enough until Kira sidetracked them from talking about politics because she wanted to hear how things with Danielle were going. Of course, his mom had to repeat her overstated opinion that he shouldn't be dating. Kira came to his defense, but it didn't appease Karen.

No matter, he thought. He wasn't going to let the argument with his mom ruin his last night with Danielle. He had heard from the seasoned veterans that the days and nights were about to get long. James had two bills up for passage, and he was hoping they would pass so he could show his constituents he was a man of action.

The porch lights went on as he pulled into Danielle's driveway, and when she opened the door, he greeted her with a long, lingering hug.

"I missed you," he said as he felt her slender frame in his arms.

"You just saw me on Friday night," she giggled, pulling away.

"Yes, but I didn't see you last night," he replied.

"How are your parents?" she asked as they walked into her kitchen. She had a mixing bowl on the counter along with a bag of flour, sugar and a carton of eggs.

"Same as always." James crossed to her sink to wash his hands. "My mom wants to talk politics non-stop. Local. National. Doesn't matter. Gets old."

Danielle peeled the parchment paper from a stick of butter and put it in the glass bowl.

"What's your dad doing while she's talking politics?" she asked.

"Listening. But he'd rather hear about how Kira's classroom is running or talk about cycling."

"He likes to bike?"

James wiped his hands on the towel by the sink before coming over to stand by Danielle.

"It's a new hobby in the last couple of years."

James stared down at the recipe card on the counter. "Our last night together before May madness, and you want to make cookies," he chuckled. "Okay, so what do you want me to do?"

"Can you crack two eggs?"

"Sure, where do you want me to crack them?"

"Ha ha," she said without laughing. "That was bad."

James laughed. "I know. Get used to it. I'm known for my bad jokes."

"My mentor, Paul, was too."

"How'd you get paired with him?"

Danielle measured a teaspoon of vanilla extract and poured it into the mixture.

"When I first started, they put me with him to be my mentor. Now, we don't have enough experienced caseworkers to pair new employees. Callie, my best friend at the agency, was paired with me when they were still doing that."

"I'd like to meet Callie someday."

"And she'd like to meet you," Danielle said with a grin. "I need to find the chocolate chips," she said crouching down to open the drawers on the island.

She pulled up a can of pineapple chunks and set it on the counter, followed by a jar of jelly. Moving things around, she set a can of tuna on the counter before announcing she found the chocolate chips. Just as she did, Tinkerbell, who had been resting on the top of the refrigerator pounced onto the counter. As she sailed over Danielle's head, she hit the mixing bowl with her back legs, causing the buttery egg mixture to dump onto Danielle's hair and drip to her shoulders.

"Oh my," Danielle laughed, swiping the yellow goop off her forehead.

James stared at her in horror and then broke out into a broad laugh. "Why did your cat do that?" Tinkerbell spooked when she knocked the bowl, and she landed on the floor before slinking out of the room.

"She saw the can of tuna," Danielle said between giggles. "I'm going to go clean up," she said as she grabbed the towel off the sink and started wiping her hair.

When James heard the shower start, he began cleaning up the mess, and by the time she returned to the kitchen he had the recipe restarted. Seeing her in jeans and a sweatshirt, with her wet hair against her shoulders, he longed to take her in his arms again.

"Well, aren't you efficient," she smiled. "Thank you for taking care of Tinkerbell's disaster. Sorry you've got to see me like this."

"You're beautiful," he said sincerely. Danielle sat down on a bar stool at the counter and was pulling a brush through the back of her hair when it got stuck in a tangle. "Oww," she muttered.

"Here, let me do that for you," he said, taking the brush from her hand and beginning to tenderly comb out the problem spot.

"I guess I didn't get all the butter out of my hair after all," she sighed. She sat enjoying the soft movement of the brush on her scalp. "One of my nannies used to do this for me. Miss Brenda. She was my favorite."

"You had nannies?"

"Quite a few. My mom and dad worked so much when I was young, and I guess they thought that was better than a daycare."

"Did you drive them all away?" he teased?

"No, I was a perfect angel. Can't you tell?" she teased back.

"That I would believe."

"Miss Brenda was with me for a few years. I think I was five when she started and seven when she left. She got married, and she and her husband moved away. Something like that happened with each one. Maybe that's just how it goes with nannies?"

"All done," James said. He pulled her hair to one side and gently kissed her neck. He swiveled the bar stool so they could face each other. Leaning towards her, he drank in the floral scent of her hair as he pressed his lips against hers. Losing all train of thought but the moment, James burned with passion. He didn't know how long they would have stayed there, had it not been for Tinkerbell.

She jumped onto Danielle's lap, and she laughed. "I guess Tink was getting jealous of all the attention I was giving you."

James brushed a loose strand of wet hair away from Danielle's eyes.

"I love you," he whispered.

Booker and Layla had moved. That was not uncommon with clients who dealt with addictions. Landlords could only handle so many months without receiving rent until they got fed up and kicked the tenants out. Danielle typed the new address into her phone's mapping system.

As the calm, female voice fed her directions, Danielle prayed for the conversation she wanted to have with Layla. How could she motivate and encourage her? Help her realize she'd be better off without Booker's control and fellow-addiction problems?

"Turn left on twenty-first street," the voice of the GPS dictated.

Danielle's thoughts then went to James. It was May first, and he sent her a May Day gift basket, filled with candy and flowers. It had arrived at her office in the morning, along with a note about how happy she made him. And it was signed "love James." He had said the words aloud the night before, and she hadn't returned them. But he didn't seem phased. Maybe he knew she couldn't. Or wouldn't.

"In five-hundred feet turn right at Lowell Avenue," the voice interrupted. *"Your destination is on the right."*

The little rental house was in a rough part of town, and with it being so nice out, there were many neighbors on their front porches. As Danielle put the car in park, she noticed two men smoking on the steps of the neighbor's house. One looked particularly tough, with a sleeve of tattoos and muscles that showed, thanks to his white tank top.

For some reason, Danielle's heart began to race, and apprehension filled her body like a rushing, white-hot fire. That was abnormal. She always walked tall and kept her eyes on the job at hand. She didn't engage hecklers, and she prayed profusely. She wasn't usually nervous, even in situations where she probably should be.

Looking at the clock in her car, she saw she was right on time. Layla should be ready to go. As she opened the car door, she slipped her cell phone into her pocket before locking the car doors.

Walking up to the front door of the dilapidated, small white bungalow, the men on the porch began shouting to her, and a dog began barking. *Hey good lookin'. Why don't you come over here? We'll buy your girl scout cookies.*

Danielle prayed. *God, please help me. Protect me and keep me safe.*

Danielle rang the doorbell, but it didn't appear to work. Then she knocked. The heckling and barking continued. *Hey baby. They're not home. Come over here. We'll help you out.*

Danielle heard a still, small voice.

Leave.

She ignored it.

Making a snap decision, she decided to head to the back. She always tried the back at their old place, and once Layla was there but hadn't heard the knock at the front. While she walked around, she noticed a third guy come out on the porch. Bigger than the other two, but quiet, he didn't enter the shouting competition.

The quiet, inner voice came again. *Turn around and go.*

Danielle shook it off and kept going. As she neared the backyard, the barking grew louder. Keeping her focus on the back door, Danielle noticed out of the corner of her eye that Booker's pit bull was making the racket. He was tied up on a stake, like before, but he looked skinnier than usual.

He growled and bared his teeth when she walked onto the cement patio, but he was a good ten feet away. Danielle just wanted to get this visit done. Before she had even knocked once, she heard something snap and the pit bull charged at her, tearing the leg of her pants, and knocking her over.

"Help," she cried out. "Help! Help!" She shook the pit bull off her leg and tried to stand up. The dog charged again, this time for her face. With an unearthly scream, she felt her left cheek being torn downwards, as a muscular gray weapon jumped up and sunk his teeth into her skin. With that her head hit the cement, and everything went black.

Chapter Nineteen

Danielle's eyes fluttered open, and her face felt heavy.

"Callie?" Danielle questioned. She tilted her head slightly to the left and saw her friend standing at the side of the bed.

"Linda's here, too," Callie said, and Danielle saw her boss sitting on the guest chair in the corner of the hospital room.

"What am I doing here?" she slurred, feeling like she could barely move her lips to form words.

"Do you remember going to Layla's house this afternoon?" Callie asked gently, rubbing her hand.

"Layla's house?" Danielle mused, trying to get her foggy brain to focus. She shut her eyes, trying to remember, but all she could feel was an intense tiredness and the stirring of head pain.

"We'll let you rest," Callie said.

When Danielle woke up next, she was surprised to see her mom sitting in the guest chair, and she wondered if she was dreaming.

"Mom?"

"You're awake," Hillary said, putting down her laptop and looking up.

"How long have you been here?" Danielle asked, feeling anxious because she felt so confused.

At that moment, the door to her room opened and a doctor walked in, followed by a nurse. "Hi, Danielle, I'm Doctor Dohan. How are you feeling?"

"I can't remember what happened to me," Danielle mumbled.

The middle-aged doctor with short, light-blonde hair came near the bed and took her temperature. "You were attacked by a dog this afternoon. You hit the back of your head on the concrete patio, and you have a concussion."

The doctor pressed lightly on Danielle's cheek. "Do you feel anything when I touch you?"

Danielle started to shake her head 'no,' but recognized the pain in her head when she moved it. "No," she said softly. "Why do my lips feel so huge?"

"You've had maxillofacial trauma. The soft tissue of your lips, cheek and nose were torn. Thankfully, there were no broken bones. However, because the laceration to your cheek was so deep, we had to do two layers of stitches." As the doctor talked, the memory of the pit bull grabbing her leg and then knocking her over came rushing back.

"How did I get here?"

"A neighbor heard your cries and came to your aide. From my understanding, he fought the dog off you and ran you to his porch, where he called 911."

"What happened to the dog?" Danielle asked, partly out of anger and partly out of concern for the safety of others.

"The only piece of information I received was that the dog took off through the neighborhood."

"How long will she be here?" Danielle's mom chimed in. Danielle had forgotten she was in the corner.

"We need to keep her overnight to make sure the wound isn't carrying infection."

"I'm assuming that the I.V. is administering an antibiotic of some sort?" Hillary asked.

"Yes, we're doing ampicillin–sulbactam."

"And, what sort of care will she need at home?" Hillary continued, matter-of-factly. "I need to get this all set up before I have to go."

"Well, ma'am, if she is infection-free tomorrow, she'll be able to go. Because her concussion was mild, we'll observe her through the night, but if she lives alone, she'll probably feel more comfortable having someone with her for a few days. This has been a traumatic event."

"Okay, thank you, doctor."

As the doctor and nurse left, Hillary began talking into her phone. "Home health care aides in Springfield, Illinois," she said.

"Mom, what are you doing?" Danielle asked, with her eyes shut, feeling tears beginning to trickle into her ears as she lay flat on her back.

"I'm in the middle of a trial right now, Danielle, and I really can't be away."

"I'm sure Callie would stay with me. Or, I've got a neighbor. He could always check-in, I imagine, if I needed him too."

"I'd feel better if you had a trained medical professional with you," Hillary said scrolling down the list of names with her finger, not noticing Danielle was crying.

"Where's Howard?" Danielle asked, still silently shedding tears.

"Oh, he's in the middle of trial research. I've been texting him. I've told him it's nothing a little plastic surgery can't fix. We can hire a good lawyer to cover your case. You shouldn't have to pay for anything."

"Is it that bad?" Danielle said softly.

"You haven't seen yourself?" Hillary gasped.

"No."

"Well, you might as well get it over with," Hillary replied, setting down her phone and looking around for a mirror. Not seeing one, she used the intercom to call the nurse. "Nurse, could you please bring us a hand-held mirror?"

Hillary went right back to her phone, and Danielle looked around for a tissue.

"Hello, Tonya? This is Hillary Hunt. I'm looking for a home health care aide for my daughter, starting tomorrow."

As Hillary continued to work out details over the phone, a nurse came by with a mirror. Hillary waved for her to give it to Danielle. Danielle slowly shifted her weight upward, feeling a bandage on the back of her right calf for the first time. The nurse looked at Hillary and then back at Danielle and decided to stay. She held the mirror out, so Danielle could look at her face.

When the mirror was angled just right, Danielle could see the purple bruises under each eye, and a clear picture of the pit bull's bite around her lips. Stitches also ran along the right side of her nose and in two circular lines on her cheek. Blood was seeping from the stitches around her upper lip. There were also stitches on her forehead.

The nurse put the mirror down and looked into Danielle's eyes. "I'm so sorry for what happened to you. You sound like a really caring young lady," the older woman said. "The surgeon took some of the skin from your forehead to fix your nose. You've got 100 little pieces of thread on your face to remind you that God still has a plan for your life."

Danielle started to sob. She hadn't ever considered herself a vain person, but she barely recognized the woman in the mirror. She wondered if she would ever look normal again.

"Oh, honey," the nurse said softly, giving Hillary a wicked stare as she continued to chat away on the phone, asking the health-care aide questions about her education background. "I'm sure you need some time to process all that has happened today. We have a few counselors on staff. Would you like to meet with someone tomorrow?"

"Sure," Danielle said, knowing her mom wouldn't be any help.

Her mom caught the tail-end of their conversation as she hung up the phone. "Danielle doesn't need counseling," she said coldly. "She's going to be fine. This is all fixable," she said sweeping her hand in the general direction of Danielle's face.

"Ma'am, she's been through a very traumatic event. The healthier she can go home the better. And mental health is a key component to a person's overall health. After all, this young lady is a social worker herself, I'm sure she sees the benefit in this service," the nurse continued, giving Hillary an icy glare.

Looking back at Danielle the kind nurse said, "if you need anything, I'm your nurse on duty for the next few hours, so please let me know." She patted her hand before exiting the room.

"Well, Tonya, will be taking care of you for three days," Hillary replied, as if nothing had happened. "She's got an associate degree at the local college here, and she's been working in the field for twenty years. I think you'll be in good hands."

"Are you leaving tonight?" Danielle asked, wishing her mom had a motherly bone in her body.

"I need to be back by nine tomorrow morning, so I'll sleep here. I did tell your dad about this, but you know him. I doubt he'll come."

Danielle noticed it was dark outside. "What time is it?" she asked.

Hillary checked her phone. "Seven."

"I think I'm going to try to sleep," Danielle replied, wearily. Danielle wasn't completely tired, but she needed to be alone, in her head. This was too much to take in. Her mom, here, complete with a cold heart. Her dad had been contacted. Would she have to encounter him, too? Her face ripped to shreds by the backyard beast, and a mysterious rescuer who came to her aid. She wanted to sleep so she could forget everything. And suddenly she wanted James. Had he tried to call her? Did he know? How could he if she didn't tell him?

"Mom, do you know where my phone is?" she asked.

"Your clothes, phone and keys are in here," she said pointing to a drawer next to the bed. Hillary walked to the drawer, opened it, and retrieved the phone.

Danielle had four messages, twenty texts, and five emails, but after taking ten minutes to check them all, she was very disappointed. There had been no contact from James.

The clock on his car's dashboard read two-thirty a.m. James rolled his neck from side to side and sighed. He had weathered a twelve-hour debate on legalizing cannabis in the state of Illinois. They had started at two in the afternoon, and they were just getting out.

There would be more to do tomorrow, and a whole new bill to debate in the afternoon. Anyone who told him this was a part-time job was crazy. He would definitely include the day's details in his once-a-week video put out for his constituents.

James only had to go a few blocks to get to his apartment, and the traffic lights seemed extra bright against the inky black sky. The short drive didn't give him much time to decompress from the intense day. He wondered if he should have said more…or less? Some of his fellow congressmen were so long winded. Did his arguments change anyone's mind?

After parking on the second floor of the three-story parking garage, he took the steps down to the main level. Everything was so quiet at this time of night. He pulled his phone from his pocket and checked his messages. There was one from his mom, two from his administrative assistant, and one from the woman leading the fundraising campaign for the running path in Naperville.

It wasn't until he turned the key to get into his apartment that he realized Danielle hadn't called or texted to thank him for the May Day gifts. He hoped she had gotten them. It was unlike her to not send some type of response, and it was too late to call her now. He made a mental note to check on her in the morning.

It was fifty-thirty in the morning, and Danielle had already been awakened twice by the overnight nurse to check her bandages, make sure she was still alert after her concussion, and monitor her temperature. Now, her mom was rustling around in the bathroom. The mirror was still on the bedside table, and she wondered if she should check her appearance again?

Maybe the swelling had gone down. She held the mirror up to her face and felt her heart sink. The bruises under her eyes were darker, and her nose looked twice it's normal size. She noticed the stitches were oozing blood and liquid and wondered if that was normal.

Within a few minutes, her mom emerged from the small en suite bathroom looking sharp in a black skirt and blazer. Everyone said she looked a lot like her mom, and she hoped her face would go back to being as pretty as the one she saw before her.

"Are you getting ready to go?" Danielle mumbled. With her lips feeling like puffy pancakes, it was hard to talk.

"Oh, sorry, Danielle," Hillary said as she put her make-up bag into her small suitcase. "I didn't mean to wake you up. At least now I won't have to worry about being so quiet."

"I don't feel so good," Danielle said as she lay her head back onto the pillow. A wave of nausea came over her.

Hillary looked at Danielle, and her eyes widened. "I better call a nurse. I've never been good with vomit." Hillary pressed the intercom and requested a staff member, pronto.

Danielle had hoped to talk with her mom before she left, but she felt too sick to worry about it. A nurse came in with some medicine to calm Danielle's stomach. After the nurse left, Hillary, who had been focusing on her cell phone, came to Danielle's side.

"I'm sorry I've got to go. With this delay, I'm running late. I'll make sure to call you every day, to check on you. Do you want Howard and me to come this weekend?" she asked, not so sincerely.

"It's okay," Danielle muttered, feeling queasy.

Hillary patted her hand succinctly. "Well, I know you're going to be fine. Really, this all will be behind you before you know- it."

Then she grabbed the suitcase handle and rolled out of the room.

Chapter Twenty

At eight a.m., Danielle awoke to the sound of footsteps in the hallway. Her pain medicine must be wearing off, she thought. Her head pounded and every part of the right side of her face felt like it was on fire. As she pushed the button to make the bed move to a sitting position, she saw Callie come into view.

"They caught the dog," Callie said quietly from the chair where her mom had been sitting a few hours earlier.

"What's going to happen to him?" Danielle asked as the bed stopped moving.

"Unfortunately, nothing. I guess, in the state of Illinois, unless a person is killed by a dog, the owner gets to make the decision about what to do. And, Booker decided to keep the beast."

"Wow," Danielle replied softly.

"The good news is that the police recognized how emaciated the dog was, and they called the Animal Protective League to get involved. So, he'll probably get the dog taken from him."

"Just like his daughter," Danielle said to herself.

"Do you know if Layla was there when the police brought the dog back?"

"Linda stopped at their rental last night. She said Layla was high as a kite when she got there."

Tears stung Danielle's eyes. She was not normally a crier. Maybe it was the anesthesia, she thought. She had heard that its effects could make you feel weepy.

"Why do I care so much? It's not worth it," Danielle replied sadly. "My face is ripped up. I can't reunite this family, and I think I'm ready to retire in Florida with Bruce."

"Oh, Danielle," Callie said, coming to her side. "It's going to be okay. Your mom told us she thought that plastic surgery would take care of everything."

"What does she know? She believes what she wants. And really, she just wanted to get out of here as fast as she could. She put in her time. The mandatory appearance, you know."

Callie got a tissue and wiped the tears that were running into Danielle's ears.

"Oww," Danielle groaned, as Callie touched the stitches on her cheek.

"Hey," Callie said brightly. "That's a good sign. The doctor told us if you started to feel again in your cheek it meant that your nerve endings were still intact, or something like that."

There was a knock on the door, causing the ladies to shift their gaze.

"Good morning," said a bald man dressed in blue dress pants and a plaid shirt. "Are you Danielle Davison?" he asked, with a warm smile.

"Yes," Danielle replied.

"I'm Paul Johnson, the hospital chaplain. I was told by your night nurse that a visit would be welcome."

Danielle's face wanted to contort in question, but the natural instinct hurt, and she winced. "I think I was supposed to see a counselor this morning," she replied.

"Oh, well, the wrong person must have gotten scheduled. Would you be open to talking with me?" he asked politely.

Callie looked at Danielle, "I'll leave you be," she said. "The flowers are from the whole department. Oh, and I fed Tinkerbell for you." Danielle scanned the room and then located the bright bouquet of spring flowers on the table next to the guest chair.

"Thank you, Callie," Danielle replied sincerely.

"I'll be back later." Callie brushed past Pastor Paul, as she said goodbye to both.

Paul remained by the door frame. "Is it okay if I come in?"

"Sure," Danielle replied, disappointed to not have a counseling appointment. There was much on her mind.

"I'll leave the doctors and nurses to ask you how you are feeling physically," he said as he sat down in the chair next to her bed. "I'm wondering how you are doing emotionally. An attack like you encountered yesterday is very intense."

"I don't remember anything after I hit the concrete. I only remember the dog charging at me and biting my pants leg. I remember shaking him off, and I kind of remember him coming back at me and leaping for my face, but that's it."

"Maybe that was God's way of protecting you from the trauma," Paul replied, and Danielle noted his eyes were very blue.

"Maybe," Danielle said uncertainly.

"What are your biggest concerns this morning? If our counselor, Pam, was here, what would you want to talk with her about?" Paul asked.

Danielle sighed. "There are so many things. I don't know where to start."

"How about you start with whatever bubbles to the surface first."

"My face looks so...so horrifying," Danielle sighed with embarrassment. "What if it never heals."

"What has the doctor told you about your long-term prognosis?"

"I haven't asked. My mom said something about plastic surgery."

"When your doctor comes in again, I think it would be a good idea to get the facts. Sometimes we can jump to conclusions when we don't know all the details," Paul said kindly. "Is your mom still here? It might help her to be a part of the discussion, as well."

"No, that's another thing. My dad and I don't really have a relationship, and my mom...well let's just say she's not the motherly type."

"How so?"

"She had to leave for a trial, so she was only here for a few hours, if that gives a glimpse into the picture." Danielle laid her head against the raised bed frame.

"So, she has a history of not being really present for you?"

"You hit the nail on the head."

"Have you ever told her how you feel?"

Danielle's cheek felt itchy, but her instinct told her not to scratch the stitches, so she twitched her nose instead, hoping that would help. "I went through some extensive counseling about ten years ago. One of the things my counselor had me do was to talk to my mom about the kind of relationship I needed."

"Did you do that?"

"Over the phone, once, back then. I told my mom I hoped our relationship could get stronger, closer. And I asked her if we could try to have more regular contact, either with visits or phone calls."

"How'd she respond?"

"Like she thought that it was a good idea, but then nothing changed. I tried to call her more regularly, for a while after that. But she rarely answered. It would go to voicemail and then I wouldn't hear from her for weeks. When she did call back the conversations would be short, like usual, and very surface-oriented."

"So, your relationship hasn't changed, and it leaves much to be desired."

"You seem to be a good counselor, Pastor Paul," Danielle smiled the best she could with a drooping face.

"The role of chaplain is often similar to the role of a counselor," he replied, returning the smile. "Would it have been better if she hadn't come?"

"Yes...well maybe," Danielle replied. "I mean, I appreciated the effort. I know how busy she is. And at least she came, even if it was for less than twenty-four hours. But her lack of empathy, her coldness...I don't know, it feels so hurtful."

Pastor Paul let the silence rest in the room.

"Ever since I became a Christian, I've clung to Psalm 27:10. Though my mother and father forsake me, the Lord will take care of me. And here I am in the hospital," she added softly.

"Being here doesn't mean God's stopped taking care of you."

"I guess not, but I sure feel alone."

"Do you know the twenty-third Psalm?" Pastor Paul asked, looking into Danielle's eyes.

"Yes."

"The Lord is our..."

"Shepherd," Danielle replied.

"The Lord is a good shepherd. As our caretaker, He goes where we go. So, He was with you yesterday during the attack. He was with you through the night, and when you woke this morning. He is Immanuel. God with us."

Pastor Paul let the words rest in the air, as he waited for Danielle to respond. When she didn't, he continued.

"I read in the paper this morning that a neighbor rescued you."

"It was in the paper?" Danielle said with astonishment.

"Yes, I can bring you a copy, if you'd like."

"I'd like that."

"God sent someone to help you. And maybe He even gave you a warning not to go on that path yesterday, and you just missed His voice."

Danielle thought about the impending doom she had felt before going into the backyard, and the voice that had told her not to go. At the time she dismissed it as silly, irrational fear.

"I did have a sense that something wasn't right. I just thought I was being overly sensitive."

Danielle wiggled her nose again trying to relieve the ever-present itch.

"Pastor Paul, to be honest, I feel let down. For the last nine years I've been pouring into others. I've given up my own interests, not that I even know what they would be at this point. I've given up sleep. My own safety and health. And look where it's got me."

"Danielle, the rain falls on the just and the unjust," Pastor Paul replied. "God never promised us we wouldn't have pain. But He did promise us we'd always have his peace. If you are His child, you have all of His great power inside you."

Danielle leaned her head against the pillow behind her back and sighed wearily.

"It might be a good idea, in this time of recovery, to use this space to allow God to speak to you afresh, to draw near to Him. And, maybe you could seek out a mentor to be a father figure in your life. It might feed a part of you that is very hungry. I'd like to see you again tomorrow, if you're still here."

"The doctor implied I'd get to go home this afternoon, but if I'm still here you are welcome anytime," she said kindly.

The Stratton Building's cafeteria was offering the usual pre-packaged salads, sandwiches, soups, and made-to-order hot sandwiches. James had been hungry for over an hour, as he sat through a committee meeting for items dealing with the state budget.

He was planning on taking his ala-carte items to his office and knocking out a few emails and phone calls when a fellow congressman approached him as he carried his bagged lunch to the door. After a fifteen-minute impromptu discussion about the clean energy act, James tried again to exit the cafeteria, still hungry.

This time he was stopped by a committee member who wanted to drum up support for an idea he had pitched during the morning meeting. With his stomach practically barking, he did his best to hurry the conversation along.

When he finally got to his office, a half-hour later, he noticed he only had fifteen minutes to eat before it was time for the afternoon debate. He was still tired from the previous night, so he prayed for endurance before he chomped into this turkey and cheese sandwich.

Opening his email account as he ate, an online bill from the flower company appeared on the screen. Danielle, he thought. He had forgotten to contact her. Swiping his phone, he checked his texts and voicemails. Still nothing from her. James regretted not having enough time to call her, so he sent her a quick text message.

Hi Sweetheart, he began. Then he wondered if they were at the 'sweetheart' stage yet. He erased the word and inserted her name instead. *Hi Danielle. I hope you're okay. I didn't hear from you yesterday, and I had a late night. Didn't get home until two-thirty. Long debate. Did you get the flowers and candy?*

With only five minutes left before he had to get going, James quickly scanned the rest of his emails, and scarfed down the rest of the sandwich. Turning his phone on vibrate and sliding it into his front pocket, he was thankful for the beautiful May weather that poured sunshine into his office. He wished he could walk outside, but he needed to take the tunnel, it would be faster.

Chapter Twenty-One

Hawk didn't get the weekly newspaper, but there were plenty at Walmart. Someone on his mom's shift had read the front-page article about a pit bull's attack on a young social worker. No names were given, but his mom remembered Danielle's profession, and she called Ethan with concern. At first, he hadn't thought much about it, but then he remembered he hadn't seen her come home the night before.

Since she parked her car outside the garage, it was easy to look out the front window and see her car was not there. Maybe he just missed her coming and going. He didn't track her every movement, he told himself. He just spent a lot of time in the front room where it was easy to notice when she came home and when she left.

However, when he was working in the backyard after work, he heard a car pull into her drive. Peering through a small slat in the fence, he quickly realized it wasn't her vehicle. A petite, brown-haired woman helped her out of the passenger side. Hawk moved to get a better look at Danielle, but she was walking towards her house with what appeared to be a slight limp. It was then he became concerned.

"I'm so sorry. This is so unprofessional," the plump lady, dressed in light blue scrubs, said as she stood at Danielle's front door. "My name is Tonya. I'm the home health care aide your mom hired to help you the next few days. I just got a call from her saying you were home. Unfortunately, I was in the middle of taking my dad home from a doctor's appointment, and we live in Girard. Would you mind if he came in until my sister-in-law can pick him up?"

"No, that's fine," Danielle said tiredly. She was so worn out from the trauma, her hospital stay, and heightened emotions, she just wanted to lay down.

"Okay, I'll just go and get him," she replied hastily as she retreated down the steps.

Danielle went to sit back down in the living room. Everything felt so different, even though she had only been away from home for a little over twenty-four hours. Her stitches were itchy again, and it was a constant battle not to scratch them.

"Well, your mom said you don't have any sign of infection from your wounds," Tonya said, perkily as she escorted her dad through the door. He had a walking cane, and Danielle noticed Tonya guided his hand over the wall as they walked. "Danielle, this is my dad, Joseph. Diabetes took his eyesight from him about four years ago, but we're not letting it take anything else, are we, Dad?"

"That's right dear," said the elderly man with white hair lining the base of his head, leaving a bald circle around his forehead. His khaki pants were baggy, and he shuffled when he walked.

Tonya sat her dad down onto the couch and had him feel for the oval coffee table in front of him.

"Thanks for letting me come in," he said kindly, feeling the fabric of the floral couch. "I'm sorry to hear you were in an accident."

"Thank you," Danielle replied, glad he couldn't see her face.

Tinkerbell had fled to her bedroom when she heard the doorbell ring, and now she slunk out to meet the company. She hopped to the couch and sniffed Joseph's hand.

"Sorry," Danielle chuckled. "My cat, Tinkerbell, is saying hello."

Joseph felt for the cat, and tried to pet her head, but she jumped down in fright.

"She can be skittish," Danielle said as Tinkerbell ran down the hall.

"Let's see here," Tonya said, taking charge. "I need to take your vitals. Temperature. Blood pressure. And see what scripts I need to pick up. Your mom said you had two things I needed to get at the drugstore."

Danielle was thankful her mom was so diligent. She always had been good with details. If only she had been equally good with emotions. After Tonya had done her nursing duties, Danielle told her that she could find the prescriptions on the counter.

"So, they want you to continue taking an antibiotic and keep taking some pain killers," Tonya said returning from the kitchen. "My sister-in-law isn't answering her phone, so I guess my dad gets to keep you company while I run out and get these for you."

She grabbed her purse from the floor. "Your mom left instructions for me to take care of your meals. What are you wanting tonight?"

Danielle had only liquids while at the hospital and she craved something she could chew, but she didn't know how the stitches inside her mouth would handle the stress. "I think I'm supposed to stick to a liquid diet for another day or two," Danielle replied reluctantly. "But I sure would like a burger."

"That might be because you lost a lot of blood due to your injuries," Tonya replied. "Red meat is high in iron, and your body may be craving it due to a deficiency. How about a fruit smoothie with spinach? Spinach is high in iron too."

"Okay, but how about some soup to go with it? Is that too many stops?"

"Taking care of you is what I'm here to do," Tonya said with a kind smile. "Dad, do you want some soup?"

"I'll have a little of whatever you're having, Tonya," he said sitting forward on the couch.

"You can lean back and get comfortable, Dad. It looks like you're going to be here, at least through dinner," Tonya said, continuing to take charge. "I'm just going to run these errands. I'll be back in under an hour."

"Okay, dear," Joseph replied.

"Oh, one more thing," she said hurrying back into the kitchen. "You both need to drink lots of water. Recovery happens faster when you flush all the anesthesia and toxins out of your system. And, Dad, you haven't had anything to drink since before your doctor appointment," she called over the sound of running water. Bringing them each a glass, she yelled a quick goodbye as she hurried out of the house.

There was silence as the door closed, and they heard the car back out of the driveway. Tonya was like a tornado with legs, Danielle thought, as she left. As they sat in the stillness of the quiet house, Danielle had no energy to exude her usual friendliness, and she began to feel sorry for herself. Her first few minutes at home were now being shared with a stranger. She didn't want to be rude, but she just wanted to be alone.

As if Joseph read her thoughts, he said, "I bet you're awfully tired. Hospitals are not really relaxing. You'd probably just like to rest."

"I would, actually. I think I'll just go lay down until Tonya gets back. Can I turn on the television for you?" she asked as she got up.

"Sure," he replied. "This time of night, there's bound to be a game show on."

Danielle found *Wheel of Fortune* and handed Joseph the remote before heading to her bedroom. The sun was still bright, so she shut the blinds before pulling back the white comforter and laying down on the cool pale sheets. She wondered if she should get a towel since her face was still oozing, but she didn't have the motivation to get up again.

She lay on the side of her face that wasn't stitched up, not feeling as tired as she thought she was. She had taken a short nap at the hospital late morning, which meant sleep probably wouldn't come. Danielle was tired mentally and emotionally as much as she was physically. Pastor Paul had recommended refreshing spiritually. Before he left, he talked about compassion fatigue. It wasn't the first time she had heard the term. Her boss, Linda, was the first to share the term with her.

When you give out to others who are very needy, you can get drained. It was a simple concept, in some ways. Paul suggested reading the Psalms to recharge. So, she opened the Bible that lay on the bedside table. She didn't read it every day, but it always went to church with her on Sundays. Now, she found Psalm 1 and began reading, but her mind drifted.

Why hadn't James texted or called? It had been two days. Since they had begun dating their communication was regular. He had warned her May would be busy, but she needed him. Where was he? Her phone had been untouched for a few hours. Maybe he had tried? Where was her phone?

The sound of clapping floated in from the living room, and she realized it was on the kitchen table by her purse. She'd have to go by Joseph to get it, and she probably should check on him anyways. Why, God, Danielle cried in her head, do I always have to take care of people? Even when I'm trying to recover from a dog attack, you bring me a blind man to take over my couch, she huffed silently.

If I'm quiet, will he still hear me, Danielle wondered as she tiptoed through the hallway. The wheel was spinning, as she slipped into the kitchen. Stealthily she rummaged through her purse. Retrieving the phone, she tried to glide back to the bedroom when Joseph called out, "Everything okay, Danielle?"

"Oh, yes," Danielle said, stopping in her tracks. "I was just getting my phone. Everything okay with you?"

"Just fine, dear," he replied kindly, staring straight ahead. "If you can't sleep, please come join me."

"Okay," Danielle said hesitantly.

He pushed some buttons on the remote, making the television go up in volume, then down, then back to blaringly loud.

"Would you like help with that?" Danielle called over the din.

"Sure," he replied sheepishly. "I was trying to find the mute button. I know which one it is on my remote at home, but this must not be the same kind."

Danielle muted the television, and it became quiet. "Do you want me to find a different show for you?" she asked, trying to be polite.

"Oh, no dear. I just wanted to see how you were doing."

The way he talked without looking at her was odd, but strangely welcome due to the discomfort she felt about her appearance. "I couldn't sleep," she replied, not knowing what else to say.

"Probably a lot on your mind."

Danielle sat down on the wing back chair that sat beside the couch and stared at the letter being turned by Vanna White. "I guess."

"Tonya told me you were attacked by a dog. Got pretty scratched up."

"You could say that," she laughed. "The dog did a lot more biting than scratching."

"Tonya said it happened at work. Do you think you'll hang up your hat and find more peaceful pastures?"

"I don't know. I am pretty burned out at the moment."

"I sure wish I could still work," Joseph said wistfully.

"What did you do?" Danielle asked, leaning back into the chair, wanting to check her phone, but wanting to be polite. Even though he couldn't see, he would be able to tell if she was distracted.

"I was a postman."

"Did you like your job?"

"I must have. I did it for forty years."

"Wow. That's a long time."

"I've only been retired for six years, but it feels like a lifetime ago."

"Has it been hard to adjust to your new way of life?" Danielle asked, thoughtfully.

"Being retired or being blind?" he asked with a smile.

"Both, I guess."

"Retirement was harder than going blind. Probably because I knew for some time, I was going to lose my sight. The waiting was difficult. But I've learned to adapt. And Tonya is a big help."

"She seems like a take-charge type of person."

"That's Tonya," Joseph chuckled. "She's always been like that. It makes her good at what she does. You'll be in capable hands with her."

"That's reassuring. Thank you."

"Thank you- for letting me stay here. I'm glad I didn't have to wait in the car. I'm sure my daughter-in-law will be here soon. I'll need my next dose of insulin before too long."

"I bet managing diabetes is challenging."

"I've had it since I was a young child, so I don't really remember life without it. And being blind has taught me a lot about how judgmental people can be," he said, rubbing the handle of his cane, which was leaning against the couch.

"What do you mean?"

"It's just so natural for us to judge someone by their outer appearance. Now, I can tell a lot about a person just by their voice, their actions."

"Well, I'm glad you can't see my face because it's pretty hideous. I think I'd prefer the world to be blind to me for a while."

"Maybe this will be a good test of character."

"How so?"

"You'll be able to see who loves you for who you are on the inside."

Danielle's phone vibrated in her hands.

"It sounds like you got a text," Joseph said.

"I guess I did," Danielle replied, surprised at how much his ears could pick up. "Do you mind if I take a look?"

"Oh no, please go ahead."

Danielle swiped her finger over her screen.

How are things going? Did Tonya make it there? If not, I can come over.

Danielle saw Callie's picture next to the text. She quickly replied. *Tonya's here. Well, technically she's not here, she's picking up my prescriptions and dinner. But her dad is here…long story. Everything's okay. Thanks for checking.*

With her phone open, she went on to check her other texts. She scrolled through her unread messages. At least ten were from clients, but there weren't any from James. Danielle glanced at Joseph. He was still staring straight ahead. She needed to know if he had left her a voicemail. Dialing the mailbox, she heard "no new messages," so she pushed the button to end the call.

Chapter Twenty-Two

Hawk rarely wore polo shirts, but he wanted to look nice for his visit to Danielle. Recent word from his mom confirmed that Danielle had been the victim of the vicious attack. In an interview for the local paper, Danielle shared she didn't remember much about the incident, but the one-hundred stitches on her face were a constant reminder.

She wanted to thank her mysterious rescuer when she recovered, and he wished he could have been that man. All he had to offer her were the books she loaned and a beautiful bouquet of flowers. And his heart. But that would be offered when the timing was right.

It was twelve-thirty, and he had texted her to see if she was up for a visitor. He was thrilled that her response was favorable. There was nothing more he wanted to do but be with her, even for a moment.

Hawk was thankful for a flexible work schedule. As he walked over to her house on a Wednesday afternoon, the spring sunshine felt fantastic. He mentally noted four things he needed to do in his backyard later in the day. After ringing the bell, a plump lady in nursing scrubs answered the door and introduced herself.

Danielle was facing the television as he entered her living room. When she turned to face him, he was shocked to see her lovely face looking so puffy, bruised and riddled with stitches. In that instant, Hawk realized Danielle now knew, in a small way, what it felt like to be him.

"I brought you these," he said offering her the bouquet of purple, yellow and white crocuses.

"They are beautiful," she replied, from her seat on the couch. "Tonya," she called, "would you mind putting these in a vase? You can find one in the cabinet above the microwave."

"Sure, honey," Tonya said, entering the living room. "I'll be in the kitchen if you need anything. And don't forget to drink your water."

"Yes ma'am," Danielle replied with a hint of a smile. "Have a seat," she continued.

Hawk chose the wingback chair next to the couch, and Danielle angled her body, so they were facing one another. Like a schoolboy, Hawk held out the books he had placed on his lap.

"I wanted to return these. Thank you for sharing them."

"You're welcome. I hope you enjoyed them."

"I did. Especially *Mere Christianity*."

"I never did answer your questions about the book," she said, taking a sip of her water.

"I don't want to wear you out today. Maybe I could come back in a few days with my notebook."

"Sure."

"How are you doing?" Hawk asked quietly, with deep sympathy in his voice.

"Well, I've been better. But I'm trying to look at the positives. I get paid time-off. I'm catching up on my favorite tv series, reading a book, and Tonya has been a great help."

"I'm so sorry," Hawk said sadly.

"Could've been worse," she shrugged.

"Has the dog's owner contacted you? Apologized?"

"Booker? No, he's not responsible enough to do either," she said cynically.

"Does it make you mad?"

"Mad that he hasn't apologized or mad that it happened?"

"Both, I guess. I wish I could go back and redo those few minutes before going into their backyard. I knew it was a risk. My boss, Linda, reminded me that I didn't follow proper protocol, and I know that. It was stupid of me. But I should've listened to the Holy Spirit."

"God was talking to you?"

"Yes."

"How do you know God's voice from your own?" he asked with genuine curiosity.

"Obviously I'm still working on that," she chuckled, "But I've heard the Holy Spirit speaking to me before, and looking back, it felt the same. There was a sense of urgency. A sense of guidance."

They sat in silence for a moment, as neither knew which direction to take the conversation.

"So, what's your recovery going to be like?" Hawk asked, staring at Danielle's face and wondering if she would have to live as he had for so many years-disfigured and ashamed of his appearance.

"My mom says she thinks plastic surgery can fix most of it. However, Tonya says if I don't have feeling in my cheek, my nerve endings may be so damaged that I'll need surgery to repair them. And I'm not sure how well they can repair my upper lip. We'll see. It's hard not to know, but all I can do right now is wait and see how my face heals."

"How'd you hear about this?"

"My mom. She read a few articles in the paper. So, I guess all of Springfield knows now."

"Maybe not everyone," Danielle replied coldly, thinking of how James still had not contacted her.

"I would've thought you would have lots of people from church come by... or friends," Hawk said, fishing for information about the mysterious good-looking stranger with whom he was in competition for her devotion.

"I live a pretty sad existence," Danielle said, trying to wryly smile, but failing because of her damaged cheek. "My life has been wrapped up in my work. And the people I help are not often able to think past their own needs."

"What about your church?"

"I come in and go out each Sunday. I haven't really worked to make any connections. Wish I would've."

"Well, then I vow to be a regular visitor, just like you were for me."

"You are recovering well," Danielle replied, now realizing Hawk had walked in without a cane...or a limp.

"I have about 75% mobility in my knee. It's getting close to normal."

"That's great. So, you'll probably be getting your house ready to be sold then?"

"Not likely. I've had a change of plans," smiling softly at her. "I'll be here for about a month, then I'm going away for a little while."

"Really? Where are you going?"

"Let's just say a long vacation."

The committee meeting had just adjourned, and it was time for lunch. James walked through the cool marble hallway of the capitol, in stride with committee member, Robert Wisekoff.

"I'm afraid that our education reforms are going to die a slow death," Robert said as his fancy dress shoes clicked along the ground.

"Unfortunately, as much as I want to be an optimist, I have to agree. There's too much opposition from the other side right now. Maybe next year we can craft something that's more workable."

As they walked past a newspaper vending receptacle, Robert said, "Sorry to hear about that girl."

"What do you mean?" James asked, nodding to some visitors who passed them.

"I guess you didn't read the paper yet today? I thought she was your date at the governor's mansion."

"What are you talking about?" James questioned, feeling an alarm going off in his mind. "That late night debate session meant for another night of little sleep. I got up fifteen minutes after my alarm, and I've been running ever since."

"She seemed like a nice young lady," Robert said.

"Seemed? What happened to her?"

"It appears that she got attacked by a pit bull while on the job."

"Oh my," James said, stopping in his tracks and pulling out his cell phone. "You go ahead, I've got to do something," he continued.

"You okay?" Robert asked. "You look a little pale."

"Yeah, go ahead."

"Okay. Do you want me to order you something for lunch?"

"No, it's okay. Thanks, though," he said in a daze as he sat down on a bench on the main floor.

Robert walked through the tall doors, leading out towards the Stratton building as James swiped his phone. He had sent Danielle a text yesterday. Why hadn't he checked it? His afternoon committee meeting was followed by another debate until two a.m., that's why, he thought.

He clicked on his text messages and scrolled past the most recent ones until he found the one he had sent the day before. No, he screamed silently. *Message not sent. Tap to send again.*

The tunnel, he thought with fury. Sometimes when he went through the tunnel right after sending a text the message would fail to be delivered. Why hadn't he checked? He berated himself again. Frantically searching his pockets for coins to put into the newspaper receptacle, his pockets held no change. Running towards the security guards he asked them if they had a spare paper, or if they could break a five.

With no success, he turned to the office where the tour guides for the building were stationed. Sprinting to the open door, he saw one of the ladies that led the tours sitting at her desk. He asked if she had a paper, and he practically hugged her when she handed him a copy.

Returning to the bench, he saw the headline on the front page. *Pit bull Attacks Springfield-area Social Worker.* No, no, no, his mind railed. Monday afternoon. At West Twenty-First Street. Neighbor Saved her. 100 stitches to face. Social worker unsure if she will continue in field after she recovers.

My dear, sweet, beautiful Danielle, James thought. Why, God? He cried without waiting to hear an answer. Oh Danielle, I told you I would be there for you, and I've failed. Just like your parents. A tear slid down James' cheek, and he wiped it away quickly with the back of his hand. I've got to see her, he thought.

Pulling up a calendar with his afternoon schedule, he saw he had another committee meeting, followed by a conference call with Banks. The clean energy bill was getting close to being voted on, so he knew Banks would be intensifying his pressure to confirm he would vote against it. He would happily cancel the latter. He had to see her.

Chapter Twenty-Three

The sun had set, and the room was dark. Callie had arrived at Danielle's in time to watch a rerun of *American Idol* with her. Danielle had already returned a phone call to James and had her afternoon visit with Hawk by the time she arrived.

"So, you just told him he couldn't come over?" Callie asked from the wingback chair.

"In so many words, yes," Danielle replied, longing to scratch the stitches on her cheek. The constant itchy feeling was exasperating.

"And, his excuse again was what?" Callie questioned, absentmindedly twirling the bracelet around her wrist.

"He *said* he had two late night debate sessions. And he *said* he tried to send me a text sometime when he hadn't heard from me and it didn't go through."

"You don't believe him?"

"He told me he loved me," she confessed to Callie. "If he did, would he really go almost three days without talking to me?"

"He told you he loved you!" Callie exclaimed. "Did you tell him you loved him?"

"No, and I'm glad I didn't. He's like all the others."

"I don't know," Callie said scrunching her face in thought. "He seemed different."

"I never knew debate sessions could go until two a.m.," Danielle said cynically.

"But have you ever dated a congressman before? How could we find out if his story is true?" Callie sighed as they both heard Tonya washing dishes in the kitchen.

"Well, he told me I could watch his YouTube video on Friday. I guess he makes one every week to let his constituents know what's going on."

"You should do that," Callie said excitedly. "He wouldn't lie to you *and* his voters, would he?"

"I hope not."

"If you find out his story matches up, then will you let him come see you?"

"I told him once I got my stitches out, he could come and visit."

"Good, because if you think this relationship is going to go the distance, then it's all-the-more reason to let him in right now."

Callie's phone buzzed, and she checked her text messages. "I forgot to tell you," Callie said, after she was finished, "Layla contacted me today."

"Really?"

"She wanted you to know she's going to get away from Booker once and for all. She said she couldn't bring herself to call you, because she feels too bad. She thinks your accident is all her fault."

"Linda assigned you to the case while I'm out of commission?"

"Yes," Callie sighed. "You've got to get back- no pressure or anything. It's just that you know how hard our caseloads are, and now Linda's doled out all your clients until you are able to come back."

"I don't know if I will be," Danielle said softly.

"What?"

"I don't know if I will be coming back," she continued, propping her bare feet on the coffee table in front of her.

"Danielle, if you leave, I don't know if I can make it. You're my rock."

"Everything's too tough right now, Callie. I don't feel like I'm really making a difference. I'm burned out. And I have all these scars as a reward," Danielle replied gruffly.

Callie sat quietly in the chair.

"So, did Layla give a reason for not being there on Monday?" Danielle asked, switching topics.

"She said she had spent the night at a friend's house and had forgotten the appointment."

"And did she say what they've done with the dog?"

"I guess Booker is fighting for it. He wants to keep it. The Animal Protective League said he wasn't fed enough. That could have been the reason for the attack. That, or being chained up. Layla said they're letting him be an indoor dog now, but it's not going well. The poor thing isn't used to the new environment. He's chewing everything up and peeing on the floor."

"It's amazing how a man will petition for a dog but not a child," Danielle sighed.

Hawk's surprise for Danielle was almost complete, and during their last visit she had shared that her birthday was in two weeks. It was the perfect opportunity to reveal what he had been planning for months. All he needed was for her to say 'yes' to the invitation and a night without rain.

He was going to ask her to come over on her birthday, and he determined he would ask today. Danielle had seemed despondent the last few visits, and he wanted to do something to cheer her up. Somehow, he convinced her that they could pot plants for her back deck.

Every day, since she had come home from the hospital, he visited after work. Tonya had been present for the first week, but then it was just the two of them. At first, he was unsure what they would talk about, but as the days passed, he found being with her was as comfortable as sitting in his favorite recliner at home.

The first few visits he asked questions about her faith. After that he began to ask questions about her life. As she shared about her past, he wondered how she could have turned out so kind and compassionate. She seemed to have been a lost soul, like himself. But she said her faith in God made her whole, when once she had been broken. Hawk found this beautiful creature fascinating. Even with her injuries she was still beautiful to him.

Her facial muscles were still not working properly, and when she smiled, the bottom of her cheek didn't raise like it normally would have. Her stitches had been removed only days earlier, and the lines where the dog's teeth had done damage looked bright red.

There was a triangular scar above the right side of her upper lip and a fang-like mark below the lip. She also had an 's' shaped line curving around her cheek. The crude wounds were bound to humble any pride she had about her appearance, and if she had remorse over her appearance, she didn't share it with him. Somehow it made her even more approachable, and he found he could be completely himself around her.

He freely opened up about the social traumas he had in school, the shame he felt because of his face, and the hopes he had to do more with life. The only thing he hadn't shared was the biggest part of himself, and the most secret. Only his mom knew what his backyard meant to him-it was his future. And he was ready to share it with her.

But he had the pots for her deck to do first. He had promised to bring all the supplies. After scouring a few of his gardening books to get new ideas for her planters, he constructed a plan for four large, round clay pots. He had chosen some unique plants, and he was thankful to be able to find what he needed at two small, local nurseries. Unfortunately, he had to shop in the daylight, and he was met with the usual stares. But he was willing to go to great lengths for her.

Now, he stood at her doorstep with two large containers of canna plants. Their bold colors and towering height would be a great focal point for the biggest two clay pots. When he stumbled across a licorice plant, he scooped up two containers of light-green, trailing plant that would let off a slight licorice smell.

Hawk prided himself on being able to delight the senses with his choices of plants, and while the interior of his house didn't speak to his ability with colors, he had a knack with it and used it exclusively outdoors. As he waited for her to answer the door, he hoped she would like the choices he selected.

Chapter Twenty-Four

"Joanne brought me a loaf of banana bread yesterday," Danielle shared with Hawk, as she sat on the taupe patio chair watching him pour a bag of soil into a large circular pot. "I don't think she meant to stare so long, but I actually broke into a sweat."

"Welcome to my world," he chuckled from one knee. He was quietly thankful that his leg could bend so well, only four months after his injury.

"Not everyone stares though, right?" Danielle asked, watching his arm muscles flex, and wondering how he developed such a built upper body.

"No, but it seems like for every nine people that walk by without reaction there will be one that really is inappropriate."

"Don't you get lonely being by yourself so much?"

"I don't know anything different. I've never really had anyone to hang out with- besides my mom. When I started homeschooling, I was alone, but my life got easier because I stopped comparing myself to other people and dealing with the rejection."

"Well, I'm getting lonely, and I've only been doing the hermit thing a few weeks."

Hawk worked silently, scooping out a hole to make room for the first plant to slide into its new home.

"Why are you doing all this for me?" She asked, noticing beads of perspiration on his brow.

"Maybe because you told me we're not that different, and now that we have matching faces, I guess you are right," he turned to her and chuckled.

Coming from anyone else, the joke would hurt, but she laughed along with him, her lopsided cheek drooping down as she chuckled.

"At least I can fix mine…I think," she sighed, feeling the warm rays of sun soak into her bare arms.

"I could do something about my birthmark, too," he replied, taking the canna plant carefully out of its black container.

"What's held you back?"

"It was too expensive when my mom learned about it a long time ago. Then I didn't care. And now I could do it, but it would mean postponing my dream. I want to move onto some property at the edge of the city. I've been eyeing the land for a few months. I finally have enough saved, and if I spend it on laser treatments then I won't be able to afford the property for a while and it could sell."

He gently placed the plant into the open hole he had made for the red flowers.

"Sorry I'm not helping. I had a bad headache earlier, and even though the pain meds seemed to dull the pain, I don't have any motivation to do things these days."

She took a drink of the glass of water resting in front of her on the patio table and continued. "I always thought if I had an extra-long vacation from work, I'd get so much done on the house. Put up blinds in the guest bedroom, clean out the junk from my garage. Now all I do is lay around and watch movies."

"Maybe your body and mind just need a break," Hawk suggested as he took the licorice root plant from its container.

"Maybe," she replied.

"I think I know something that would cheer you up," Hawk replied, keeping his eyes on the plant he was pushing into place.

"Yeah?"

"You mentioned your birthday is coming up, and I have a surprise for you. Something I've been working on for a while."

"Really?" Danielle said, not sure how she felt.

"Would you be willing to come over for dinner that night? It's May thirtieth, right?"

"Good memory," she replied with reserve.

"It would just be dinner at my place. Actually, in my backyard," he replied, hoping to entice her by making it sound casual.

"I don't know. It sounds like a lot of trouble for you."

"I already asked my mom to do the cooking," he laughed. "I'm not very good in the kitchen."

"You already asked your mom?"

"I guess I was hoping you didn't have anything planned with Mr. Titanic."

"Mr. Titanic?" Danielle asked, confused.

"You know... that guy that looks like Leonardo DiCaprio who's been seen coming in and out of your place the last month."

"Have you been spying on me?" she asked, raising an eyebrow, and wondering how concerned she should be.

"No, it's just that I sit in my living room most nights, and I can see your driveway from my window," he said, eyes cast down on his work.

"Mr. Titanic is actually James Patton, and no, we don't have any plans that night. He doesn't even know my birthday is coming up," she said with disappointment.

Weeks earlier, Banks had threatened James- yet again. If they had been playing chess, Banks would have said, "check." Banks said he had the power to undo HB2210-Social Work Reform.

James had put hours of hard work into drafting legislation that would provide social workers with an assistant for every three workers and terminate parental rights earlier when drug abuse was present. It would all be undone, Banks said, if he didn't vote against the Clean Energy Act.

Banks represented the forty percent of his district who didn't want the Clean Energy Bill to pass. However, James, along with the majority of his constituents, represented the opposite view.   The morning of the vote for the Clean Energy Act, he walked with trepidation down the maroon carpet to his seat in the House of Representatives. He looked at the digital board where the electronic votes would be tallied, and he wondered how everything would play out.

An hour later, after six bills were voted upon, and all the Yeas and Nays had been accounted for, the Clean Energy Act passed. James was thrilled, but a feeling of dread washed over him thinking of Banks wrath being unleashed against the Social Work Reform Bill. James had made a personal vow to stand firm in the face of political pressure, and now his beliefs needed to become action.

Maybe Banks wouldn't be able to get the congressmen he controlled to turn against the Social Work Reform Bill. Did Banks really have that many people in his pocket? The bill needed sixty votes to pass, and he felt secure that he had fifty-eight. A few congressmen were still deciding if the budget could handle the cost of adding additional state payroll.

James thought about how the past few weeks had brought so many changes, as he put on his dress shoes for work. He was so busy, he felt like his childhood pet hamster, Fluffy. Whenever Fluffy would exercise in his wheel, he would go so fast his whole body would flip over, but he just kept going.

Yet, even though he was in the midst of May madness at the Capitol, every free thought was on Danielle. She had been home almost two weeks since her accident, and she finally said he could come for a visit. Most days, during their hiatus, he was buried in work and couldn't even call. When he found a few free moments, she didn't answer. So, he prayed. He petitioned God for her health and recovery, for their reconnection, for His will to be done in their lives.

James looked around his apartment for his cellphone. Eyeing it on the coffee table, he walked over to retrieve it. When he opened his calendar, he saw the reminder to get flowers for his visit with Danielle on Saturday.

Last weekend it had been hard to be in Naperville, having local meetings, while Danielle was recovering without him in Springfield. When Saturday night rolled around, and it was his first break in weeks, he didn't know what to do with himself. Since his argument with his mom over the relationship with Danielle, their daily conversations had cooled.

He hoped Karen hadn't been right when she said having a relationship would make him too divided. Did his service to his district have to keep him from having a family one day? Afterall, he saw other congressmen and women balance family and work-albeit often poorly. He knew one of his fellow congressmen was having an affair with a lobbyist and most worked ten to fifteen-hour days.

But dating Danielle was different. He could make it work. Afterall, he worked in Springfield part of the year, and he could drive to see her on weekends over the summer. Plus, she worked long hours, too. They seemed equally matched. But did she still want to pursue a relationship with him?

He had told her he loved her, and he meant it. He just had to show her he could be counted on, and he was determined to find a way. What would her face look like now, he wondered as he grabbed his briefcase. All he knew was from the article in the paper, and it said she had extensive injuries to her lips, nose and cheek.

James thought about how he had cupped her beautiful face in his hands and kissed her sweet lips the last time they were together. He didn't consider himself a supercilious man but seeing Danielle would put him to the test.

As Danielle washed her face with the prescription cleanser, she wondered why she invited James to come over tomorrow afternoon? She felt so anxious and uptight. Perhaps she should text him and tell him she changed her mind, or maybe she should say she didn't feel well.

Toweling off her cheeks, she studied her reflection in the mirror. The scar on her forehead was the smallest, since it was the only incision not made by the dog. The skin grafted onto her nose looked like a different shade than the skin around it, making it look more bulbous than it was. As her gaze traveled to her lips, she saw the triangular red marks above her lip, and the fanglike pattern below.

Then there was her cheek. She tried to smile. The top of her cheek still wouldn't lift. Frustrated, she grabbed the lotion and a Vitamin E capsule to apply the two to minimize the scarring. If only she could wear make-up tomorrow, it would be better, she thought. But she wanted her skin to heal properly, and she didn't think it was quite ready to take on even the most natural cosmetics.

I should cancel, she said again to herself, as she gently rubbed the lotion onto the scar on her forehead. No, she countered, you told him he could come and visit when your stitches came out, and that happened two days ago. She was in a war with herself. Danielle longed for him to come as strongly as she wanted him to stay away.

She had gone through enough therapy to know the reason she picked so many poor partners in the past was because of her dad's rejection. Yet now she had someone who truly seemed to care about her. It shouldn't matter that James hadn't been there for her right after it happened, she had to cut him some slack. He had legitimate reasons, and he hadn't meant to let her down.

She rubbed the lotion on her cheek, wincing as she applied it. Danielle had always longed for love from someone like James. Someone honest and kind. A follower of Christ. Handsome. If only he could be there for her. She was giving him another chance to come through, and she hoped he would prove faithful.

Callie had said that allowing him in right now would be the truest test of his character. Tonya's Dad had said the same thing. When she thought about her faithful friends, she thought about Callie, then Hawk. Hawk had certainly proved there were no barriers to their friendship. Actually, she thought, he seemed more comfortable with her since the accident.

Maybe God wanted her to be near Hawk, not just to share her faith, but possibly for more? He had invited her to his backyard for dinner on her birthday, and he had come over every day without fail. Hawk said their faces matched. His birthmark was on the opposite side of her scars. It was like they were two pieces of a broken locket. Was friendship just the beginning for something more?

Chapter Twenty-Five

James awoke to the sound of rain outside his apartment window in downtown Springfield, but he still felt like singing a happy song. He looked at his alarm clock. It was six. Even on a day when he could sleep in, he was so used to getting up early that he naturally awoke. But even his early start wasn't bothering him. He just couldn't wait to see Danielle. Hold her. Tell her everything would be okay. And pray with her.

Slipping his feet out of the covers, he padded barefoot down the hall. One thing he liked about his place in Naperville was that it had an en suite bathroom. As he was washing his hands, he heard his cell phone ringing.

Quickly running back to his bedroom, he caught the call on the final ring.

"Hello," he said breathlessly.

"You exercising?" his mom asked.

"Oh, it's you."

"Who were you expecting at six in the morning?" she said curiously.

"Why are you calling so early?" he groaned as he sat on the edge of the bed and ran his fingers through his wild hair.

"I need a huge favor."

"What is it?" he sighed.

"Did you remember Joliet Junior College's graduation is this afternoon?"

"No, not really, why?"

"Well, our commencement speaker got appendicitis late last night and is recovering from surgery, so he obviously can't come."

James was silent, already knowing what was going to come next.

"I can't mom. Sorry," he replied, hoping she wouldn't press it.

"Why not, James? Everyone on the staff knows my son is a congressman. And, Dean Stillwell actually was the one who texted me last night asking if you would be willing to step in?"

"Well, you'll have to tell Dean Stillwell that I have a pressing appointment here in the capitol city that I just can't miss."

"What is it? I thought you had today and tomorrow off."

A crack of thunder shook the apartment.

"I do, it's just that Danielle was in a horrible accident, and I haven't been able to see her since it happened almost two weeks ago."

"Oh," his mom's voice dropped. "This is about *that girl.*"

"Mom, we've been dating for the past six weeks. To tell you the truth, I really see a future with her. So, you need to get over the hang-up you have about her."

"Let's get back to priorities here, James. Could you please just reschedule with Danielle. Couldn't you just see her on Sunday night? You could speak this afternoon, spend the night up here, and drive back after our Sunday brunch. *We* haven't seen you in two weeks."

"Mom, I'm sorry. I just don't feel like I can cancel with Danielle."

He could hear his mom let out a huff.

"Fine, James. Fine. I'll see if Dean Stillwell can find someone else. But if I can't, I'll be calling you back and expecting you to get on the road to help me out."

"Thank you, Mom. I'm sure you two will be able to find someone."

Danielle woke to the sound of light rain on her roof. She looked at her phone. It was eight o'clock. As she laid in bed, adjusting to being awake, she felt her hands begin to get clammy, and her nervousness about seeing James returned. Saying a silent prayer for peace, she pulled her phone out of the charging cord and sat up in bed. Opening her text messages, she saw she had one from James already. Her heart skipped a beat.

Hey, Danielle. I'm so sorry to say this, but I won't be able to come this afternoon. My mom is a professor at a junior college in Joliet, and their commencement speaker got appendicitis. I told her I couldn't fill in, but they've tried five other people and couldn't get anyone. I even asked my mom to do it herself, but she said the new programs were already being printed with my name on them. How can I make this up to you? I can be back by Sunday afternoon. Could I see you then?

Danielle sighed. It sounded legitimate, but it would only prolong her agony and nervousness. Yet, she needed to test his character, see how he would respond to her "new look."

Sure. See you tomorrow.

"James, that was a fantastic speech," Karen said, putting her arm around her son as they walked to their cars in the auditorium's parking lot.

"Thanks, I had that three-hour drive to come up with something," James said, loosening his tie.

"How many programs did you get asked to sign?"

"Only a couple."

"What do you mean?" she exclaimed. "I saw a whole group of young ladies gathered around you afterward-some cute ones, too."

"Mom," James groaned, watching the tall light flicker on as the sky went from navy blue to a light charcoal. "I'm dating Danielle. Well, I was-until *you* called, and I had to postpone my plans."

"You'll see her tomorrow," Karen said, her heels clicking on the blacktop.

"Actually, I think I should head back tonight."

"Why?" Karen questioned, as she pushed the button to unlock her sports utility vehicle.

"I don't know. I just have a feeling that I should."

"Your sister and your dad haven't seen you in two weeks. I promised them you'd be at brunch tomorrow."

"I'll be coming home at the end of May. It's not like we haven't gone a whole month without seeing each other before."

"But James, it's almost nine o'clock already. You wouldn't be back to Springfield until midnight. I don't want you driving on the interstate that late. You could get tired."

James thought about what his mom said. It had been a long week, and sleep had been sparse. Maybe she was right. Driving this late might not be the best idea. He didn't really know why he felt like he should head back anyhow.

"Okay, Mom, you win. I will see you tomorrow at eleven for brunch. But I'm leaving right after we eat."

"That's fine, dear."

James began to walk to his car, one row over from his mom's vehicle.

"Oh, James," she called. "Thank you *very* much. You saved the day."

"So, James," Kira said as she dished a heaping scoop of egg casserole onto her plate the next morning. "Mom told me Danielle was in a serious accident."

Sitting next to Kira at the circular wooden kitchen table in the Patton's cozy home, James dished himself a bowl of fruit salad.

"She was picking up a client for an appointment when a pit bull attacked her, tearing up the left side of her face."

"That's horrible," Kira replied. "How bad is it?"

"Unfortunately, I haven't been able to see her," James replied giving his mom a cold stare. Then he passed the plate of French Toast to his dad.

"How come?" Kira asked.

"Well, it's been insanely busy with a bunch of late nights, and then Mom called," he said, throwing her another look.

"Your mom told me you gave a great speech," James' dad, Myron, interjected, trying to ease the discomfort between mother and son.

"Well, I hope she'll be okay," Kira continued, ignoring her dad's response.

"Me too," James said softly.

"When's the Social Worker Reform Bill going to vote?" Karen asked.

"This week, but did I tell you what Banks threatened?" James replied.

"No," his mom replied.

"He said he has the power to get the vote to swing the other way. To shut it down."

"Do you think he does?" his dad asked.

"I don't know."

"He works for a petroleum company, right?" his mom questioned.

"Yes, Harshaw Petroleum."

"Well, then he means it," his mom continued. "That's a billion-dollar business."

"I don't doubt people can be swayed by his power, money and influence. But I guess I'll find out if I can really trust the congressmen and women around me, or if they're going to be bought out."

"And at least it's not a bill that your constituents really care about," Karen replied.

"Why would you say that?" James asked.

"Well, you know it's not a bill that's going to appeal to the general public. And the Joe Schmo's are the ones you need to worry about. They're your voters."

"You made a lot of voters happy when you voted for the Clean Energy Act," Myron said, once again trying to keep a brawl from happening.

"How long have you been dating Danielle?" Kira asked, circling back to her own topic of interest.

"About six weeks," James said, more at ease with the change in conversation. He scraped the last of his egg casserole onto his spoon.

"And things are pretty serious?" she continued.

"From my view, yes."

"How can you even know that James?" Karen asked. "I mean, what can you really know about a person in six weeks?"

"We've been getting to know each other since January, Mom. Plus, I think you can learn a lot about a person in a short amount of time, if you ask the right questions."

"I agree," Kira said, coming to his aid. "I think you know a lot about a person's character pretty quickly."

"Thank you, Kira," James said, giving his sister a smile, bringing out his dimple.

"Have you been getting to know anyone lately?" James asked impishly.

"No," Kira sighed. "I have no life, outside of my students, and grading papers."

"Know anyone for me? Any cute, single congressmen?"

"Sorry, Kira," he laughed.

"That was delicious, Mom," James said as he pushed his chair back from the table. "I think I'm going to go take a quick power nap," he replied, looking at his watch, which read noon.

"Didn't sleep well last night?" Karen asked.

"I did until someone with a very loud motorcycle decided to peal past my house at five a.m."

"Sorry, son," Myron replied, "You're welcome to lay down in the guest room for as long as you like. The weather is supposed to be nice today, so you should have a good afternoon for travel."

"Mom, could you wake me up in a half-hour, if I'm not awake?" James asked getting up from the table with his plate, bowl and silverware.

"Are you sure you don't want to rest longer?" she asked.

"No, I want to get on the road as soon as possible. But if you want me to help with dishes before I lay down, I can."

"No, no," Karen replied. "Your dad, Kira and I will cover it. You go lay down."

"Oh, I see how it is," Kira said. "My famous big-shot brother gets out of everything. Kira can do his load."

James laughed. "Sorry sis. I'll stay and help."

"I'm just teasing," she replied, winking. "Go get your power nap on."

James faintly heard the television from the downstairs as he awoke to the afternoon sun and looked at his watch. Four o'clock.

"Mom," he bellowed.

Quickly he jumped out of bed, threw on his dress shoes, and ran downstairs to find his mom sitting on the couch, watching the news.

"Mom, why didn't you wake me up?" he growled.

"You were so tired," she replied, keeping her eyes on the television.

"Mom, I told you I wanted to get on the road."

"You'll still get back by seven- if you leave now. Everything's fine," she replied, turning to give him a smile. "I'll feel better knowing you are well rested."

"Where are dad and Kira?" he asked, noticing that no one else was around.

"Your dad had to go to a drama awards ceremony at his school, and Kira went home to grade papers. Both said to tell you goodbye."

"Well, I'm taking off," he replied in a huff.

"Don't be mad," his mom replied. "It doesn't sound like Danielle is going anywhere in her condition."

"I don't want to argue about it," James said. "I just want to get going. Thank you for brunch. Tell everyone I love them, and I will see you all in a few weeks." He grabbed his car keys off the table by the front door and headed to his car.

Chapter Twenty-Six

As James merged onto Interstate 55, he was pleased to see that the traffic was light. He almost felt like rolling down his window to get some fresh air. After driving in the rain all morning yesterday, he was thankful it was beautiful, warm and sunny for his return trip to Springfield.

James turned on a Christian music station and said a prayer for safe travels. After his amen, his thoughts turned to seeing Danielle. In an instant he realized he had forgotten to pick up a bouquet of flowers on his way out of town. Should he go empty handed? That didn't feel right to him, so he reasoned he'd pick some up on his way into Springfield.

How would he react to her face? James had always been squeamish around blood. Working in the medical field was something he ruled out when he was about five. But she wouldn't be bloody…he hoped. They hadn't found time to talk since her accident, and he just wanted to encourage and comfort her.

He lifted up another silent prayer for words of wisdom and for strength, no matter what the situation would entail. As the miles rolled along, he was surprisingly thankful for the nap. There was no tiredness in him, and he hummed along with the radio. Maybe his mom had been right to let him sleep. His only concern was that he had been in too much of a hurry to text Danielle before he left.

As he passed the city of Dwight's water tower, the traffic began to slow down ahead of him. Within a mile, all traffic came to a complete standstill. He was sorely tempted to pull out his cell phone and check the google maps app to see if there was an accident ahead. Ever since becoming a congressman, he never used his cell phone in the car. Sometimes he even put it in the trunk so it wouldn't tempt him.

Fifteen minutes later, traffic was still completely stopped, and the line of cars behind him was now so long he couldn't see an end. Two drivers from the cars in front of him got out of their vehicles, presumably to find out what the hold-up was. James fiddled with the stations, hunting for local news with information.

The two men were walking back when James got out of his car to get an update. Unfortunately, one of the men said he hoped James packed dinner because it was going to be a while. There had been a bad accident involving a truck and a motorcycle. Police and medical personnel were on their way, according to the report.

Another prayer went up to God, this time for the accident ahead. As he sat back into the cloth seat, he let out a huge sigh. Not again. It was as if something was continually keeping him from Danielle. James needed to let her know about the delay. Could he text while he was in a standstill? Surely that wasn't against the law?

Taking his phone out of the center console, James texted Danielle.

I've got bad news. I'm stuck in traffic. There's been an accident. I don't know how long I'll be. Unfortunately, I took a "power nap" this afternoon, and it set me back, too.

Within minutes James heard his phone ding.

It's okay. I'm sorry to hear about the accident. I will pray.

James saw a woman in the minivan behind him lean back to give a child in a car seat a snack.

Thanks for being so understanding. I'll text again, after I am through this.

Two hours later, James was finally past the wreckage. There was an eighteen-wheeler in the median, and two policemen were directing traffic into one lane around the site of the accident.

When he finally got to the next exit, he turned off and headed to the roadside gas station. Pulling into a parking spot by the convenience store, he blew air through his lips with force. The last two hours of sitting, and the inchworm pace of stop-and-go movement created a ball of frustration in his stomach.

He had to call Danielle and tell her he wouldn't be to Springfield before nine. Would that be too late? There was only one way to find out.

The dawn of Danielle's birthday proved to be a lovely spring gift. Turning thirty-four had been uneventful, except for the visit from Callie at lunch. She was thankful they didn't talk about whether she would be returning to work when her medical leave was up in a few weeks. Callie mentioned that Layla wanted to meet with her, and she wondered why she didn't want to talk to Callie, since she was her temporary social worker.

Callie brought over cream of broccoli soup for lunch, and gave her a thorough ribbing for seeing Hawk, instead of James, on the night of her birthday. But when she explained all that had transpired the previous weekend, with James missing both of his scheduled dates with her, Callie understood.

Maybe she should have told James he could come over after nine, but at that point she was tired. The waiting had worn her out. Being let down by James took her back to high school when she would wait to see if her dad would show up for her debate team matches. When he didn't, she felt the same ache and sadness on Sunday night.

But she didn't want to think about James anymore, she reasoned as she slipped on a light blue sundress for her date with Hawk. She had thirty minutes to get ready for her date with Hawk. She decided to curl her hair, for the first time since the accident, three weeks ago. What made her want to she didn't know. Maybe it was because it was her birthday, or maybe it was because she was going out, and that was something she hadn't done since she arrived home.

After bounce and body were added to her blonde locks, she carefully applied a few layers of mascara. Danielle was still going make-up free where her scars were healing, but her eyes were fair game. Finishing with a light lip gloss, she looked in the mirror and was moderately pleased with her appearance, which was another first since the attack.

Sure, she was still scarred, and the swelling on her lip and cheek weren't altogether diminished, but she saw a glimpse of her former appearance and that made her hopeful. When she first moved in, Hawk had been a big bully. Her dad had been one too, and somehow that felt…comfortable, in a predictable sort of way.

When he had his accident, she felt obligated to help him when she could. But since her injuries, he had tried to repay the favors, and his kindness was blooming like the beautiful potted plants in her backyard. Danielle realized he had moved from a moderately annoying neighbor to a fine friend. She wondered if his invitation to come over on her birthday signified something else. Was he wanting more than just friendship?

His appetite for matters of faith had been growing, so she never felt like they ran out of things to talk about. And she looked forward to seeing the secret he'd been keeping for weeks. She assumed it was something in his backyard. The noise behind the house couldn't be hidden, although the tall shrubs managed to block her view.

Danielle picked up her cellphone and stuffed it in her purse before stopping to scratch Tinkerbell before she left. With only twenty steps between their houses, Danielle was to Hawk's front door by two minutes until six. Hawk opened the door, and Danielle noted he looked very handsome in khaki pants and a short-sleeve light green polo, accented with a brown belt and matching loafers. His beard was more tame than usual, and his hair was shorter than she'd ever seen it before.

"Happy Birthday, Danielle," Hawk said with a grin on his face.

Danielle didn't see Hawk grin very often, and his joyful mood was contagious.

"How old are you? Is it wrong to ask?" Hawk questioned as he closed the door behind her.

"No," she laughed, her cheek still disagreeing with the upward movement of the muscle. "34," she replied, bending down to scratch Chewie. "How old are you?"

"I turned 31 in the fall."

"I thought we were pretty close in age," she said, standing back up.

"Let's start with the surprise," he said, like a child itching to open a gift.

"Should I sit down?" she asked.

"Oh, no. Sorry," he said, shaking his head. "It's in the backyard."

"The backyard?" Danielle gasped in mock surprise. "I thought you didn't allow anyone back there," she teased.

"That's actually true," Hawk replied matter-of-factly. "The only other person who gets to visit it is my mom."

"Wow," Danielle said softly, "How come?"

"Maybe you'll figure it out once you see it."

Hawk led her through the living room and kitchen. The patio blinds were closed so she couldn't see anything.

"Okay," Hawk said. "Close your eyes and give me your hand."

He had looked forward to the last part of that statement since he thought it up days ago. Danielle covered her eyes with one hand and lifted the other towards him. Feeling her slender fingers against the roughness of his own hands, Hawk lingered in the moment. Then he swiveled the blinds to one side with his free hand and slid the patio door open. Carefully helping Danielle step out onto the patio, Hawk said, "You can open your eyes."

As Danielle's eyes fluttered open, she let out a small gasp. The backyard was the most beautiful oasis she had ever seen. The first thing that caught her gaze was the lattice pergola sitting atop four tall wooden pillars. The cream-colored slats that framed the top were strung with twinkling white lights. Leading to the pergola, gray stones patterned in the grass created a whimsical walkway. In the middle of the pergola was a circular stone fire pit, where a small fire flickered. A wicker couch with rust-colored seat cushions looked inviting.

Danielle noticed that next to the couch a glass-covered side table held drinks and a tray of appetizers, but before she could think about dinner her eyes caught sight of a color-changing waterfall that pleasantly bubbled to the left of the pergola. To the right side of the pergola a well-manicured semi-circle of blooming flowers and tall grasses, and path lights in the shape of small lanterns were strategically placed throughout the area. Several tall shrubs hid something with a roof behind the flower bed. But Danielle didn't have time to ask about what was hidden because Hawk's words pulled her out of her head.

"What did you say?" Danielle asked, shaking her head slightly, as if in a dream.

"Look down," he repeated. "This was my project last year."

Danielle glanced at the purple, taupe and gray stones that laid under her feet.

"You laid this?" she asked.

"Took about two weeks."

"How did you learn?"

"Youtube can teach you almost anything," Hawk laughed.

"Really? That's how?"

"Well, that's how I learned the technique. The design was my own."

"It's stunning," Danielle said sincerely, noting the beautiful, intricate pattern.

"Your birthday gift was that," Hawk said gesturing towards the pergola.

"What?" she questioned, not understanding.

"I'm getting ahead of myself," Hawk said with a hint of embarrassment. "I meant to talk about it later."

"Talk about what?" she asked again.

"I'm going to be leaving for the rest of the summer. So, I'm giving you a key to my backyard."

"I didn't think you had a gate."

"I didn't until now. I put one in before your accident. You were at work." He pointed to the gate that was now fashioned on the side of the fence next to her house.

"You were planning all this before then?"

Hawk shrugged, sheepishly.

"It was an exceptional coincidence that you mentioned your birthday."

Hawk opened the palm of his hand and extended it towards the covered porch. "My mom made some appetizers for us."

Danielle led the way to the couch slowly, taking in the enchanting space. When she sat down, Hawk took the wrought-iron chair next to the side table.

"This is really amazing," Danielle said breathlessly, taking in the beautiful view from a new angle. "How is it that I've never heard you doing any of this work?"

"The flowers are pretty quiet," Hawk teased. "Those impatiens and hostas are new this year," he said pointing to a grouping of plants under a tree near the side of her house.

"Sure, but what about all of this?" she asked, pointing to the wooden construction around her.

"I prefer to start early. Less people around." Hawk replied, taking the pitcher of water with lemon and pouring some into her clear glass. "I hired someone to cut the pieces at his garage, and he helped me put it together."

Hawk poured himself a glass of water. "Brad, the guy who helped me cut out the pieces, even managed to follow my blueprint so well that the pergola can actually do this."

Hawk stood up and walked over to the corner of the pergola where he took hold of a crank attached to the wooden board. He turned the crank slowly for about thirty seconds, and all the boards that had been open now gently closed.

"Wow," Danielle muttered.

"Now, if it's too sunny or rainy, you can still be outside," Hawk replied.

"I still can't believe you could make this...this fairy wonderland without me knowing."

Hawk sat back down. "You've had a lot on your mind," he said. "It's not like you were looking to see what I was doing in my backyard. Do you like it?" he asked softly, busying himself with putting two small meatballs on a plate.

"It's absolutely amazing," she said, touching the top of the hand that was ladling the food. Hawk felt fire in her touch.

"Thank you."

"How long have you been landscaping back here?" she asked, taking the small plate from his outstretched hand.

"It started with the flowerbed, ten years ago. The next year I added the tall shrubs around the fence line- for privacy. Then, each year I've added something. The patio. The waterfall. The Hotel-" Hawk stopped himself.

"Hotel?" Danielle asked.

"Nothing," he said, shaking his head. "Just a mix-up of words."

Chapter Twenty-Seven

"These are homemade," Hawk said, pointing to the meatballs on his plate. "My mom's recipe. She usually only makes these once a year at Christmas. She obviously likes you."

"Please tell her they are delicious," Danielle replied as she finished the last one on her plate.

"How come you haven't gone into landscaping?" Danielle asked, leaning back against the cushion, watching the fire.

Hawk laughed cynically. "I'd love to, but do you think anyone would want to do business with a monster?"

"Is that really how you think of yourself?"

Hawk didn't reply, but instead picked up his plate and her empty one as well.

"I'm going to go get our dinner," he said.

"Do you want help?"

"No, it's your birthday. You just sit and enjoy."

As Danielle waited for him to return, she watched the fire spit sparks onto the concrete patio. She tried to lift her left cheek. Several times a day she practiced raising the muscle. Again, she felt its resistance to the upward movement. Would she ever regain strength in her cheek, or would it always droop?

Maybe if she lived with a disfigured face for as long as Hawk had, she would feel like he did. An outsider. Self-conscious. Bitter with the world. Danielle shook her head, as if to cast off the thoughts. No, she told herself. She knew that inner beauty meant more than anything external.

Poor Hawk, she mused. He probably didn't know that Biblical principle, she realized. Danielle heard the fire pop, and her eyes caught sight of the shingled roof that could be seen towering slightly taller than the shrubs it hid behind. What was the thing he called the hotel?" And why was he so secretive? Danielle got up to explore the back corner, but then she caught sight of Hawk carrying two plates of food.

"Need help?" she called.

"No, I've got it. Everything okay?"

"Yeah. Just stretching my legs," Danielle replied, moving back to the couch.

Hawk set her plate on the glass table, and then sat down, putting his plate on his lap.

"This isn't homemade, but dessert is."

"Well, it looks delicious," Danielle said, as she took in the smell of garlic.

"I ordered the lasagna and garlic bread from the Italian-place downtown- Saputo's."

"I love that restaurant."

"Me too," he replied.

Over dinner, Danielle found herself caught up in Hawk's stories about his backyard and forgot all about the hidden hotel, and she didn't think about her appearance for over an hour. The outside of the logs in the firepit grew white with ash, and the stars and fireflies came out to share the sky.

"Thanks for a lovely evening," Danielle said, as she felt a weariness come over her from the rich meal, causing her to want to take a nap.

"You can't leave yet," Hawk interjected. "You haven't had your birthday cake." Hawk stood up, picking up the two nearly empty plates in the process. "Plus, I have to give you your gift."

"I thought that this was my gift," Danielle replied raising her hand to the pergola.

Hawk laughed. "It is, but you can't take it home." Hawk started walking towards the house. "Be right back. Sit tight," he called, hurrying inside.

Danielle had her second moment of silence, as she waited for him to return. Thoughts of her facial disfigurement returned. Did Hawk see her differently, or was he now immune to her appearance as she was to his? If James ever saw her, what would he think?

James wasn't going to see her, Danielle reasoned. They were over.

When he called last Sunday, Danielle felt surprisingly sorry for him. He sounded so distraught. Somehow, she knew all the delays weren't entirely his fault. His mom didn't wake him from his nap, and the accident postponed him even more. But James didn't know how much she had wanted him to come, and how stressful the waiting had been. She had longed for him to see her. To look at her and pass the test. No grimacing, stuttering, or turning away.

She had *needed* him. For weeks her arms had ached for his comfort, his touch, his presence. All her life she had needed what no man had been able to provide- an unconditional love. For the first time in her adult life she had courage to wage the war inside of her to try to trust someone that might actually prove trustworthy, and James had failed.

Over the course of the week, she tried to forgive him. In her training to become a social worker, she learned about seeing things from the other person's perspective. She tried to apply that to James, but when it came to visualizing a future with him, she kept circling back to the busy lifestyle he would have in politics. And becoming president was his goal. This pace would never end, and she didn't want to be along for that ride. It was easier to get out now, before her heart was completely captured.

Hawk stepped onto the stamped patio outside the back door with a platter holding a candled cake in one hand and a gift bag wrapped under the elbow of his other arm.

"Happy Birthday to you," he began singing, slightly off-key.

Danielle smiled lopsidedly.

"Blow them out," Hawk said, after the laborious and slow journey of walking the distance to the pergola, not wanting any candles to extinguish before their time.

"I hope you wished for this," Hawk said. He handed her the gift bag from under his arm and set the cake down on the side table.

"You didn't have to-"

"I know, but I wanted to."

Danielle dug through the white tissue paper to discover what was inside. Reaching down she pulled out a box of chocolate truffles.

"Those are from my mom. I told her you liked that kind we had at Christmas-time, and she found some more."

"That was so thoughtful," Danielle replied, "Please tell her thank you." She rustled the paper again and pulled out a journal and a set of colorful pens.

"Those are to go with this," Hawk said, smiling. Danielle could tell he was enjoying every minute of the night of surprises. He handed her a key. "Remember how I said I was giving you a key to my backyard? Well, this place is where I find peace, and I hope you will, too. The journal and the pens are for you to work through your thoughts while you sit back here and relax."

Danielle was touched by his overwhelming kindness.

"Why are you going away?" Danielle asked.

"I have some," Hawk paused looking for the right word, "business to do that can't be done while I'm here."

"When are you leaving?"

"Monday morning."

"Wow. That's only a day away."

"I hope you'll use the space often."

"I will," she said sincerely. "It's… beautiful. This is truly the best gift I've ever received. Thank you."

Hawk looked like he wanted to lean in for a kiss, and Danielle didn't know how she felt about that, so she busied herself getting a plate of cake. She grabbed a small plate and fork and took a bite.

"Delicious," she sighed enjoying the sweet vanilla flavor melting on her tongue. "Why did you do all this for me? A few months ago, you could barely stand me,"

Hawk grimaced remembering how he had treated Danielle when they first met. "I could barely stand myself," he said softly.

Hawk went over to the firepit. Crouching down, he struck the wood with a poker, so he didn't have to look at her.

"You're my first true friend." Hawk said, keeping his gaze on the fire. "Do you ever think," he began and then stopped.

Hawk had planned on asking Danielle if she would consider pursuing a relationship when he got back, but now, in the moment, he didn't have courage to ask. He poked the fire again, sending sparks flying.

"I know I'm not the best-looking guy, and I certainly am not the kindest. I still don't like to think about the way I treated you. But I think you know now why I was like that. It kept people away, but I don't want to wear that armor around you anymore. You've made me want...more."

Hawk paused. He had so much more to say, but he couldn't bring himself to say it.

"I'm going to go get another log for the fire," Hawk said. He walked to the barrel holding pieces of wood. He wasn't ready to face rejection from Danielle. He needed the hope of her love to propel him forward with his surgeries. Maybe when he came back in three months, with a new face, he would be bold enough to ask if she could love him, like he loved her.

Sine Die. James had heard those words thrown about by many of the elder congressmen. They were words he had been longing to hear for the last seven days, and finally they had been spoken. The legislature was adjourned.

Back at his office, James had little to pack up. He'd be back in October, but three months seemed like a long time to leave his potted plant without water, so he figured he'd take it back to his Naperville office. He was setting the African violet into the brown box on his desk when Logan Cunningham, Representative for District Two, knocked on his door.

"Hey, rookie," Logan said with a grin. "I wasn't sure this day would come."

"Me neither," James said with a sigh.

"You got off easy," Logan said, resting his hand on the silver door handle. "Four years ago, we had to come back the first two weeks in June."

"Believe me, this was plenty." James replied, putting some folders into the box.

"Your Social Work Reform Bill took a good beating," Logan said solemnly. "I was surprised."

"Me too," James said with a cynical laugh.

"Well, you know I voted for it," Logan said with innocence.

"You're one of the few that didn't get bought by Banks."

"That guy's a manipulative bully."

"It's too bad a few more of our fellow voters didn't feel the same way."

"Are you leaving this afternoon to go back?"

"Most likely. I've got a stop to make in town, but then I'll be headed home."

"Well, have a safe trip, and I'll see you at that fundraising barbeque in July," Logan said, turning to exit.

James finished putting the paperwork he needed to take with him in the box, next to the plant, and then sat down at his desk. Pulling the phone from his pocket, he swiped the screen, entered his password, and checked his text messages. Still nothing from Danielle.

The last time they talked he had been at a gas station on the side of the highway. She made it clear she was done waiting for him. She said she was taking the stress of a relationship off his plate. James was irked that Danielle made the choice sound like a favor. He was also irritated at his mom, so their relationship had been limping along, too. Then, of course, there was underlying anger with Banks.

Nothing he proposed this session had passed-thanks to Banks. He tried not to blame the Education Reform failure on him too, because that wasn't his fault. Everything he had worked to accomplish, hoping that it would change lives for the better, disappeared like smoke. It was hard not to blame someone.

James was overtired, overworked, and irritable. This was not the way he thought he would feel at the end of his first calendar session. And it was not the way he wanted to see Danielle. Not that she even wanted to see him, but he couldn't leave for three months without attempting to say goodbye. Determination had gotten him far in his career. He hoped it wouldn't be the undoing of his personal life. He was going to stop by her house on the way out of town- even if it would be a surprise. He didn't trust she'd let him come if he asked.

When he drove up to Danielle's house, he was nervous. He had the air-conditioner on, to fight the afternoon heat, but he was still sweating. As he pulled alongside the curb, he saw a large sports utility vehicle he didn't recognize parked in the driveway.

However, as he turned off his car and took a closer look at the vehicle, the back plate held a plastic frame from a Naperville car dealer. Maybe Danielle's mom had come for a visit, James mused. He debated taking off and heading home, but he knew he'd regret it, and at least, he reasoned, she was home. Even a brief meeting would let her know he cared -and that he wasn't going to give up easily.

James stepped out onto the road and headed for the sidewalk when he heard Danielle's voice. He stopped to make out which direction it was coming from. She was clearly outside.

"Really beautiful," a deep male voice bellowed.

Who was she with, James wondered? Walking towards the sound, he found himself at the gate of the neighbor's backyard.

Chapter Twenty-Eight

James knocked on the gate, and the backyard conversation silenced. Within seconds, Danielle was before him.

"James," Danielle gasped.

James took in the sight of Danielle. She was wearing a floral chiffon sundress with tall taupe sandals. Her hair was curled, and she looked beautiful. James was surprised at how well she looked, given it had only been one month since the accident. There were scars across her cheek and by her lips, but she still was a woman worth beholding.

"James Patton?" a tall man, with a head-full of gray hair questioned, as he moved to stand next to Danielle.

"Yes. Have we met?" James asked with apprehension.

"Why, of course," the man replied jovially. "I'm Danielle's dad."

Daniel Davison reached his hand out to James.

"You almost beat my daughter out for her second-place finish at Naperville North, but it looks like you've done well with yourself," Daniel said flatteringly. "I've followed your political career, and you're going places, young man."

James felt like a stiff-robot, unsure of what to do or say. He remembered all the unflattering stories Danielle had shared about this man. She was right, he was smooth on the exterior.

"Thank you," James muttered.

"Well, Danielle, I'm sure James didn't come here to see me, so I'll go check into the hotel. I'll pick you up for dinner around five-thirty, if that's okay?"

"Good to see you again, James," Daniel said, patting James on the back as he exited next to him.

When Daniel was clearly out of range, Danielle sighed, "I need to sit down."

Hawk laid on his back, staring at the ceiling. The doctor must make a massive amount of money, he thought, turning to look again at the state-of-art laser machine that would soon be activated for his first pulsed dye laser treatment. As he had entered the building, he was impressed with its modern design, plush waiting room, and the cream-colored leather chair where he now reclined.

With no facilities of their kind in Springfield, Hawk had scheduled his care through the Laser and Dermatology Center in St. Louis. His mom had wanted to come with him, but he felt silly being a thirty-one-year-old man with his mother along for an outpatient surgery that would require no anesthesia.

From what he had learned about the procedure, the numbing lotion he had applied before he came would help take the edge off the pain, and the laser would just feel like the snapping of a rubber band.

Dr. Reeza, an aging gentleman with a bald head, would be in to perform the surgery any minute, and Hawk didn't feel the least bit nervous. When the doctor met with him a month ago for his consultation, he asked him why he hadn't done it sooner. The three surgeries would cost a few thousand dollars, and finances had been his answer.

However, as he reflected on his response as he drove home that day, he realized that he had needed a motivator. Hawk had been going through the motions of life for so long, enjoying his gardening projects, planning the future move, and living as if he'd never associate with the human-race, he saw no reason to change. Honestly, he didn't even think about doing life any differently.

The plan was to do one surgery at the beginning of each month. By mid-August, the healing should be done, and he could see Danielle again. The recovery process took a week to ten days, and blueberry-sized purple dots, which would look like a plague from times past, would cover every area touched by the laser. He'd have to stay out of the sun and wear sunscreen, but since he wouldn't be gardening it wouldn't be too hard.

Hawk heard a rap on the door, and Dr. Reeza entered.

"Good to see you again, Ethan," Dr. Reeza said as he extended his hand. "You ready for this little guy to become your savior?" he asked, holding the laser wand.

Hawk thought *there's only one Savior*, and as quickly as his mind registered the statement he wondered where it had come from.

The fountain gurgled quietly in the background, although Danielle didn't notice. She was too shocked to pay attention to anything but her swirling thoughts. Two hours earlier, her dad pulled into her driveway, unannounced. She hardly recognized him. Sixteen years brought with it gray hair, age spots and a slight hunch to his back.

He said he didn't call in advance because he didn't think she'd give him permission to come. When she opened the front door, she didn't know what to say, and that is how the rest of the two hours had gone. Danielle had spent a long portion of their conversation relaying the details of her accident. She seemed to be able to talk about the present more easily than the past.

Then Daniel offered her legal counsel asking if she wanted to sue Booker for the damage done to her face. She declined. She knew Booker didn't have enough to live on himself, let alone pay for her facial reconstruction.

After that topic had been exhausted, Daniel asked about her career and life in Springfield. Danielle tried to be polite and ask him questions in return, but she was so in shock, she had a hard time appearing calm and confident when her limbs felt like jelly.

Somehow Hawk's backyard oasis had come up in conversation, and when her dad asked to see it, she hadn't refused. When James showed up, also unpredictably, it was almost too much to bear.

"Whose backyard is this?" James asked as he sat down in the same seat Hawk had occupied just a few days earlier.

"My neighbor's," Danielle said in a shaky voice.

James laughed. "I gathered that."

Danielle giggled, and she felt shamefully embarrassed that her cheek wouldn't rise with her mouth's movement-yet again. This is the test, she thought. Will he stare at me with pity, now?

James saw her cheek droop and wanted desperately to reach out and caress her scar, but he didn't know how she would take it. He could tell she felt uncomfortable, and he quickly pulled the conversation back on track.

"Are you plant-sitting for your neighbor?"

"No, he just gave me a key, so I could enjoy his backyard while he is out of town."

"Oh, that's nice. It really is peaceful back here," James said, feeling the sweat under his armpits, and hoping it wasn't showing through his shirt. "I'm sorry to surprise you like this. I just didn't think you'd answer if I asked to visit you in advance."

"You're the second person to say that today," Danielle mused softly as a moth fluttered by the firepit.

"Maybe I'm more like your dad than I realized," James replied, reading into the comment. "He sure seemed outgoing."

"You both have never met a stranger," Danielle replied flatly.

"Obviously with your dad's visit, you've got a lot on your mind."

Danielle chuckled sarcastically. "You can say that again."

"I had no idea–"

"I didn't either," Danielle interjected. "I haven't seen him in sixteen years. And now here he is. He just showed up on my doorstep two hours ago."

"Has he changed?"

"I don't know," she answered honestly.

"Why'd he come?"

"I don't know?" she replied with confusion.

"Well, I hope when you go out to dinner, you'll get the answers to those questions."

"Me too. This is only my second trip out of the house since the accident."

"Really?"

Danielle pointed to her face and gave a smug, lopsided grin.

"You're still beautiful," James replied sincerely. He took her hands in his, but she pulled them away.

A cool breeze blew through the pergola.

"Do you want me to go with you tonight?" James asked.

Danielle pursed her lips and felt the scar tissue pull. His offer was tempting. James was so outgoing, and he'd be a great buffer for them both.

"No," she said, shaking her head. "I'll be fine."

"Are you sure? Are you sure you want to be alone with him?"

"No, not entirely. But you don't owe me anything, James."

"You'd be doing me a favor by letting me come. I know you're not happy with me. I know my schedule kept me from you when you needed me the most, but I'm here now."

"But I can't count on you after that, and that's the trouble," Danielle replied tender-heartedly.

"My schedule is slowing down."

"I know, but you'll have campaigning to do on top of the workload this fall, and we both know how many hours you put in already."

James was quiet. He knew what she said was true. Campaigning last fall had been exhausting, and with two-year terms, working to get elected was a big part of his job.

"James, you're a great guy," Danielle sighed knowing what she had to say. "Thank you for proving to me that your kind does exist, but even if we wanted to make this work, I can't see a future with someone who has to sacrifice so much for his career. And that's saying a lot coming from me."

"You worked as many hours as I did."

"I know, but I've realized a few things in the past month. I gave up so much for my job, I didn't really make time for anything else. Do you realize I've gone to the same church for nine years, and I don't really have any friends there? And, I just started clearing out my garage last week. I never even had time to take care of things here."

"But you can help me change. I'd like to be more balanced." James persisted.

"Don't you want to keep climbing the ladder politically?"

"I might not have a choice."

"What do you mean?" she asked, as she noticed a bead of perspiration run down behind his ear.

"Let's just say my efforts didn't really pay off this year for my personal platforms."

"You mean the Social Work Reform Bill didn't pass?" Danielle asked in alarm.

He shook his head sorrowfully.

"Neither did the education reform bill."

"I'm sorry to hear that," Danielle said. They had talked extensively about the Social Work Reform Bill, and she was sincerely sorry it didn't pass.

"I may not have any support left."

"That sounds extreme. I highly doubt most of your constituents pay attention to which bills pass and which don't."

"Maybe. But I didn't come here to talk about my dismal political career. I came here to tell you I've won a fair number of elections in my life, and none of the wins compare to the feeling of complete joy that I have when I'm with you. Not even when I was voted by my third-grade class to be hall monitor for the month of May."

Danielle let out a musical laugh, and James drew himself nearer to her body. He ran his finger along her scars tenderly.

"Oh, my sweet Danielle, I am so sorry," he whispered, his lips inches away from hers.

Tears began to fall from Danielle's eyes and ran onto the hand that caressed her cheek.

"My beautiful Danielle, would you forgive me for letting you down? For not being there for you when you needed me the most? If I could go back and redo all these days, I would."

James brushed the tears from her cheeks with his hands, and then tenderly kissed her lips. Danielle didn't stop him. James continued to soak in the taste of her mouth. How he loved her. Desired her.

A strong breeze blew and the gate to the backyard swung shut with a loud thud. Danielle pulled back.

"James," she exhaled.

"Danielle," he interrupted. "This fall, after I won the election, I knew something was missing. I was surrounded by people, but I was still lonely. I could go back to living without you. I could go on with my life, but I don't want to. I love you, like I have never loved anyone or anything. Not even my political career."

"James, you've worked too hard to-"

"I don't care, Danielle," he said, trying to control the anger he felt for being unable to make her understand. "All I care about is you."

"I wish you would've been with me at the hospital to tell me that, or when I was recovering at home," she said quietly.

"I know. I know," he said gruffly.

James stood up and felt the breeze blow through his dress shirt. It felt cool and refreshing.

"Give me another chance," he said, keeping his eyes on her.

"I don't think I have it in me to try again," she replied, returning his gaze.

She rose to her feet and enveloped him in a hug. At first, he wouldn't give in to the embrace, but he felt the pure, soft skin of her back and he relaxed. Then he held her until he felt her shoulders shaking. Pulling away, James could see she was crying. He kissed her gently on the lips, tasting her salty tears.

"I'm not ready to let you go," James said softly.

"I'm sorry," Danielle said, and then she turned and fled out of the garden.

Chapter Twenty-Nine

It had been five weeks since Danielle had entered the DCFS building. Linda would have given her a few more weeks off, but Danielle felt an obligation to return. She knew how much extra work her absence had placed on her co-workers, and although Danielle's career plans had shifted, she still needed a job.

Just days earlier she had been accepted into an online degree program so she could earn a bachelor's in elementary education. It wasn't a decision she made lightly. Danielle had been praying for direction since she left the hospital, and an answer had come in a surprising way. Tonya's dad, Joseph.

He had asked if he could meet with her weekly, when Tonya went to help a client on the same side of town. Danielle felt unsure at first, when he called. She barely knew Joseph, but minutes after telling him she'd think about it she realized she'd be pushing away a blessing from God if she'd didn't take him up on the offer.

So, that began their Wednesday evening dates. The two hours they had together never felt like a chore. Joseph was a man with deep-faith and great wisdom. Sometimes they sat in her living room talking and sometimes they went to Hawk's backyard. Joseph asked so many wonderful questions, he naturally drew out her worries-one of which was the decision about her career.

She had helped hundreds of kids through her years with the agency. And she shared that work was hard, often unrewarding and emotionally exhausting, but she wanted to make a difference in the lives of children. Joseph asked if she had ever considered teaching. It wasn't something she had ever thought about pursuing, but Danielle recognized the potential to fulfill her goal in a new environment.

In the meantime, there were still bills to pay, and she wanted to transition in a way that would be helpful to the agency and her clients. Entering her office, she found her desk the same way she had left it. As she sat down in her chair, she saw the scripture jar James had given her so many months ago. On the wall behind her computer, she glanced at pictures of foster kids and families she had helped in the last few years.

Feeling nostalgic, she pulled down a hand-drawn note. *Thank you for changing my life. Bree.* Danielle recalled how thirteen-year-old Bree had been placed with a couple that decided in their fifties to foster. In less than a year's time Bree was officially adopted and thriving in their home. A knock on the door drew her attention away from the note.

"Hey, girl," Callie said as she rested her elbow against the door. "You ready for this?"

"I hope so. I feel a little rusty."

"Don't sweat it. It will be like riding a bike," Callie replied as she moved from the door to sit down in the chair across from Danielle.

"I haven't seen Layla since before the accident."

"You'll be fine."

Danielle sighed and smiled her lopsided grin. "Thank you for handling this case, and so many of my other ones for the past month. I can't imagine how hard you've had to work while I was away."

"That's what any of us would do for each other, you know that. Linda said you're officially starting back in one week."

"That's the plan."

"Well, I'm super excited to give you back your work," Callie laughed. "We'll all be doing a happy dance around here."

"You know it's only temporary."

"I know, you told me," Callie said, frowning. "You're only taking one class at a time though, right? And that could take years," she said hopefully.

"If I find I can handle the workload, I may speed it up, or maybe I will decide to become a full-time student. We'll see."

"Miss Davison, elementary teacher," Callie replied, trying out Danielle's future title.

"Someday, but for now it's Miss Davison, case worker. I better get to the conference room. Layla probably won't be on time, but at least I will."

Danielle wasn't surprised that Layla was fifteen minutes late. When she arrived, she reeked of smoke and her hair was pulled back in a messy bun. But she had come. Danielle hugged her, and Layla began to sob. When Layla had recovered enough to talk, she expressed deep sympathy for the accident and Danielle's scars. After reassuring Layla that it wasn't her fault, another torrent of tears began. Layla admitted she needed to give up Nevaeh.

Despite the strong smell emanating from a woman that needed a shower, Danielle held Layla until she had calmed enough to talk. Pushing a box of tissue closer to Layla, they sat down at the table.

"What brought you to this decision?" Danielle asked.

Layla wiped her eyes. "I just can't seem to get my-" catching a cuss word from flying, she continued, "act together. It's been two days since I've had a hit and look at me." Layla held out her shaking hand. "Nevaeh deserves more. And I've seen her with the Worthingtons. Debbie seems like the perfect mom," Layla said with a hint of jealousy.

"This decision takes a lot of courage," Danielle replied.

Pulling in Callie for back-up, the three ladies talked through this major choice for the next half-hour. By the end of their meeting, Layla said she didn't have the courage to meet with Nevaeh again to say goodbye, but she had written her a note. She asked Danielle to read it after she left. Hugging Layla one last time and letting her know she'd be in touch, Layla walked out, and Danielle opened the letter.

Dear Nevaeh,

I'm so sorry I couldn't be the mom you needed me to be. I'll love you always and forever. With the Worthingtons, I'm giving you a chance to succeed. Maybe you'll have the life I always hoped for but couldn't seem to achieve.

I never told you how I picked your name. Nevaeh is heaven spelled backwards. When I saw you for the first time, you were like a glimpse of heaven, and I knew that had to be your name, too. Heaven is hope of a better future, and Nevaeh, that's what I'm giving you.

I hope you know how hard this is for me. How I'll think about you always. I love you.

Mom

"Thanks for bringing me lunch, Kira," James said as he unwrapped the paper from a ham and cheese sub sandwich.

Kira sat down in the office chair across from James and started unrolling her turkey and swiss.

"I love summer," she smiled. Her brown skin reflected hours of sun.

"How are you passing your time without all your students?"

"Laying out at the pool at the apartment complex, reading, catching up on sleep. It's delightful."

Kira flattened the paper and laid her sandwich on top.

"You look down...or tired?" she asked.

"Is it that obvious?" James sighed. "It seems summer "recess" is almost as busy as the month of May. Meetings, speaking engagements, tours of hospitals, schools. I am exhausted."

"Is it worth it?"

"I honestly don't know." James ran his hand through his hair. "I lost Danielle because of the hours. That was a steep price to pay."

"Do you still think about her?"

"All the time."

"You used to say a politician could balance work and a relationship. Have you changed your mind?"

"Both of Danielle's parents put their careers in front of her. Maybe the case would be different with someone else. She needs someone who will show her she has value by being there for her consistently."

Kira took a sip of her water bottle.

"Maybe she's not the right person for you then," she said.

"I would ask for counsel about finding "the one," but you're as single as I am," he chuckled.

"Hey, just because I'm single doesn't mean I can't give advice," she said with an indignant grin. "This may not seem very intellectual, but I think deep inside you just know. There's a settled feeling."

She picked up a piece of lettuce from the paper holding the sandwich drippings and popped it in her mouth.

"And that is why I am still available," she laughed. "No one I've dated has passed that test."

"Danielle passes those standards," James replied.

"What?" Kira erupted.

"I don't have any reservations. I could spend the rest of my life with her."

"Then you know what you have to do next," she said excitedly. "James, you've always been an "all in" type of person. When you wanted to run for representative, you cashed out the savings account from Grandpa without question. You went for it 100%. Now you've got to do the same with Danielle."

"You mean quit my job?"

"No, not now. Finish your term, but then take a hiatus to show Danielle you can be who she needs you to be."

James pursed his lips in thought.

"You don't have to be done with politics forever. Just because you change paths now doesn't mean you're locked into staying that course forever. Plus, there are always school board and park district positions to run for."

James' eyes flickered with hope. "I'll pray about it."

Hawk stared at his reflection in the mirror. Half of his face looked like it had a plague. He was thankful to be staying at his mom's apartment, so there would be no chance encounter with Danielle.

His second treatment had been as uncomfortable as the first, but now he knew what to expect so he anticipated the visit more highly. While the little stings of pain were temporary, the hundreds of purple dots took weeks to fade.

However, after the healing period of his first treatment was over, Hawk was thrilled to see how the rosy appearance of his birthmarks had diminished drastically. As Hawk applied the special cream to his cheek, he thought about Danielle.

It had been five weeks since the backyard birthday. Was she using the journal he gave her and sitting under the pergola? He missed doing his outdoor projects almost as much as he missed her, and Hawk wondered if his irrigation system was working.

When he got back, he planned to share the vision he had for his future with her. Starting Adams Landscaping and living in the country with rows of trees and greenhouses filled with shrubs and perennials was the ideal life for him. He hoped she could catch his vision and be willing to go along for the ride.

His mom had warned him to take things slowly when he returned, but he was too excited. Everything he had ever dreamed was falling into place. A new face, a new love, and a new dream awaited him.

Hawk thought about texting Danielle to see how she was doing, but he knew she would ask about him, and he couldn't bear to be dishonest. The next six weeks couldn't pass quickly enough, he mused. Soon he would be going home, and he was full of hope.

Over the course of the past few months, Hawk read the Bible his mom had gotten him, and the word "hope" graced many pages. Hawk still wasn't "all in" like Danielle appeared to be. He now believed Jesus really walked on earth over two-thousand years ago. Enough extra-Biblical sources confirmed that, but he wasn't sure Jesus was as powerful as He claimed.

He had recently finished the book of Psalms, and chapter 121 said God would keep his foot from slipping. Yet, he had fallen on the ice, and the stiffness in his knee still reminded him of his kneecap injury. How could a loving God, who declared His ability to shelter His children, let him fall? Why would a benevolent Father let him face rejection and the pain of humiliation because of his birthmarks?

Hawk closed the cap of the facial cream and wiped his hands on the navy blue towel in the bathroom. Maybe he would ask Danielle these questions one day. Until then, he would keep searching for answers.

Danielle had become so comfortable on the couch in Hawk's backyard that she now considered it "her spot." She had thought about Hawk many times over the course of the past two months. So much had transpired. Although Hawk had said she could text him if she needed something, nothing that called for his attention had arisen.

Hawk had installed an irrigation system to take care of the plants while he was gone, and she offered to water the potted ones. Danielle found herself gravitating to the peaceful oasis at least three times a week, and on a Saturday night in late July, she made her way there again.

She had already started a fire, and she sat quietly for a few minutes watching the sparks fly. The first few times she had tried to make a fire, she couldn't get one going. She had to use her phone to research how to start one. But almost eight weeks later, she was a pro.

At nine-thirty, the stars were just beginning to come out. Danielle loved the long days of summer. As she stared at the sky, she heard a noise and looked to the back corner of the property. A rabbit darted across the backyard. Danielle caught the sight of the shingled roof tucked behind the bushes in the back.

She was thankful she now knew what it was. On her first solo visit, she went straight to the mysterious spot. There she found a sign that read "Hawk's Hotel" on the tall, metal cage. Inside the cage, there was a tire swing, a hollow log, and climbing planks. Obviously, it was for animals, which was to Danielle's relief. When he had mentioned a hotel, she just didn't know.

No furry critters were inside at the moment, but Danielle figured Hawk had taken care of many animals in the past. He had been as confident as a veterinarian when he fixed Tinkerbell's paw many months ago.

She was thankful she was a cat person. The two major repercussions from her accident were having to explain the story about her scars over and over, and a new-found fear of dogs. Linda allowed her to trade the five cases where she would have to encounter them. But that didn't completely solve the problem.

Sometimes the neighbors of a client would have a pit-bull, and that would send her heart racing. However, the most intense fear she faced was going back to the scene of the accident. No one asked her to, but she wanted to thank her rescuer. She had journaled about it, and as she flipped through the pages to get to the nearest blank one, she ran across her account of that afternoon.

I met D'Shawn Williamson today. I didn't know what kind of gift you would give someone who saved your life, so I opted for a plant and a hand-written note. That doesn't seem like enough, but he seemed grateful. I was glad I had called ahead. D'Shawn only visits occasionally. I guess his cousins live in the house. He had been visiting on the day of the attack. He told me he had gone out to the porch for a smoke and heard my cries. His cousins followed him to the backyard, but they were too scared, and they ran to call for help.

D'Shawn told me he had to kick the dog really hard to get it off my face. But once it stopped attacking, it didn't go after him. It just ran towards the front yard. D'Shawn said he had nightmares over the images of my torn-up face, but he was glad to see me looking so well. I hope the nightmares will stop now. I thanked him as many times as I could fit into our fifteen-minute conversation, and I'm glad I went, even if it was hard.

I was half tempted to go into the backyard to see if any of my blood remained on the concrete patio. But I couldn't bring myself to do it, even though there are no new tenants living there now. What would be the point, anyway? The blood that was spilled is behind me.

Danielle found the next blank page. She picked up the pen to write but noticed the fire was dwindling, so she put down the journal. Grabbing the poker, she pushed the logs around.

Her mind went back to the night of her birthday when Hawk had stirred the fire. Setting the poker against the pergola, she ran her hand along the smooth wood pillar. What had made him create this for her? Sure, she had been kind to him, especially through the recovery of his broken kneecap, but she'd never been one to see a need and not try to help.

She had been concerned that night that he was going to ask for more out of their relationship. There had been a few guys in college that took her kindness as interest in more than just friendship, and she had to explain to them that she was just being friendly. Hawk said he'd never had a friend, and she was glad to be his first. But she hoped she hadn't led him on.

Where had he gone? He'd always been secretive but leaving for three months seemed odd. There was only one more month without him. Part of her would be glad when he returned, the other part would miss the exclusive use of his backyard. She knew he would likely welcome her to use it anytime, but it wouldn't be the same. She didn't have to share it or wonder if he'd come out to visit. Now it was perfectly private. And perfectly healing.

Walking back to the couch, Danielle heard a noise by the gate, and she turned to look. Maybe it was the same silly rabbit. Nothing appeared in the dark. Staring at the gate, she thought about how James had rested his arm against it the last time she saw him.

Not a day had gone by, since she ran from him in tears, where James didn't cross her mind. She tried to remind herself why it wouldn't have worked. She was striving to find balance in her own life. James could claim he wanted that too, but she knew his career would make it very challenging. She'd already spent too many years hoping those that she loved would make her a priority.

He was the first, and only, man she had envisioned herself marrying. She'd heard people say that once you know- you know. And it was true. Maybe someday, someone would come along who would make her feel the same way James had.

But in the meantime, she was learning to embrace a quieter, deeper part of herself.

The fire pit sizzled, and before sitting down Danielle moved the couch closer to the fire. Then she opened her journal to the nearest blank page and began to write.

My dad has continued his Sunday phone calls. I have to say, I'm pretty surprised. He told me at the restaurant, two months ago, that when he found out about the attack, he was devastated, but he couldn't bring himself to see me until I had some healing time behind me.

He still hasn't said anything about my appearance. However, both my mom and dad have offered money for plastic surgery, seeing that I wasn't going to sue Booker. He also hasn't been anything but kind. It's been unnerving. I keep waiting for the "shoe to drop." But he told me he had a bout with prostate cancer a year ago. I think that may have mellowed and humbled him. But I'm still taking things cautiously.

He's asked if we could do another visit at some point. I told him maybe after my plastic surgery. I've decided to go through with it. The muscle in my cheek needs some reconstruction, and the doctor can use a laser to lighten my facial scars. With the treatment and some make-up, they should be almost unnoticeable.

Tonya's dad, Joseph, doesn't think I need to do the surgery, but I guess I'm vainer than I realized. How much have I judged people by their outer appearance my whole life? I feel like I'm constantly being assessed by my appearance. Before the accident, I didn't mind because the feedback was positive. Now, there are so many questioning stares.

I always thought I never judged people by their looks. Even Hawk. I didn't care about his birth marks, but I definitely felt sorry for him. I know people have been feeling sorry for me.

It's strange having people pity you. I've prayed about the surgery, and I feel God's peace.

My life is forever changed because of the accident, but at least now I can see glimpses of good- in my character, in my renewed relationship with my dad, and a greater appreciation for those that don't judge by outer appearance. Like Joseph. Being blind actually helps him truly see.

Joseph has made me recognize that I can be loved unconditionally. After Paul left the agency, I felt the loss of that father-figure influence. But Paul was really only a work friend. We didn't talk about faith, relationships, hopes and dreams. With Joseph I can talk about anything, get advice. He genuinely seems to care about me. And we pray together every visit.

In the hospital, when the chaplain told me to seek out an "adopted dad," I thought that was a far-fetched idea. But God with you nothing is impossible. Nothing.

Chapter Thirty

I'm coming home tomorrow. Can I see you? My backyard, around eight? Should be cooled off by then. It was supposed to be in the low nineties, Danielle thought as she read the text from Hawk as she sat in the wingback chair, enjoying a quiet Saturday night at home.

She'd been going to a small group Bible study every other Sunday night, made up of people from her church. Danielle found these new friendships to be life giving, and the bi-weekly gatherings had become a high point on her calendar. Thankfully, Hawk was coming home on one of the Sunday's they had off. So, she texted her consent to meet. She felt confident Hawk would notice the change in her appearance.

Only three weeks earlier, she had sat behind a laser having her scars treated. After the first six days of dealing with peeling and itchy skin, Danielle could see that it had been very successful. Even without make-up she couldn't see scar lines on her cheek, and there was only a slight line on top of her lip that could be remedied with foundation.

The muscle in her cheek still didn't have complete mobility, but she decided it would be a mark of God's faithfulness in her life. She could have died if D'Shawn hadn't come to her rescue, and she knew who had sent him. Danielle looked forward to seeing Hawk. They had three months of news to share with one another, and she felt her former energy and confidence returning.

Hawk loaded up his car with the cat carrier, Chewy, and two baskets of clean laundry. He couldn't wait to be going home. At first, living with his mom hadn't seemed too bad. But as the days passed, her need to clean up around him became annoying. If she worked the night shift, it seemed to help. He'd do his transcribing in the day, and she would be gone most of the evening. Then, he'd have the whole apartment to himself.

When they both had the day off, that's when the apartment felt small. He missed working outdoors, working with his hands. And he missed Danielle. He wished their relationship had been a closer one when he left, but he hoped that his new look would cause her to see him in a new way.

At the beginning of August, he had his third pulsed-dye laser treatment. With two procedures behind him, it still stung, but now he knew what to expect. The blueberry-colored stains covered every portion of his birthmarks, and it took about a week, after each treatment, for the small circles to fade. Besides putting on ample lotion and wearing sunscreen in the brief moments he was outside, the recovery-effort was minimal.

After the third surgery, when the bluish-purple dots disappeared completely, Hawk went to get his shaggy hair cut and his beard trimmed. It was the first time, since his mom had taken him as a child, that he had gone to a barber. He'd always grown his hair out, and trimmed it himself, to keep from having extra contact with the world. This was the first test of how successful the procedures had been.

The barber, a graying gentleman in his fifties, passed the exam. As he walked Hawk back to the chair, he chatted about the weather and what Hawk wanted done to his hair. There were no stares and no questions asked about his skin. When Hawk looked at himself in the mirror, as he sat in the chair, he could make-out a wisp of pink coloring in his eyebrow and on the side of his nose, but the marks were barely detectable. And the good news was that as long as he kept going for laser-treatments once a year, the results would last.

When his mom arrived home from work, the day he got his haircut, she cried when she saw him. The natural body in his hair meant that the long-on-top style worked well for him, and his chiseled cheekbones could be seen now that his birthmark and beard no longer covered his face. He looked totally different, and he liked the way it made him feel.

Closing the backdoor to his car, he wondered why he hadn't done the treatment sooner. He hoped Danielle would be pleased. Eight o'clock couldn't come fast enough.

Rain swept through in the afternoon and cooled off the day. By evening, the grass was still wet, but the temperature was comfortable. A few minutes before eight, Hawk took out a towel, to dry off the couch and chair under the pergola.

As he was drying the couch, he heard the key in the gate's lock, and he turned to see Danielle. Even fifty feet away, Hawk could tell something was different. Her floral sundress was light blue, and she wore a wide-brimmed white hat, but that wasn't it. Bellowing a hello, she approached carrying something wrapped in foil.

Hawk put down the towel, and stood up straight, squaring his shoulders. He smiled broadly. Confidently. She gasped and nearly dropped whatever she was carrying.

"Hawk," she exhaled. "What have you done with yourself?"

"Like it?" he asked confidently.

"You look amazing," she gushed. "Your hair. Your beard. Your face," she exclaimed, and then quickly raised her hand to her mouth in embarrassment. "I'm sorry," she continued.

"Don't be," Hawk smiled. "I'm glad you noticed."

"Noticed? It would be impossible not to. You look...incredible."

"You look different, too. And yet the same." Hawk said, patting the couch. "It's dry."

Danielle was happy to return to "her spot," and she handed Hawk the foiled package as she sat down. "I made you a blueberry-crunch loaf."

"Thank you," Hawk replied, picking up the towel he had dropped on the concrete and proceeding to wipe off the side table.

"I had laser surgery a few weeks ago to lessen the appearance of the scars," Danielle said. "If only my cheek would do its thing," she replied, unconsciously rubbing her fingers over it in a massaging motion. "The doctor says the muscle may respond with time, otherwise I'll be having surgery at some point to graft in a new muscle."

"That sounds intense," Hawk replied, setting down the towel and placing the bread on the table.

"Tell me more about you," Danielle bubbled. "How hard was your surgery?"

Hawk shared the journey to recovery over the next fifteen minutes, with Danielle interrupting only to ask questions when she didn't understand something or wanted more detail.

"So, I'll have another laser surgery in six months, and then just one a year for maintenance," he finished.

"You were really brave," she said sincerely. "Does this mean you won't be in hiding anymore?"

"I still have to wear lots of sunscreen when I'm outside, and a hat. I should be wearing yours," he teased.

Danielle reached up and fondled the brim of hers. "I think we had the same instructions," she laughed.

They were silent for a moment, as the conversation lulled.

"Thank you for letting me use your backyard while you were away," Danielle began, breaking the silence. "It was the perfect oasis, and I used it quite often."

"You don't have to stop now that I'm back."

"I know, Hawk, but-"

"I've changed my name," Hawk interrupted. "No more Hawk. It's just Ethan, now."

"How come? New face, new name?"

"Old name, really," Hawk grinned. "Nah, not really the new face. Just new things happening in me."

"That's great...Ethan," Danielle smiled. The new name would take time to roll-off her tongue.

"But, really, I'd love to see you enjoying the backyard anytime you want," Hawk said. His mom warned him not to come on too strong, but he was like a tea kettle, ready to explode.

"Sure, but it's your space."

"Couldn't it be *our* space," he asked. "I'd like to spend more time with you, now that I'm back, Danielle."

Danielle was quiet.

"You mean like talking about the Bible or something?" she asked hesitantly.

"Well, we could. I know Jesus is real now, and I've been reading the Bible, but there's still a lot I want to understand."

"Hawk...Ethan...that's great," Danielle said excitedly. "I'd love to study the Bible with you." She paused. "I'm just not looking for anything else right now, if that's what you were implying."

"Is it Mr. Titanic?" Ethan asked, his voice dripping with jealousy.

"Who?" Danielle said, confused. "Oh, James," she replied, remembering the nickname he gave him. "We're not together anymore-"

"But you wish you were," Ethan replied angrily. "I can see it on your face."

"I think you and I are better off as friends," Danielle said as kindly as she could.

"And that's why I loved you," Ethan said in a huff. "You were my first real friend. You saw past my appearance." He stood up and went to the edge of the patio, staring at his animal habitat.

"You think I'm weird, don't you?" he asked, still facing the cage. "You saw the cage, and you think I'm weird."

"No," Danielle replied, getting up to stand next to him. "I did see Hawk's hotel," she smiled. "But I liked that you would take care of animals. At least that's what I think you do with that big thing."

"When you first moved in," Ethan began, "I was taking care of two baby rabbits. I accidentally ran over the hole their mom had made for them with my lawn mower and one of them didn't make it. The day you moved my garbage can for me was the day I disposed of it. I was always afraid you saw it."

"I never saw anything," she replied. "But you were really good with Tinkerbell. I just put two and two together."

"I have other goals," Ethan continued, trying to advocate for himself. "I want to run a landscaping business. I have stacks of notebooks filled with ideas."

"And I think that's great," she said, staring out into the backyard, shoulder to shoulder with him.

"Then it's because I was mean to you."

"You apologized."

"Then what is it?" Ethan asked, turning to face her. "What more could I have done?" he asked, fighting back tears.

"I'm sorry. There's not a formula," Danielle said, gently putting her hand on his shoulder. "You've become a great friend to me, too. You really helped me through one of the toughest times in my life-when I was home and recovering. I will be forever grateful for your friendship. And I'm excited that so many new things are happening in your life. You look amazing, but your appearance doesn't matter. It never has. It's just that I fell in love...with Mr. Titanic. And I can't "will" myself to stop feeling, even though we are not together."

Ethan shook off her hand, and Danielle noticed the tears in his eyes.

"I've been reading about this God of yours. I kept wanting to hope," he laughed cynically. "But it's like I thought. He set the world in motion, but he's not in the details of my life."

"Just because this conversation isn't going as you planned, doesn't mean God's not for you," she rubbed her hands together in thought. "I haven't told you yet, but I've been working on reconciling with my dad."

"That's great," he said quietly but sincerely.

"That's been a wound waiting to be healed for sixteen years. More than ever I believe God *is* in it all. His timing just isn't always our own."

"Then where was He when I was born with my hideous red face? Or when Lewis Fotana kept calling me names on the bus every day for a year? Or when I slipped on the ice six months ago?" he said angrily.

Danielle paused, praying for the right response.

"Where He is right now. He's Immanuel. God with us. He gave you a mom that loves you unconditionally. He made you strong through the taunting, and I found you after you fell."

"I just wish He gave you to me for more than a one-time rescue," Hawk replied as his shoulders slumped in defeat.

"You are really special to me, Ha-, Ethan, and believe it or not, I pray for you. One of my prayers is that God's best plan for you will prevail. That you'll be fully committed to Him, like He is to you. I believe you're going to see God do a lot of new things in your life."

"Maybe he's stopping with my face," Ethan sighed, feeling a sad resignation.

Every time Ethan walked past a mirror he paused. The reflection that stared back at him didn't seem like his own, but he liked what he saw. It was an unusual feeling.

When he was in third grade his mom purchased him a pair of expensive brand-name sneakers. With money always being tight, she had never done that before. Whenever he put on his new shoes, he couldn't help but look at them over and over again. And his new appearance was novel, just like the Nikes had been.

Ethan finished washing his face, and as he headed to bed for the night, he picked up his stack of landscaping notebooks. Earlier in the day he had walked the twenty-three acres of land on Farmingdale Road. The land had been rented to a local farmer for many years. The farmer was now retiring, and he decided to put the land on the market. Ethan hoped it would be his by morning.

The real estate agent had put in an offer for $150,000 which was ten thousand dollars under the listed price. If he sold his house for a top-end valuation of $69,000 and added in the $100,000 he saved over the last ten years, he'd have enough for the property and a used trailer to park on the premise until he could afford to build a home.

He'd seen shows like *Tiny House Nation* which featured dramatic downsizes. Ethan wondered how he'd like living in a compact twenty-five square foot trailer compared to his current 1,200 square foot house. But then he thought about all the land he'd own, and he felt like a child eyeing the best Christmas present ever.

Opening one of the notebooks, he eyed the sketches he made detailing what plants he put in each of three hoop houses he planned to construct. Hoop houses wouldn't need to be heated, which would save him a huge monthly expense, but would still provide extra protection from the cold winter weather and harsh winds. For his new landscaping business, he envisioned filling them with barberry, boxwoods, burning bushes, rhododendron, hydrangeas, and other popular Midwest shrubs and plants.

Flipping a few more pages, he saw the lists he'd made of trees he'd grow behind the hoop houses. American redbuds, emerald green arborvitae, and sugar maples were just a few of his choices for the rows he hoped to plant.

Ethan anticipated that one day he'd be able to sell annuals and perennials along with the shrubs and trees, from a storefront on his land. He'd also design and implement beautiful plans for customers. With his new appearance, he felt more confident working with people, but if he ever got wealthy enough, he'd hire someone to handle the marketing end, and he'd be happy to do the labor.

Knowing he was about to jump into a whole new adventure, he waffled between nervousness and excitement. A few days earlier he'd hoped he'd be looking at these books filled with his future ideas alongside Danielle. She said she trusted God was going to do new things in his life. He'd only wished these firsts would be with her by his side.

How could he have thought she'd be interested in him. Who would want to date a guy that was about to move into a trailer? Sure, he planned to keep his transcribing job until he could pay the bills with the landscaping business alone. But his plans seemed so speculative. For all he knew, a tornado could rip through and ruin everything.

Maybe he'd come on too strong? Maybe he should have given her some warning before he blurted out his feelings? What did it matter now, he questioned. He wasn't confident enough to try again or wait it out, and he certainly didn't want to be around if Mr. Titanic appeared back in the picture.

No, he needed to move. The expenses of his surgery had been under two-thousand dollars, and he wondered why he hadn't done it earlier. He looked normal for the first time in his life. He didn't feel normal, but perhaps he never would. All that he cared about now was starting over.

A "for sale" sign went up in Ethan's front yard within a week. Danielle was surprised, but she was even more shocked when a "sold" sign was pasted on top within two days. Houses in their neighborhood were popular, but it was rare to see one sell so fast, especially when the public schools had already begun, and the prime selling season in Springfield had passed.

One evening, when Danielle drove home from work, she saw a moving truck in Ethan's driveway. The day had been warm, and as she stepped out of the car, she felt a humid breeze blow her blonde curls. Grabbing her purse and locking the car, she heard Ethan in his backyard.

Walking over to the gate, she knocked.

"Did you forget your key?" he asked as he opened the gate.

Danielle still wasn't used to his new appearance, and she thought to herself, "he won't have a hard time finding someone new."

"I'll have to bring that back to you," she replied. "I saw the truck," she said pointing to the front yard.

"Can you believe there was a bidding war for this place?" he said, moving back to the patio, where he had been cleaning the glass-topped furniture. Danielle followed him.

"That's great. It's a nice house."

"It wasn't the house that sold the place. It was the backyard."

"That makes sense," she said, sensing his cool edge. Every time she had talked with him since their conversation two weeks prior, the intonation was the same. "I guess you're off to the country?"

Ethan sprayed the table with cleaner and began wiping vigorously. "I got the asking price for the house, so it made it possible for me to get the property I really wanted all along."

"I'm so happy for you," she replied sincerely. "I'll have to hire you… if I can afford you."

Ethan just kept scrubbing.

"I hope we can still be friends," Danielle said.

"I suppose I was looking for more than just a friend," Ethan replied.

"Then I hope you find what you're looking for," Danielle said. Before she turned to go, she put her hand on Ethan's shoulder. "I'll be praying for your business."

James never knocked when he went to his parents' house. The garage door had been open, and he went in through the kitchen entrance.

"Hey mom," he called as he opened the door.

"I'm in the office," she bellowed back.

James found her at the computer reading an email.

"I brought the book that I was talking about on Sunday." James set the hard-cover textbook on the desk.

"Thanks," she replied, pushing her glasses onto the top of her head. "You could've just dropped it off at the next Sunday brunch."

"I know you're busy preparing for your new classes at the college, and I figured you'd want to look it over before then."

"That was very thoughtful. Have a seat."

James sat down in the black leather desk chair across from Karen.

"This time last year, we would've been out knocking on doors with this kind of weather," she said looking out of the window at the sunny August afternoon. "I sure miss that."

"You do?" he asked incredulously.

"I still can't believe you're not going to run again," she said. Karen pulled the glasses back down and looked back at the computer.

"If you enjoyed the process so much, maybe you should run," James said with a hint of fire in his voice.

"I don't have time," she said coolly.

"You wanted to though, didn't you?"

"Wanted to what?"

"Be a politician."

"No, I just like politics. I don't have your bravery or courage."

"What do you mean? You teach students all year long. You could make the necessary speeches. And you obviously didn't mind knocking on doors or attending fundraisers."

"I don't have your personality. You're so outgoing. You're a natural leader."

Karen stopped looking at the computer and gazed at James.

"As much as you may think I am trying to live out a goal of mine through you, I am not. I just believe in you. I see no limits on your potential, and all I've ever wanted was for you to achieve your dreams."

James smiled. "Thanks, Mom."

"Don't be mad at Kira, but she told me that part of the reason your goals have shifted is because you found a new dream to pursue."

"Danielle was only a portion of the equation, Mom. As I prayed about the decision, I recognized the situation with Banks wasn't an isolated one. So many good ideas get blocked because of corruption in the system."

"But you're a world changer, James."

"So are you. Moms are world changers. Dads. Teachers. Nurses. Pastors. Foster parents. There are so many ways to influence our corner of the earth for good. And I can do that through educational law again. I can do that by being a good husband and father one day-I hope."

Karen was quiet.

"You're so important to me, Mom, and I want to respect you, but in the end this is my decision."

She smiled.

"James, I don't want to be angry about it anymore. Danielle's accident, and your acceptance of her despite her appearance, made me realize your feelings for her are strong. I've certainly never seen you so committed to anyone. A few weeks ago, when I was taking a walk with your dad, I started thinking about you and how you seem ready to have someone walk beside you. You are an amazing young man. You've opened my eyes to see that your job doesn't define you. It's your character that counts."

"I'm glad you understand. That means so much." James got up, walked to his mom's side, and wrapped her in a hug. "I love you. Thank you for supporting me, wherever my path leads."

Danielle must have been at work the day the house was reoccupied. She knew there was a new owner, when she saw a rattan welcome mat appear on the step. But besides the new mat, the house became like a bat cave at night- dark and empty. For the next week, she eagerly watched for the new neighbor but saw no sign of anyone.

The following weekend, she saw the front windows were open, when she drove home from the grocery store, so she decided to take back the key. She had forgotten to do it the night she talked with Ethan, and the following morning he was gone.

After unloading her groceries, she rummaged around her kitchen looking for something that could be a welcome gift. She didn't feel right going empty-handed. Opening the freezer door, she saw she had frozen banana bread on the bottom shelf. Grabbing a ribbon from a box in her guest bedroom, she wrapped the foiled loaf and headed over with the key.

As she walked, she took her free hand and massaged her cheek. Improvement was being made, but the droop was still noticeable when she was tired. Not that she was now, but she was conscious of meeting someone new. Danielle was thankful she had on blue jeans and a red blouse, and not just workout pants and a sweatshirt, like she often wore on Saturdays.

Almost at the door, Danielle said a silent prayer that she could be God's light to her new neighbor, or neighbors. Maybe there was a family in Ethan's old home, she pondered. Ringing the doorbell, she thought about the many times she rang Ethan's bell, only to have him avoid her. He had come so far in such a short time.

She heard the shuffling of feet and the lock click.

"Hi Danielle."

"James! What are you doing here?" she said breathlessly.

"You look fantastic."

"Laser surgery," Danielle replied quickly. Her mind was in comprehension mode.

"I thought you had a house in Naperville," she continued, completely confused.

"You want to come in?" he asked, ushering her inside with a cool confidence.

"Where's your car? I didn't see it," Danielle replied, flustered.

"It's in the garage. Can I take that from you?" he asked, noticing how she was moving the loaf of bread from one hand to the other.

"It's cold," she replied, as he took it from her hands and brought it to the kitchen.

As he stepped out of the room, she scanned the place with his furnishings in it. It looked sophisticated and well put together with the black couch, gray chairs and dark end tables.

James returned and sat down onto a gray chair.

"Sure you don't want to sit?" he asked.

"No," Danielle replied, still baffled. "Oh, here," she said, taking the key in her hand and pushing it towards James.

"You can keep it," he replied.

"But it's a key to the backyard."

"I figured."

"You bought Hawk's...I mean Ethan's place."

"That I did," he grinned.

Danielle felt weak. She sat down on the black couch, staring at James. It all felt like a dream.

"I heard there was a bidding war," Danielle said, still stunned.

"This backyard is going to make Ethan famous," James replied.

"What do you mean?"

"Do you know how many offers he had on this place?"

"No."

"I think he told me there were fifteen. I just happened to bid the highest. The pictures of his backyard were on every realtor's website."

"What'd you do with your place in Naperville?" Danielle asked again.

"It's still there," James replied, enjoying the cat and mouse game, and secretly wishing it was over with so he could kiss her.

"Don't you need to live in your district?"

"I do. This is my vacation home," he teased.

"How come I didn't see you move in?"

"I hired a few men to help me unload my stuff. You were at work."

Danielle sighed in exasperation, and James knew it was time to give her some real answers.

"I decided not to run again next fall," James said seriously.

"What?"

"I'm going to try to get work as an educational lawyer here in Springfield after my term is up this May."

"I thought you were doing what you loved?"

"I was, until I realized there was something I loved more."

"A beautiful backyard?" Danielle asked, cocking one eyebrow, certain that wasn't it.

"No, a beautiful neighbor," James smiled, bringing out the cute dimple in his cheek.

James moved to the middle seat on the couch, next to her, found her hand, and rested his on top.

"This past year in office taught me a lot about politics. There are other ways to be influential besides holding a seat in the legislature."

"You're giving up so much...for me."

"Not giving up. Just redirecting my efforts."

"But one day you might regret it."

"Well, one day if we both decide *together* that there's a need for me to enter a political race, then we'll be unified in the choice."

"I don't know what to say," she said, looking down.

"Then say you love me, because I know that I love you," he said huskily, keeping his eyes on her face.

"I don't know if I'm worth the redirection."

"I guess I'll have to spend the next thirty-years showing you that you are."

James took both of her hands in his, and she looked into his eyes.

"That's how long the mortgage is," he said with a playful grin.

Then he leaned in and gently kissed her lips.

Epilogue

One Year Later...

"Okay, now Callie and Danielle jump in," bellowed James from behind the camera. "Callie, lean in a little closer. I can't see you. That's better." James snapped a picture. "Do you want to make sure it looks okay, Mrs. Worthington?" he asked.

"Sure," she replied, hurrying forward in her heels.

"You look really pretty today," Danielle said, leaning down towards Nevaeh. "Who picked out your dress?"

"My mom," Nevaeh replied. "She even bought me these new shoes," she said, tapping her feet outward to show off her sparkly silver shoes.

"I'm happy that so many people who love you were here today," Danielle said, smiling at the Worthington family. "Was it scary to talk with the judge?"

"No, she was really nice," Nevaeh said. "Maybe one day I'll be a judge too, and help new families say 'I do.'"

Danielle laughed. "That could be a great job for you."

Mrs. Worthington came over to Danielle and Nevaeh, and Danielle stood back up.

"Thank you for all the help you've given our family over the last year and a half," Debbie said. "You gave us courage and hope when we really needed it, and now you've forever changed our lives...for the better."

Danielle hugged Debbie.

"Now, I need to see that ring," she exclaimed, pulling back from the hug.

Danielle extended her left hand.

"That's beautiful," Debbie gushed.

"Let me see," Nevaeh said, pulling Danielle's thin fingers down, level with her eyes. "It's sparkly, like my shoes."

"Which house have you decided to keep?" Callie asked, joining the crew at the back of the courtroom.

"Neither," Danielle grinned, her left cheek muscle only drooping slightly. "We're going to start fresh. Look for something closer to James' new job at the school district's office."

"Then, I'll put the first bid on it," Callie replied. "I want that backyard."

"You know Ethan's business is booming," James said. "I'm sure he'd be happy to landscape your current place."

"Good point," Callie said. "I saw his picture in the paper. I wouldn't mind hiring him," she said with a twinkle in her eyes.

"You'll have to contend with my dad for the house, Callie," Danielle said as they began to exit the courtroom.

"Really?"

"He's fallen in love with the backyard, too."

"Or, has he fallen in love with being closer to his daughter and his future grandkids?" Debbie asked as she held open the door for the group.

"I can't quite picture my dad as a grandpa," Danielle replied. "But then again, I couldn't ever picture him moving to live by me, so who knows?"

"Now, where did Chris and the boys go?" Debbie asked as they started down the hallway.

"They went to get the car," Nevaeh said. "Dad told me he was going to pull it up to the front."

"Dad?" Danielle whispered in Debbie's ear.

"She just started that a few weeks ago. Forgot to tell you," Debbie whispered back.

"See you at lunch," Nevaeh waved, as she took Debbie's hand and began to walk to the main doors.

James put his arm around Danielle and whispered in her ear, "You're amazing."

She kissed him on the cheek.

"Okay, you two lovebirds," Callie said, walking behind them. "I'll see you at the restaurant."

Discussion Questions

1. Danielle's past effects how she views relationships with men. Have you seen something from your past effect your relationships?

2. Classmates were mean to Hawk when he was growing up. Why do you think people pick on those who are "different?"

3. James didn't want to be funded by political action committees or organizations that would "pull his strings." Do you think some politicians in today's society live with those same standards?

4. Danielle and James both found their lives were overly controlled by their work. Do you ever feel that way? What could you do to change that?

5. Danielle felt a check in her spirit when she was entering Layla and Booker's backyard. Do you think that was the Holy Spirit? Have you ever had a similar experience?

6. Ethan begins to learn about God but closes himself off when things don't go his way.
   Do you think most people expect God to make their lives perfect?

7. If God is perfect, and has power to make our lives perfect, why do you think we live with imperfection?

8. Were you happy with who Danielle chose in the end? Why or why not?

Preview of Book Two

Adams Landscaping is broke. Ethan's marketing skills are non-existent, and he fears he'll be stuck forever transcribing medical records from his tiny trailer, the Artic Fox, while he stares at the twenty-three acres of blooming dreams in his backyard. Then a miracle happens that makes him, and his business, an overnight success.

When his phone won't stop ringing, he hires Claire Rogers, the sweet elementary school teacher who lives with her parents on the farm next door, to be his receptionist.

While Ethan struggles to hone his interpersonal skills for the first time, kind-hearted Claire becomes the voice of his business earning the customers' trust and appreciation. As Ethan moves into the local spotlight, seductive bartender Jezmeen Williams sets her sights on the handsome landscaper who visits Finnegan's Taphouse regularly-and no one ever forgets a glance from Jezmeen.

Claire finds herself unsettled with Ethan's choices and Jezmeen's grasp on her employer, so she makes a drastic change that leaves Ethan without the one he has come to depend on. When Claire returns, she finds much has changed-including herself. Why is a talkative thirteen-year-old girl living with Ethan? Who's forcing Claire's family farmhouse to be sold? In book two, *Finding Home,* discover where Ethan turns when he's about to lose it all.

Made in the USA
Monee, IL
01 October 2020